‖‖‖‖‖‖‖‖‖‖‖‖‖‖‖‖‖‖‖‖‖

W9-BCP-424

HIS QUESTION ANSWERED

"No!" the thug screamed. "I ain't gonna die!" Wildly, he threw a shot over his shoulder.

He turned to face his opponent, raised his revolver to put the man away. Then a bright, white light dazzled him, and immense pain assailed his gun hand. He stared in horror. No one could be that fast.

Then a rocklike fist slammed into his stomach. He started to double over, only to be straightened up by another enormous pain in his chest. He wound up on his back, staring up at Smoke Jensen holding a Peacemaker in a steady, level grasp.

The hard case used the last of his breath to ask his most pressing questions. "Wh—what are you, Jensen? Who are you?"

A tiny mocking smile lifted the corners of Smoke Jensen's mouth. "Some people have called me the gunfighters' gunfighter."

BOOK YOUR PLACE ON OUR WEBSITE AND MAKE THE READING CONNECTION!

We've created a customized website just for our very special readers, where you can get the inside scoop on everything that's going on with Zebra, Pinnacle and Kensington books.

When you come online, you'll have the exciting opportunity to:

- View covers of upcoming books
- Read sample chapters
- Learn about our future publishing schedule (listed by publication month *and author*)
- Find out when your favorite authors will be visiting a city near you
- Search for and order backlist books from our online catalog
- Check out author bios and background information
- Send e-mail to your favorite authors
- Meet the Kensington staff online
- Join us in weekly chats with authors, readers and other guests
- Get writing guidelines
- AND MUCH MORE!

**Visit our website at
http://www.kensingtonbooks.com**

ORDEAL OF THE MOUNTAIN MAN

William W. Johnstone

PINNACLE BOOKS
Kensington Publishing Corp.
http://www.kensingtonbooks.com

PINNACLE BOOKS are published by

Kensington Publishing Corp.
850 Third Avenue
New York, NY 10022

Copyright © 1996 by William W. Johnstone

All rights reserved. No part of this book may be reproduced in any form or by any means without the prior written consent of the Publisher, excepting brief quotes used in reviews.

If you purchased this book without a cover, you should be aware that this book is stolen property. It was reported as "unsold and destroyed" to the Publisher and neither the Author nor the Publisher has received any payment for this "stripped book."

All Kensington Titles, Imprints, and Distributed Lines are available at special quantity discounts for bulk purchases for sales promotions, premiums, fund-raising, and educational or institutional use. Special book excerpts or customized printings can also be created to fit specific needs. For details, write or phone the office of the Kensington special sales manager: Kensington Publishing Corp., 850 Third Avenue, New York, NY 10022, attn: Special Sales Department, Phone: 1-800-221-2647.

Pinnacle and the P logo Reg. U.S. Pat. & TM Off.

First Printing: August 1996

20 19 18 17 16 15 14 13 12 11

Printed in the United States of America

One

Dust rose like a brown shroud around the rumps of a long string of shiny coated horses as they trotted, tails high, away from the lush pastures of Sugarloaf, Smoke Jensen's ranch. Smoke and a dozen hands, including Utah Jack Grubbs, Jerry Harkness and Luke Britton, had set out to drive a herd of two hundred remounts north to Fort Custer on the Crow Indian Reservation in Montana. It would turn out to be a much longer and harder journey than Smoke would have believed, becoming a grueling ordeal for Jensen and every man with him.

At the lower pasture fence, Sally and young Bobby Jensen sat their mounts and waved at the departing backs. Sally thought uneasily of the many times Smoke had ridden away on far more dangerous missions. Over the nearly ten years they had been married, after Smoke's first wife and son were brutally murdered, Smoke had strapped on six-guns, and frequently a badge, and had gone off to right the wrongs done to himself, or more often to others, even strangers. Smoke didn't see himself as any sort of Robin Hood, though he had read the legends as a youth, learning from the old mountain man, Preacher, what he had abandoned when he strayed from his parents' wagon as a half-grown child. The family had been bound for the Northwest Territory when he got lost in the wilderness.

Sally had first seen Smoke Jensen as a ruffian, a barbarian a *gunfighter*. She was teaching school at the time. Smoke came to town and cleaned out a gang of gun trash and saddle tramps, leaving a wide wake of bodies along the way. At first, his blood-thirsty conduct disgusted and frightened her. She had soon learned better, when he rescued her from the clutches of the gang boss. After that, she knew him as a tall, handsome man with longish, reddish brown hair and a ready smile. Now, she brushed aside such reflections and thought about the three hands who rode with him.

Jerry Harkness had been with Smoke, ever since he changed from cattle ranching to raising blooded horses. Jerry knew more about horses and their ailments than most veterinarians. He had grown up on a Thoroughbred farm in Kentucky. Lean and tall, Jerry was in his mid-twenties, with the bowed legs of a jockey, his muscles bunched and corded. He was, as their cook, Zeke Thackery, put it, smack-bang loyal. Jerry rode for the brand and would die for it if need be.

Another cut from the same mold was Luke Britton. A year or two younger than Jerry, he was an easy-going, even-tempered young man with a high school education, which was an exception for the times. Barrel-chested and broad-shouldered, he was frequently mistaken for a bare-knuckle boxer. Which he wasn't, but he could hold his own, much to the regret of many a proddy drifter who challenged him. Luke was a man to ride the river with.

Jack Grubbs was a short, bow-legged, salty horse expert with a checkered past. When the Sugarloaf foreman had interviewed him only three months earlier, he had been troubled enough by what he learned to turn Jack over to Smoke to question. Later, after he had hired Grubbs, Smoke told Sally that Jack had been in prison. A streak of wildness in his youth, Utah Jack had explained, which he had outgrown. Recalling his own past, Smoke had said that all Jack needed was a chance to redeem himself. For some reason, that now came back to give her a cold shiver along her spine. She shook it off and turned to their adopted son.

"Come on, Bobby. We might as well ride back to the house. We won't see them for two months," she added with a sigh. How she would miss her beloved Smoke, she thought as she brushed a lock of black hair back behind an ear.

Bobby wrinkled his freckled, pug nose and put words to her thoughts. "I'm gonna miss Smoke awfully." His fourteen-year-old's voice croaked with the awkwardness of change. "I hope nothing happens to them."

With Luke and Utah Jack on swing, Pop Walker on drag, Smoke Jensen rode at the front of the trail herd with Jerry Harkness. They headed for Wyoming in a lighthearted mood. Jerry cracked a constant string of Indian-and-Politician jokes.

"D'you hear the one about the politician who went out to explain to the Sioux chiefs about the new treaty? He got out here with an interpreter who translated his words. After each sentence had been put in Lakota, the chiefs would grunt and say, *'Unkce!'* He told them how they would be restricted to reservations from now on, and again they said, *'Unkce!'* " Smoke was surprised that Jerry pronounced the word correctly: *Oon-K'CHAY.* "So this goes on until the end, when the chiefs all tapped their open palms with their eagle wing fans and shouted it three times.

"Then one chief got up and made a short speech. The interpreter told the politician that the chiefs thanked him for his good words and wanted to know if he wished to see some of Sioux life. The politician said that yes, he did. He had always wanted to see a buffalo hunt. It was arranged, and hunters rode out to find the bison while the chiefs and the politician started walking out on the prairie where the buffalo roamed. All of a sudden, the interpreter reached out and grabbed the politician's arm and stopped him from stepping in a big pile of buffalo bull plop, and said, 'Be careful not to step in the *unkce.*' "

Smoke groaned and held his side; he had heard it before. "Jerry, don't you have anything better to amuse yourself?"

"Oh, sure. Did you hear about the Indian, the settler, and the politician who all died and wound up outside the Pearly Gates?"

"Spare me!" Smoke wailed in mock agony.

Four days later, six pair of eyes watched while the herd crossed the border from Colorado into the Wyoming Territory. One of the men in the small party, Yancy Osburn, turned to the others.

"That's them, all right. Burk, you ride north and let Hub Volker know they're on the way."

Ainsley Burk nodded, then asked, "What are the rest of you gonna do?

Osburn pointed to the sleek remounts. We'll follow along, send back reports on their movement.

"Good enough. I'll tell Mr. Volker that." Burk walked his horse away from his companions in order not to draw the attention of the drovers.

Once out of ear-shot, Yancy turned to the others with a nasty grin. "Well, boys, now that we've got Mr. Rule Book out of our hair, I've got me an idea how to pass our time while those nags move north."

"What's that?" two chorused.

Yancy gave them a wide wink. "I know of a nice little stagecoach we can rob."

Fifty miles northwest, Owen Curtis sat in his saddle, his left leg cocked up around the pommel, eyes fixed on the brown humps of his prize Herefords. He had paid a pretty penny for the first bull and three cows that formed the base of his herd. Over the years, he had added new blood, and his stock increased by nature's decree. Although the bevy was still small, Owen modestly counted himself as a rich man.

By the lights of many who struggled against the hostilities of Wyoming Territory, the severe winter weather, summer drought, and of course always the Indians, Curtis was indeed a wealthy, successful man. The rumble of distant hooves drew his attention to the head of the grazing beefs. Three of his hands kept them in a loose gather, allowing them to move slowly through the grassy meadow, eating their fill, while subtly leading them toward water. Seven riders appeared abruptly over the ridge of the basin, riding hard toward the cattle.

Owen Curtis looked on helplessly, stunned by the sight, as puffs of white smoke blossomed from the muzzles of the rifles the intruders held to their shoulders. Two of his men went down as Owen swung his leg into the stirrup and slid his Winchester from its scabbard. More gunshots crackled through the basin, and the cattle bolted and began to run wildly across the meadow. A half dozen more rustlers jolted down the side slopes of the bowllike pasture and began to turn the cattle back on their frightened fellows.

Curtis took aim and knocked one outlaw from his saddle with a bullet through the chest. He worked the lever action of the Model '73 and sought another target. The only problem was that he had attracted the attention of the thieves. Three cut their horses in his direction and bore down on the rancher. One of them raised a rifle and fired.

A bright, hot pain erupted in Owen Curtis' chest. Debilitating numbness swiftly followed. Owen groaned and tried to line up his sights on the man who had shot him. The other two fired then, and he dimly heard a bullet crack past his head. Sheer whiteness washed through his skull an instant later, and he sagged in the saddle, lost his grip with his knees and slid to the ground.

Immediately, Hubble Volker snapped an order. "Get these snuffies under control and take 'em out of here."

"Where to, Mr. Volker?"

"Take 'em up to Bent Rock Canyon, Garth. There's plenty pines up there to build a holding corral."

Garth Evans reacted, predictably, at once. "You mean *work?* Get blisters on our hands?"

Hubble Volker laughed. "Ain't what you had in mind when you joined the Reno Jim gang, is it? Well, when you're countin' your share of the take, you'll forget the broke blisters an' sore muscles." He turned and shouted across the rumble of hooves to the others. "Get 'em under control. Head 'em up and slow 'em down."

With an anticipatory twinkle in his eye, Yancy Osburn watched the steady approach of the stage to Laramie. The heads of the six-up team bobbed rhythmically, and their powerful shoulders churned to draw the heavily laden vehicle forward. It had taken Osburn and his cohorts a day's ride to get in position. Yancy figured the herd of remounts would stay to the main trail, there being plenty of Indians roaming out there if they did not. Now they were about to relieve the Wells Fargo company of a good deal of loot. Osburn made curt gestures, directing his men to position.

He and Smiling Dave Winters remained in the center of the road, a fleshy barricade. The coach disappeared into a dip, and each of the outlaws raised a bandanna to cover his face. Weapons at the ready, they waited for the stage to reappear a scant thirty yards from them.

Pounding hooves, a jingle of harness and the creak of leather springs announced the arrival of the Laramie stage. The heads of the lead pair surged above the draw and gained the level. Quickly the rest appeared, and Yancy made out the driver and shotgun guard. He raised his Winchester and killed the guard before the driver could react to their presence in the road.

With only his six-gun for defense, the grizzled teamster hauled on the reins and applied the brake. The coach swayed to a dusty stop. Immediately the masked outlaws moved in.

Ansel Wharton had driven stages for Wells Fargo for nine years. In that time he had been robbed eleven times. He knew exactly what to do when he saw the masked bandits strung out along the road and blocking it ahead. Especially when the shotgun guard jolted backward and toppled over the side of the driver's seat. Meekly, all the while fuming inside, he hauled on the reins and brought the coach to a stop. The masked ones, like these, rarely killed everyone, he consoled himself.

"Afternoon," called the big one in the middle of the road. And Ansel could tell the sneer that had to be under the bandanna by the tone of voice. "We'll relieve you of the strongbox, if you please."

"What if I told you we don't have one?" He had to do that, company orders.

The bullet-headed outlaw in charge shook his head. "Then your wife would be a widow."

"Ain't got a wife. She died of the cholera back a ways. Now, let me see, was it in sixty-an'-four, or seventy-two?"

Anger rang in the snarled response. "Quit stallin' and hand it over."

Facing defeat and knowing it, Ansel shrugged. "I'd be obliged if you let me step down an' you had a couple of your friends remove it. It's a heavy sucker this trip."

Instantly the outlaw's mood changed. He laughed delightedly. "Mighty nice to hear. Good enough, old man, climb on down. Mind, keep yer hand clear of that hogleg yer packin'."

"Oh, I been robbed before. An' I know what to do, otherwise I wouldn't be here."

"There's some of you do learn, I do declare."

The Jovial Bandit, Ansel named him mentally. He'd remember the voice. The size, too. This one was a brute, a huge bruiser with broad shoulders, a hefty girth, thick arms and wrists. Looked like he could take on three men at once and not raise a sweat. He worked his way down the small, round, cast-iron mounting steps and walked to the headstall of the lead horse.

"Keep him from spookin', don't ya see?" he explained to the highwaymen.

Yancy Osburn raised a ham hand to the brim of his hat and pushed it back. "Now there's a smart man. Good idee. Keep 'em calm while we relieve you of everything else and ask the passengers for a contribution."

Ansel hastened to give advise. "There ain't but one strongbox." He carefully omitted the shipment of gold bars under the backward-facing bench seat inside.

"All right, everybody out of the coach. We forgot to bring any fancy steps, so you'll have to jump down."

An angry voice of defiance came from an imprudent drummer inside the coach. "You're not going to get away with this."

His sample case cost a fortune, and he had no intention of losing it. His pudgy hand darted inside his pinstripe suit coat and came out with a nickle-plated Baby Smith .38. Hastily he fired a shot that grazed the shoulder of one of the outlaws to the side of the coach.

A roar of gunfire immediately answered him. Riddled by five bullets, the salesman slumped back in the leather of the seat and bled all over the coach and other passengers. Two women began to shriek and hug one another. Unfazed by the disturbance, Yancy Osburn motioned to the door again with his rifle barrel.

"Everyone out."

In short time, the passengers had been relieved of their valuables and herded back inside the vehicle. Osburn set two men to unharnessing the horses. Before they left, the outlaws scattered the team. Galloping off with their considerable loot— the gold undiscovered—they cast not a glance at the stranded occupants of the stage.

"We'll have to hunt down them horses," Ansel told the two male passengers. "One of you stay with the ladies and see that they are all right.

This is going to be a long day," he predicted with considerable accuracy.

Reno Jim Yurian looked down from a long slope that formed one wall of a box gorge known as Bent Rock Canyon. A satisfied smile formed under the pencil-line black mustache that adorned his thin upper lip. Not a sign of the stolen cattle could be seen. His flat, gray eyes took on an inner glow.

"We can keep them here until we have the horses as well. Then take them all in to sell. There's a livestock broker I know who doesn't look too close at brands."

"You mean your partner, Mr. Kel—" At an upraised hand from Jim Yurian, the not-too-bright Hubble Volker cut off his words before saying the name.

Always the dapper dresser, Reno Jim preferred red silk-lined, black morning coats, with matching trousers, brocaded vests and frilly, white shirts, with spills of lace at front, collar and cuff. He adjusted the latter now as he stared down his talkative second in command from under the wide brim of the flat-crown, black Stetson he habitually wore cocked at a rakish angle.

"Never mind who. The point is he will buy anything we bring him. I want you to take over here for now and wait for word on the horses. I'm going on up to Muddy Gap to see that everything is ready for their arrival."

Another branch of the Reno Jim Yurian gang had grown bored waiting for the fabled horse herd to come to them. Like Yancy Osburn's men, they chose to engage in some casual criminal activity to pass the time. The Bighorn and Laramie Line coach to Muddy Gap lumbered right up to them before the shotgun guard realized they had ridden into trouble.

"Stand and deliver!" demanded a swaggering, barrel-shaped highwayman with a gaudy ostrich plume in his floppy, chocolate brown hat.

"Like hell," roared Rupe, the shotgun guard, as he brought down his 10 gauge L.C. Smith and let go a load of 00 buckshot.

His shot column took the hat from the arrogant bandit and pulped his face with thirteen of the seventeen pellets. Immediately three of the holdup men leveled their six-guns and slip thumbed through a trio of rounds each, which shot Rupe to doll rags. Beside him, the driver slapped the wheelers' rumps with his reins to no avail as he took one of the shots intended for Rupe in his left forearm.

Muscles and tendons, strong and rangy from years of working a six-horse team, contracted and drove the broken ulna bone out of the driver's arm. He yowled and sat helplessly while two robbers caught the headstalls of the leaders and stopped the coach.

"Everybody out. Show us what you've got."

A cawing voice of censure came from inside the coach. "Young man, that's a disgusting, vulgar thought. Shame on you."

Laughing outlaws surrounded the vehicle. "You must have been a schoolmarm, 'm I right?"

Guffawing, a freckle-faced, redheaded bandit

touched the brim of his hat to the descending dowager. "It's been my experience that schoolmarms are most familiar with that famous challenge of the youngens ma'am. You know? 'You show me yours and I'll show you mine' It was a lot of fun doin' that, as I rec'lect."

Examining him with cold, blue marble eyes from above jowls made enormous by excessive, snowy facial powder and carmine rouge, she snapped in tightly controlled outrage. "You are a most disagreeable young man."

"I reckon I am. After all, I do rob stages for a livin'. Hardly a recommend to the better element of society, 'm I right?"

Looking as though she might faint dead away, she fanned herself with a black-gloved hand. "Spare me from such depraved trash."

Anger flushed what could be seen of the outlaw's face. "I ain't trash. You get that straight, you old bat."

To emphasize what he had said, the red-headed bandit stepped in close and popped her in the chops. That proved too much for one of the male passengers. He leaped forward and drove a hard right into the gut of the impudent thug, who bent double and gasped for air. The defender of womanhood followed with a clout behind the ear, which dropped the young highwayman at the feet of the woman he had assaulted. Immediately a shot cracked over the heads of the passengers and the would-be rescuer fell dead on the spot.

Sobbing, the woman turned away. The bandits worked quickly after that. They relieved the passengers of all valuables and took the strongbox,

missing the shipment of bullion the stage carried. Like the Wells Fargo team, the horses were
run off when the highwaymen left.

Two

A thin, white spiral of smoke came from the chimney of the Iron Kettle, the best eatery in Muddy Gap, Wyoming Territory. That it was the only public eating house in town, outside the hotel, the proud city fathers preferred not to acknowledge. Along the ambitiously wide main street, several prosperous business establishments had hung out their shingles. The raw wooden side walls and fresh paint of the building facades testified to the newness of this thriving community.

Among them were Harbinson's General Mercantile, the Territorial Bank of Muddy Gap, the only stone building in town, Walker's Saddlery, Hope's Apothecary and Sundries, Thelma Blackmun's Ladies' Fashions, Tiemeier's Butcher Shop, a blacksmith, the feed and grain store, and four saloons. At the north end of town stood a small, white, clapboard church. To the south, an equally miniscule schoolhouse.

Inside the school, class had been in session since eight that morning. The younger students, with the shorter attention spans, had become restless, eager for recess. The older grades, three through eight, laboriously attacked their assignments. Virginia Parkins, the schoolteacher, was listening to the sixth grade read aloud when the door slammed open against the inner wall and three large, loutish youths swaggered inside. Although she had two fourteen-year-olds and one fifteen in the seventh and eighth grades, Virginia recognized these ruffians as being considerably older, the youngest not under sixteen. She looked on them with a frown of irritation.

With expressions of blended contempt and disgust, the bullies strutted up the aisle and stopped beside the desk of young James Finch. One of them, a pig-faced boy named Brandon Kelso, spoke from the advantage of his height.

"Git outta that desk, Jimmy. You ain't got no business wastin' yer time here."

Eleven-year-old Jimmy Finch cut his eyes away from the imposing figure standing over him. He swallowed hard and spoke in a near whisper. "I gotta read next."

"What's that?" Brandon reached down with a large hand and yanked the slight, big-eyed boy out of his desk. "Your daddy needs you to help work stock. Now get yer butt outta this dump and do as you're told."

Beside Brandon, Willie Finch, Jimmy's older brother, sniggered. "That's right, Jimmy-Wimmy, Paw sent me to fetch you. Git yer skinny little ass movin'."

Thoroughly frightened, the small boy started moving his feet before Brandon Kelso lowered him to the floor. Outrage at this invasion overrode the usual quiet, nonaggressive demeanor of Virginia Parkins. She came to her feet so abruptly that her tall, backless stool toppled over and the book in her lap hit the floor with a loud bang.

All eyes turned her way. "Enough of your crude vulgarities, Brandon Kelso. You and these other louts need your mouths washed out with soap. Now, leave the children alone and get out of my classroom."

Brandon took a cocky step toward her. "Who's gonna make us, *Teacher?*" He sneered the last word.

Fat, porcine lips curled in contempt, Brandon Kelso studied the outraged young woman before him. She might make a good poke, he thought to himself, though he lacked any experience in such encounters. Couldn't be much older than himself. Those green eyes and the auburn hair, her wide, pouty-lookin' mouth, made his groin swell and ache just lookin' at her. Never thought she had any fire in her.

He had quit school four years ago, before she had come here. He got tired of doing the sixth grade a third time at the age of thirteen. Now, if *she* had been here, he might not have quit. She would have given him something to fill his . . . mind . . . with when he was sittin' in the outhouse. He made kissing motions with his lips. Her unexpected reaction surprised him.

Virginia turned sharply away and walked directly to one corner by the blackboard. She came back with a stout willow switch about four feet long. Before its purpose registered on Brandon Kelso, she began to lay about the hips and thighs of the three bullies. The limber switch made a nasty whir and sharp smack with each stroke.

When they all joined in a yelping chorus, she reached out and took the ear of the smallest in a firm grip and gave it a hard twist. Squealing, Danny Collins did a fancy dance step all the way to the door. Driving the others before her with the switch, Virginia hustled all three out onto the low stoop and hurried them down the steps. From the safety of the school yard, Brandon Kelso turned back to throw a final, ominous taunt.

"You know my father is on the school board. If you want to keep your job, you'd better watch what you do to me an' my friends."

Fists on hips, she called after them. "I'll risk that. Now, git. And don't come back."

That task completed, she returned to the schoolroom. Her expression calmed from its earlier outrage, she spoke in a soothing, quiet voice. "You may return to your desk, Jimmy. You will read next."

Riding his handsome, chestnut roan, Thoroughbred stallion down the center of the main street of Muddy Gap, Reno Jim Yurian sat tall in the saddle. He looked neither left nor right. With the schooled knees of a trained equestrian, he controlled his mount past the yapping of dogs, the shrill yells of children racing barefoot through the street and the bustle and whirl of wagons, horsemen and pedestrians. A light hand on the reins, he guided Walker's Kentucky Pride toward the tie rail in front of the Territorial Bank of Muddy Gap.

There the well-mannered horse stopped

primly on a dime and waited without even an ear twitch while Jim Yurian dismounted. He looped the reins over the crossbar and removed his black leather gloves. Reno Jim used them to flick the spots of trail dust from his trouser legs and the sleeves of his immaculate swallowtail morning coat, then stepped regally up onto the boardwalk. Without a glance in the direction of the bank lobby, he walked to an extension of the plank sidewalk that ran along one side of the building into an alley.

At its end, he began to ascend a flight of stairs that ended on a small platform outside a door that gave access to the second floor. Halfway down the well-scrubbed and highly polished hall, he paused a moment before the frosted glass pane that occupied the upper half of a closed door. Taking a deep breath, he reached out and turned the knob.

He shouldered past the gilt-edged letters that spelled out in bold face:

BOYNE KELSO
GRAIN AND LIVESTOCK BROKER

He entered and flashed a winning smile at a willowy man in his early twenties, seated at the desk in the outer office.

"Good morning, Mr. Masters."

"Good morning, Mr. Yurian. Mr. Kelso is expecting you. Go right in."

"Thank you."

Robbie Masters looked after the visitor and sighed deeply. *Oh, God, he's soooo handsome,* he thought. Then he quickly busied himself with the stack of papers on his desk. Thus occupied, he did not see the sudden, hard expression of contempt on the face of Jim Yurian. Reno Jim opened the dividing panel and stepped into the sanctum of Boyne Kelso.

"I have good news, Boyne." When he closed the door securely behind him, he went on. "That herd of remounts on their way to Fort Custer will soon be ours."

Kelso revealed his surprise. "They really exist, then?"

"Yes. Some of my men watched them cross over from Colorado. Just short of three weeks, they should be on the Crow Reservation. That is, they would be, if we didn't have other plans for them."

Beaming, Kelso rubbed pudgy hands together. "Excellent, excellent. This calls for a mild celebration. I recommend the saloon-bar in the Wilber House Hotel. They pour a fine bourbon."

Reno Jim smiled back. "That sounds fine to me."

Together, they left the office and strode out onto the main boardwalk. They talked of inconsequentials as they strolled toward the hotel. Every man who passed respectfully touched the brim of his hat in salute to Boyne Kelso. A woman in a wide, gray, voluminous dress and white-edged bonnet of the same material nodded politely.

"Afternoon, Deacon Kelso."

"Good afternoon, Amanda," Kelso responded grandly.

Reno Jim smiled behind his hand. He knew that Kelso, born to a Protestant family in the north of Ireland, was considered a pillar of the community. Throughout Wyoming Territory, his rectitude was legend. No one questioned his scales, or the quality of seed grain he sold. Considered a loving husband and father, with charming, well-mannered children, Kelso was frequently held up as a paragon of societal excellence.

What would those fine, well-meaning people think if they knew the truth of Kelso's nature? Reno Jim mused.

Most likely they'd fill their fancy drawers. Well, they needed those well-intentioned souls. Without them, they could never survive in the business of robbing and rustling. Nor could they profit any longer from the land swindles handled by their trusty underling in the land office. When the good folk lost their meekness, terrible things happened. He shivered when he recalled what had occurred recently in Cripple Creek.

Somehow, the good people of that area had found out they were being bilked, cheated, robbed and even murdered by minions in the employ of Reno Jim Yurian. They had organized a Vigilance Committee. He suppressed a shudder as he visualized eleven of his best men dangling from ropes over the limbs of brooding oak trees, so much gruesome fruit. And his own ignominious route from Cripple Creek, tarred, feathered and slung over a pole. Reno Jim quickly banished the horrible visions as they reached the hotel.

Inside, seated at a rich cherrywood table, Reno Jim eyed the softly glowing brass lamps and fittings, the dark, lustrous sheen of the mahogany bar, the muted nature of the flocked, red velvet wallpaper, and sighed in contentment. This was the sort of world he preferred to live in. A coatless bartender, in sleeve garters and a blue, pinstripe, collarless shirt, brought them a crystal decanter of premium bourbon and two matching glasses. After he poured and departed, Kelso made quiet inquiry of Reno Jim.

"How soon will your men be coming here?"

"Some time next week. Certainly before the horses get here. I want to take them farther north."

"Good. I'll be busy over the weekend with the church council."

That brought a low chuckle from Reno Jim. "You had better keep your nose clean if you want to hold on to your fine reputation. But your plans are no problem. I'll also be busy over the weekend."

They talked on for a while. During their third glass of the smoothest, sweetest bourbon Reno Jim had ever tasted, a sudden commotion rose in the street outside. Shouts to the effect the stage had been robbed brought both men to their boots. They shouldered their way through the room and out the batwings into the lobby.

A crowd had gathered in front of the Bighorn and Laramie Stage Line office by the time Boyne Kelso and Reno Jim Yurian reached there. Men in overalls and flannel shirts, ranch hands in long-sleeved yoke shirts and jeans, merchants and their clerks in wool suit trousers, collarless shirts and aprons shouted questions.

"How many of 'em was it, Sam?"

Jaws at work on a cud of cut plug, the driver replied offhandedly. "Reckon there was nigh onto ten of them."

Over their entreaties, Boyne Kelso spoke loudly. "How much did they get, Sam? The bank had a shipment on there, you know."

Conscious of the need for secrecy in transactions, especially of bullion, Sam glowered at the big broker. "Didn't touch that. Never mind, Mr. Kelso, that's between the company and the bank. What's got me riled is that they killed Rupe."

"That's an outrage," Kelso thundered. "I certainly hope your company has enough compassion to arrange for some church ladies to go along when his widow is given the news. And I say now that these depredations must cease. To that end, I am offering a reward of five hundred dollars, dead or alive, for those responsible. Any idea who, Sam?"

Sam shook his head. "Nope. They all wore masks. Didn't give me a name, like that Black Bart feller out in Californey a while back. Jist took the money, and these folks' valuables, and rode off. We'd have been in sooner if they hadn't chased off our horses."

Kelso wrung his hands and cut his eyes from one man to another. "This is deplorable. We cannot tolerate this any longer. Where's the sheriff? Why hasn't he sent out a posse?" He turned back to the coach. "You folks who were on the stage, let me offer my condolences that this reprehensible deed was done so near to our fine community. If any of you are completely out of pocket, come see me. I have a grain and livestock brokerage above the bank. The name's Kelso."

With that, Kelso turned away and stalked toward the sheriff's office. Hiding his grin, Reno Jim Yurian went the opposite way to retrieve his horse from in front of the bank. In ten minutes he rode clear of town, headed to meet his gang and see what new profit had been gained in the holdup.

Across a dividing ridge, Smoke Jensen decided the time was right to take care of what had been bothering him for the past day and a half. He reined in and motioned Jerry Harkness to take the herd on. He sat his new 'Palouse stallion, Cougar, while the remounts legged their way past. His face set in concentration, Smoke seemed not to notice the dust that boiled up.

When Luke Britton, riding drag today, ambled by, Smoke gave him a light wave and dropped back down their trail. Near the crest of the ridge, he angled into a craggy gorge and reined up. Five minutes later, three seedy-looking characters, whom Smoke had seen several times trailing them, walked their mounts into view. At once, Smoke rode out and confronted them, Cougar crosswise on the trail.

Smoke kept his voice level as he addressed them. "I think it's time you fellers stopped trailin' us."

"Who says?" the one in the middle challenged.

"I do."

Face suddenly flushed with anger, the proddy

one spat at Smoke. "That don't cut no slack with me."

Smoke cut his eyes to each in turn. "Then I'll give you a choice. You can turn around and light a shuck out of here, or you can tell me why you are following us."

Through a sneer, the mouthy thug posed a question. "What if I said we was lookin' for to hire on?"

Shaking his head as though saddened, Smoke said, "Then I'd have to call you a liar."

"That does it, by God. That surely does it," roared the aroused hard case as he dipped a hand swiftly toward his six-gun.

He had just cleared the cylinder of his Colt from leather when Smoke's .45 Peacemaker blasted the stillness of the rolling countryside. A slug spat from the muzzle and smacked solidly into the center of the chest of the saddle trash. His life shattered within him, the hard case reared sharply back against the cantle with enough force to snap the hat from his head. Then he went boneless and flopped onto the rump of his nervous, dancing horse.

By then, the other two had unlimbered their revolvers and now attempted to bring them up in line with this unnervingly fast stranger. They failed miserably in the attempt. Smoke's second round punched into the right side of the chest of the gunman nearest to him and shattered his shoulder blade. The thug's Smith American went flying in reflex to the pain that exploded in his body.

His companion thought better of further aggression. He turned his horse, spurred it to a gallop and sprinted for the top of the rise. As he disappeared over the crest, Smoke Jensen walked Cougar over close to the wounded man.

"Now, tell me. Who are you ridin' for?"

Groaning, the trash looked up at Smoke through a haze of pain. "We ain't workin' for nobody. We—we only figgered to cut out a few head and make a little money off 'em. That's all, mister."

Smoke's expression registered disappointment. "Why is it I don't believe you? Well, in the event you all of a sudden remember who it is, you can tell him the reason you got shot up is that you ran into Smoke Jensen."

His shock-pale skin went even whiter. "Oh, Jesus."

"He can't help you. You ride on out of here while I pick up that six-gun. We've got a herd to deliver."

Three

A great, bloated, orange sun hung on the eastern horizon over Muddy Gap. The smoke from wood-burning cookstoves streamed from stovepipes. Shrill voices of children, out to do their chores, could be heard in the backyards of their homes.

A small girl in a paisley dress called from the hen yard. "Chick—chick, here chick-chick-chick!"

A boy, somewhat older than she, could be heard in a low barn. "Soo-oo, Bossy. Hold still. I gotta milk you."

From a spanking-new carriage house, another boy announced cheerily, "Here's your oats, Prince."

On a hillside overlooking the town, Hubble Volker sat his mount at the center of a crescent formed by the Yurian gang. Together, they gazed down on the scene of domesticity. Volker waved a hand in the direction of Muddy Gap.

"We'll give 'em a little more time. Let the shops open up, and the bank. Then we make our move. Too bad the boss couldn't come along. He'd have enjoyed this."

Hairy Joe spoke over the rumble of his stomach. "I smell biscuits bakin'. Sure could use some of them."

Volker gave him an amused look. "Maybe you can he'p yerself to some when we clean out the town."

Pleading sounded in Joe's voice. "But, I'm hongry now. What we gonna eat?"

"Air, if you didn't bring something along," Volker told him with a snort. "Me, I've got me some corn bread from last night, an' some fried fatback. Shore gonna taste good. You gotta plan ahead, Hairy Joe."

Hairy Joe appealed to a generosity that did not exist. "Least let me have shares in some of that, Hub."

"Nope. Ain't got enough. Ask the other boys. They only brung enough for theyselves, too."

Scowling, Hairy Joe subsided. He cut envy-filled eyes to the rest of the gang while they munched on their leftovers. Unappeased, his stomach continued to growl. For solace, he rolled a quirley and puffed it to life. The smoke wreathed his head.

Two hours later, the main street began to bustle with merchants and their employees. Doors opened and shades went up. A few early customers rolled into town on buckboards or on horseback. Hubble Volker looked on, weighing the right time. It would not be long, that much he knew.

Riding in twos, as directed by Yurian's second in command, the gang entered the main street of Muddy Gap from different directions. Each pair went to an assigned business front. Hub Volker and Garth Evans entered the bank. One teller looked up and peered at them from under a green eyeshade, a welcoming smile already forming on his lips. Then he saw the weapons in their hands and the masks over their faces.

"OHMYGOD!" he blurted.

Volker took immediate command. "That's right, folks, this is a holdup. Everybody put your hands over your heads. You tellers, fill money-bags with everything in your tills. You, Mister Banker"—he gestured with the muzzle of his Merwin and Hulbert revolver to the portly gentleman seated in a glass cubicle behind the tellers' cages—"you be so kind as to step over to the vault and empty it out."

Stammering, the banker refused to comply. "You can't get away with this. The marshal will come running, and the sheriff is back in town. I'll not help you steal from these good people."

"In that case, we don't have any more use for you," Volker told him.

Hub raised the Merwin and Hulbert, and it roared loudly in the confined space. Glass bulged inward and showered musically to the floor as the bullet passed through the dividing window and struck the banker in the forehead. He flew backward out of his padded, horse-hide swivel chair and crashed noisily against a file cabinet.

Three women customers began a chorus of shrieks and wails at the sight. Volker shoved through the swinging gate that divided the lobby from the working end of the bank and yanked a bug-eyed clerk from his desk. He shoved him toward the big safe. "You'll do. Get busy stuffin' these bags with money."

"We'd better work fast, boss," Evans advised. "That shot's sure to bring the law."

Volker's bandanna masked his nasty smile. "Good. Then we won't have to waste time huntin' them down."

Muffled, yet recognizable yells of alarm came from other businesses. A man in shirtsleeves ran from the haberdashery. "Help! I'm being robbed."

A second later, a sharp report ended his appeal for aid. The clothing merchant staggered in the middle of the street, went rubber-legged and fell in a heap. From the general mercantile came the cymbal crash of disturbed galvanized washtubs and buckets. Moments later, two masked men swaggered out onto the street. One clutched a fat cloth bag. Behind them, the proprietor appeared in the doorway, a shotgun in his hands.

Swiftly he brought the weapon to his shoulder and fired. He had been too hasty. Only three pellets entered the back of the robber with the loot. Most of the shot tore into the cloth sack. It erupted in shreds; coin and paper currency flew in all directions. Three of the gang, left to cover the street, turned their revolvers on the storekeeper and cut him down in a hail of lead. Most of the nasty work had been done by then. Two-thirds of the Yurian gang had gathered in the middle of the block, ready to ride out.

At last, Hub and his cohort stepped out of the bank, arms filled with canvas money satchels. "All right, boys, mount up," Hub called.

Belatedly the law showed up in the person of Sheriff Hutchins and two deputies. Hub slung the drawstrings of his money pouches over his saddle horn and turned to respond to the warning shot and the shouted demand to surrender.

Filling his hand with the Merwin and Hulbert, he triggered a round that nicked a nasty gouge along the point of the sheriff's shoulder. To his left, another member of the gang threw a hasty shot at one of the deputies. Then bullets flew from both sides. The sheriff took cover behind a rain barrel and fired around one side.

Gundersen, a chubby outlaw originally from Norway, grunted and clutched his belly. Hub shouted to the man closest to Gundersen. "Give him a hand getting mounted. We've got to get outta here."

In the next instant, Hub Volker saw his chance and raised the Merwin and Hulbert to sighting position. He squeezed off a shot and watched in satisfaction as the bullet struck the sheriff full in the mouth. A spray of blood, bone, hair and tissue erupted from the back of the lawman's head.

By then, the shock had worn off some of the townsmen. A new crackle of gunfire rippled down the street. One of those offering resistance was the mayor, Lester Norton. Determined to contain them until the law and volunteers could act, he alternately fired and ducked from obstruction to obstruction as he steadily advanced on the gang. He was in midstride when a bullet fired by Evans smashed into his right shoulder and knocked the Winchester from his hands. Wisely, he went down and played dead. The gang had had enough. Ducking low, the final few swung into their saddles.

Firing wildly, the outlaws put spurs to their horses and thundered along the main street while citizens ducked and shot blindly back. Two men from the Sorry Place saloon ran to the side of the sheriff and knelt to give him aid. They soon saw that he needed none.

One of them immediately lost his breakfast. The other stood and cursed the outlaws as they stormed out of town. Only a scatter of stray shots pursued them. In a minute, except for a thin dust cloud, nothing marked their presence at all.

In the aftermath, while the wounded received care and the dead were carried off to the undertaking and used furniture parlor, Boyne Kelso sought out Mayor Norton. He found the mayor being patched up by Doc Vogt outside Harbinson's General Mercantile. Arranging his features into his best expression of concern and outrage, he took the mayor aside to the saloon-bar of the hotel. There, amid much hand wringing and gesticulating, he poured out his prepared spiel.

"Lester, I am deeply concerned by this. Why, only a handful of volunteers went out as a posse, led by our least experienced deputy. The sheriff is dead, and Grover Larsen is cowering at home, afraid the outlaws will come back. What I said about the stage robbery only last Friday goes double for this assault on our very homes."

Lester Norton cut his eyes to Boyne Kelso in a

sideways glance. "You mean you'll put up a thousand dollar reward?"

Kelso mopped his brow and took a long pull on his cup of coffee. "Yes, of course. Two thousand if that is what it takes. I've talked to Ralph at the bank. He's president now, I suppose. They'll put up money for the reward also. Eb Harbinson is still picking up cartwheels and gold eagles, but he offered a hundred. Got most of his back, even if they did kill his father. But the point is not that."

Norton took a swallow of coffee. "What is it?"

Kelso polished off the last in his cup and poured for both of them. "What is most important is that we must reinforce the law in this town. We have to find a replacement for Walt Hutchins immediately. We both know that Larsen is too old for his job. He's slow and the sound of gunfire frightens him. He needs to be replaced as well as the sheriff. Believe me, until we do, this town is terribly vulnerable." His warning was not lost on Mayor Norton.

Since early morning it had been building. Smoke Jensen kept a watchful eye on the towering clouds to the southwest. Slowly they progressed across the eastern downslopes of the Rocky Mountains and spread out across the high plains country. The storm had all the looks of a vicious, straight-line squall. Among land-born storms, such a phenomenon ranked second only to a tornado in ferocity. Smoke had encountered only four in all his years in the High Lonesome. One of the old fraternity of mountain men had tried to explain it to him once.

"It happens when a whole passel of cold air spills down the face of the mountains to collide with warm, moist air slidin' up from hotter country in Texas and New Mexico and the desert of Chihuahua," Smoke had been told. "When they impact it births tre—men—dous thunderstorms, Wal, boy, hail, lightnin' an' goose-drowner rains roar across the prairie. Sometimes some of them form slightly concave straight-line winds of fearsome velocity," old Spec Dawes had continued his description to a rapt Smoke Jensen. "Like their big brothers, the twisters, they can strip the roof off a building, lift a cow off its hooves and drive straws through a tree trunk.

"Anything movable, an' a lot that ain't," Smoke had been told, "is driven ahead of the powerful blast rather than being lifted into the sky. Bowled over and rolled like a chile's ball, a man can easily be reduced to a pulpy bag of broken bones."

Memory of that description, and the storms he had actually experienced, made a tiny flicker of unease in Smoke's mind. It also kept him extra watchful.

Shortly before the nooning, the light zephyrs that had brushed the manes and tails of their horses dropped abruptly, then picked up as a stronger breeze from a slightly different quarter. Smoke frowned and again cut his eyes to the dust cloud. What he saw decided him to ride ahead a ways and look for a sheltered gully or basin where they could hold the remounts and wait out the storm. His search proved harder than he had expected.

Two miles ahead he found a ravine that was too small. Determined, he rode on. Cougar began to sense the change in the atmosphere. He rolled big, blue eyes and snorted, his ears twitched, his tail swished nervously, and his spotted rump writhed as though snakes crawled under it. Another mile went by without any likely spot. Smoke had about decided to turn back after covering what he estimated to be half a mile more. Then he saw it.

Sunlight cast stark shadows over a cut in a hill. A fold, eroded into the rising mound, lay behind. Perfect, Smoke saw when he entered. The high side of the bluff lay between the direction of the storm and the small, closed valley formed by rushing water in ancient days. At once he turned back to lead the horses there.

"There's shelter ahead that we can use," Smoke told Harkness when he returned to the gather of animals. He cast a precautionary gaze at the approaching storm. "If we have time, that is."

Over the next hour the dingy brown mass swirling in the air extended upward and out over the drovers as they worked Smoke's horses toward the sheltered valley. The stout breeze stiffened into a harsh wind, chill and turbulent. Uprooted sagebrush bounded along the ground. Small dust devils formed and raised dirt, leaves, and pebbles into the air, only to dissipate and spew their content across the faces of the men and the coats of their mounts.

Steadily the force increased. Invisible hands

tugged at the sheepskin coat Smoke Jensen had shrugged into when the temperature had dropped drastically. The gale acquired a voice. Shrill and eerily mournful, it moaned around the ears of the ranch hands. Riderless, the remounts flicked their ears in agitation. It would not take much more to spook them, Smoke knew, and only a third of them had been driven into the narrow passage that led to the valley beyond.

Suddenly the western horizon washed a blinding white. Sheet lightning sizzled and crackled through the air, followed by a cataclysmic bellow of thunder. Caught in the strobing effect, the legs of the half-broken horses went all akimbo. For a second they appeared to skid in place. Then they broke in every direction. Panic reigned as the straight-line, cyclonic storm slammed into them. Rapidly the remounts ran before the punishing tumult. At once the men went after them.

With only a third of the two hundred horses headed into the little valley, the hands had no choice but to pursue. Battered by rain blown nearly horizontal, the Sugarloaf riders streamed helplessly after the frightened critters. Blinded by the huge, silver streaks that fell with sodden determination, they made poor headway against the vicious bursts of frigid air. Realizing the impossibility of it, Smoke Jensen shouted himself hoarse in an effort to call back his men.

Slowly they gave up, knowing that they would have an even harder time recovering the animals after the storm had blown beyond them. Together they sought shelter in the valley along

with Smoke. Above their heads the sky turned
an ominous black.

In half an hour the trailing edge of the storm
spattered itself out on the leaves of cottonwoods
that ringed the valley. With Caleb Noonan left
behind to watch over the sixty horses that had
not fled the storm, the rest set out to search for
the scattered remounts. Smoke had no doubt
that they had a long, hard task ahead of them.

"We'll spread out and work in circles," he
suggested. "Bring them back as you find them."

After a fruitless afternoon of search, Smoke
had a flash of inspiration. While the others
speared chunks of fatback from tin plates and
chewed glumly, he outlined his idea.

"Tomorrow morning we're going to try it another way. Luke, I want you to go back to that
valley after you eat. Bring up a couple of mares.
It would be best if you can bag at least one that
is in season."

Grinning riders cut their eyes from Smoke to
one another in knowing glances. So long as the
wind held from the southwest, that would sure
as shootin' work. Smoke came to his boots and
went to the nearby stream to scrub his plate
clean with sand. Luke Britton left with a good
two hours' light remaining.

Later, with the sun only a pink memory on
thin bands of purple clouds in the west, the
tired hands rolled up to rest until morning.
Smoke Jensen sat alone, smoking a cigar beyond
the glow of dying coals. Lost in deep thought,

his reverie was not disturbed even by the mournful hoot of an owl in a pine nearby.

Luke Britton considered himself lucky to find one mare in heat. He brought back three others, and wily horse experts, Jerry Harkness and Utah Jack Grubbs, offered advice on how to make the most advantage of this. What they came up with required a rather indelicate procedure involving some old cheesecloth from a side of bacon and a bit of messy work around the tail end of each mare. When they had finished, Smoke sent the dozen men out in groups of three.

Within half an hour, Jerry Harkness rode in with a dozen snorting, skittering young stallions in tow, led by ropes around their necks. He gave Smoke a cheery wave. "It worked, all right. What do we do with them now?"

"I'll hold them here. Go on back and find me some more. Ah—Jerry, you did good. Any more on the way?"

"Sure enough. Jeff is about twenty minutes behind me. He has a string of twenty."

Smoke brightened. "At this rate, we might be on the trail again by this time tomorrow."

Sunlight twinkled down on the puddles in the ranch yard thirty miles to the northeast of Muddy Gap. Elmer Godwin looked out from the barn, where he had been mucking out stalls. He liked working for Sven Olsen, an even-handed, fair-minded man who paid well and whose young wife set a good table. He also had a true friend in Sven's oldest son, Tommy. A gangling orphan in his late teens, Elmer had grown close to Tommy over the past nine months he had worked for the Olsens.

During that time, they had trapped for furs, and he had taken Tommy hunting, fishing, and even bare-bottom swimming in the coppery brown, shallow water of the Platte River. Still a kid at heart, Elmer had enjoyed it every bit as much as Tommy. His reflection ended when the subject of his thoughts called from inside the barn.

"Awh, c'mon, Elmer, I ain't gonna do this all alone."

Elmer turned back. "Jist catchin' a breather an' a cup of water from the pump."

Tommy Olsen appeared in the open barn door. Big for his age, he was a sturdy, stocky boy with a shock of auburn hair and a mask of freckles that covered both round cheeks. He examined Elmer with clear, blue eyes that twinkled with intelligence.

"We goin' swimmin' after this is done?"

Elmer grinned. "Sure are, Tommy. We'll take along a bar of soap, wash off this stink."

"Wheewu! You tellin' me. The pigs are worst. Be glad when that's over."

Before Elmer could make answer, he stiffened and cocked an ear to the distance. "Quiet," he cautioned. "Someone's coming."

Tommy's eyes went wide. "Is it Injuns?"

Turning his head to better hear, Elmer frowned. "Don't think so. Hoofbeats are too regular. Like soldiers riding." That reminded Elmer of something else. Over the last two months he had heard a lot of talk about bandit raids. "Tommy, let's go to the house. We have to tell your mother and sisters. Then you take a gun and go with them to the root cellar. I'll fetch your paw."

Reunited with his gang, Reno Jim Yurian led them up the lane to the Olsen ranch. When they reached the barnyard, they spread out and advanced on the house. Reno Jim raised his hat with his left hand, his right on the pearl grip of his six-gun.

"Hello the house. Your best chance is to come on out and not show any fight. Otherwise, someone is going to get hurt."

In answer, a rifle barrel slid through a firing loop in a thick wooden shutter that had been hastily closed. "Git off this place, mister, or it'll be you who is hurtin'."

It was a young voice, a boy not yet out of his teens, Jim Yurian correctly surmised. He had never met Elmer Godwin, yet he could clearly visualize him. Scrawny, scared out of his boots, perhaps his father gone for the day, his hands shaking so much he could not draw a good bead. With exaggerated slowness, Reno Jim drew his nickle-plated Merwin and Hulbert .44 and pointed it roughly in the direction of the window.

You've had your warning, boy. Now you and everyone else come out of there."

Fear pushed young Elmer to incautiousness. "You can go to hell!"

Reno Jim put a shot into the wooden shutter an inch above the rifle barrel. At once the other outlaws began to blaze away. Suddenly one of them gave a startled yell and pitched forward over the neck of his horse. The tight circle of hard cases blew apart.

Gunmen spun their mounts while others rode out to ring the house. Those who had turned saw a stocky man kneeling in the doorway of the barn, a rifle to his shoulder. He fired as his presence registered on the gang. Three of them threw shots at him, all of which missed. Sven Olsen did not.

His next round clipped the hat from the head of Prine Gephart and cut a bloody gouge along the crown of his scalp. Wavering in his saddle, Gephart let his mount amble him away from the line of fire. Dazed, he indistinctly saw the demise of the valiant rancher through a haze of red, as blood washed down his forehead and into his eyes.

Half a dozen more bullets crashed into the barn door. Two of them struck Sven Olsen in the chest and abdomen. Knocked from his kneeling position, he sprawled, his Winchester inches from his outstretched hand. A wave of dizziness swept over the rancher. He blinked and bit his lip against the pain in his belly. Gradually it numbed to a low throb. Dimly he saw the outlaws abandon him for already dead and turn back to the house. Elmer was in there alone, the dying man thought in desperation.

A rain of slugs battered the Olsen house. Chunks of wood splintered away from the shutters, and the rifle barrel withdrew. Only to reappear at another window. Impatient at this stubborn resistance, Reno Jim dismounted and gestured to three others to join him. They ran to the porch, where they were in under the field of fire from the window.

Reno Jim saw a sturdy bench against the outer wall and produced a grim smile. "Here we go, boys. Grab hold of this bench and we'll batter down that door."

With four strong men on the task, the portal rang and shuddered at each impact. After ten stout crashes, the crossbar began to yield. It splintered at first, then cracked loudly. Another push and the door flew inward.

Two outlaws, followed by Reno Jim, burst into the room. They caught movement to one side and swung their hot-barreled six-guns toward it. Reno Jim proved faster than any of his men. Coolly, he raised his .44 Merwin and Hulbert and shot Elmer Godwin through one lung and his heart.

Without another glance at the youth he had murdered, Reno Jim issued crisp orders. "All right. Clear out anything of value, then set this place afire." Out on the porch, he called to the remainder of the gang. "You boys round up all the stock and head 'em up. We'll drive them to Bent Rock Canyon with the rest."

Four

Two days after the raid on the Olsen Ranch, Smoke Jensen and his hands rode into Muddy Gap. At first they did not understand the furtive, nervous, and downright suspicious glances afforded them by the residents. They got a clearer idea when they began to note bullet holes and scars on the building fronts, and above the town, on a knoll not yet fenced and consecrated for the purpose, fresh graves in what would be the town's cemetery.

Smoke Jensen passed on his observation to Utah Jack Grubbs. "Looks like these folks have run into some trouble of late."

"Injuns, do you think?" Utah Jack offered.

"From the looks of all the bullet holes and the scared way the folks have been looking at us, I'd say white men. Outlaws from one gang or another."

Utah Jack discounted that. "Surely they have some law in this town. That the place ain't shot up worse than it is, I'd say whoever it was, they got run out real fast."

Smoke shrugged. "You may be right, Utah. We'll find out soon enough." He nodded ahead in the street, to where half a dozen armed men stood resolutely, weapons at the ready. They formed a wedge that denied passage to anyone not at a full gallop. At the head stood a man with a bandaged right shoulder.

When Smoke and his hands came within twenty feet, that man raised his arm to signal a halt. "That's far enough, strangers. Who are you?" He shifted uneasily. "And what's your business in Muddy Gap?"

Smoke Jensen did not answer directly. "Looks like you had some trouble here lately."

A frown creased the mayor's brow. "And how do we know you're not the ones who caused it? Besides, you haven't answered my question."

Smoke went unfazed. "My fault. M'name's Jensen; I'm from the Sugarloaf horse ranch in Colorado. These are some of my hands. We're driving a herd of remounts to Fort Custer."

Mayor Norton's frown deepened to a scowl. "You're going on the Crow Reservation with only four men?"

A light smile brightened Smoke's face. "Nope. The rest are holding the herd outside town."

Norton cradled the shotgun in the crook of his right arm, winced at the pain in his shoulder, and scratched his head with his left hand. "Jensen, you say? Might you be any relation to a fellow named Smoke Jensen?"

"Might be and am. Folks have called me Smoke for a long time."

Hope flickered momentarily on the face of Lester Norton. He took a step forward, extended a hand. "Mayor Lester Norton. My pleasure. It's said that you have been a lawman for many years now. A U.S. marshal?"

"Deputy, yes."

"Are you still carrying a badge, Mr. Jensen?"

"Not at the moment."

A raucous bray came from one of the saloons. On top of it came a yelp of protest in a decidedly feminine voice. Smoke cut his eyes that direction for a moment. Mayor Norton looked that way also, his glower even more thunderous. He made an inviting gesture to Smoke Jensen.

"I would be obliged if you would accompany me to the Iron Kettle, Mr. Jensen. There is something important I wish to discuss with you over a cup of coffee."

Smoke shrugged. "Fine with me. We came in for supplies. That won't take a lot of time. You boys might as well come along," he told Jerry Harkness and his hands. "Load up on some real grub for once."

Walking their horses to a tie rail, the Sugarloaf party went with the mayor to the corner cafe. Once inside, Jerry and the other hands took a separate table. Smoke seated himself across from Mayor Norton. His gaze took in the blue-checkered, lace-trimmed curtains at the window, the row of shiny copper molds on a shelf above the back counter and a sturdy potbelly stove at the center of the rear wall. A serving window under the shelf gave a view of the kitchen beyond. A still-trim woman who might have been in her early thirties brought them coffee without being told. When she had served them and gone to take the orders of the ranch hands, the mayor leaned across the table and spoke with some urgency. Smoke could smell his pitch a mile off.

"We're in trouble here. Over the five days

since those outlaws raided town, half the riffraff in the territory have drifted into town. It wouldn't take much of a spark, or a whole lot of smarts, on the part of some to make a move to take over the town. We need you, or someone like you, to clean the trash out of Muddy Gap."

"Why not have the sheriff take care of it?"

"Sheriff Hutchins was killed by the bandits. We buried him two days ago up on the hill out there."

"You have a town marshal, don't you?"

Mayor Norton looked Smoke Jensen square in the eye. "Marshal Grover Larsen is too busy hiding under his bed to help us against this glut of ne'er-do-wells."

"But, why me? I have a herd of horses to take care of. I have a contract and a deadline to meet."

"First off, because I have heard that you are a fair and honest man, a top-notch lawman, regardless of the wanted posters and what they say. Secondly, you have acquired some notoriety as a gunfighter. Third, because you are here, we don't waste time we may not have sending for someone. Lastly, because the town can pay handsomely for your services. Can't your hands take care of the horses for a while, even a few days. Surely you can clean them out in less than a week."

"I could, given some help."

Lester Norton glowed with expectation. "Then you'll undertake to do it?"

Smoke drained the last of his coffee and came to his boots. Leaning toward the mayor, he made his decision. "I'm sorry, Mr. Mayor. I'm not your man. We can't be late at Fort Custer or the army will not pay for our horses."

Smoke Jensen started for the door when a choked, frightened cry for help came from outside. The voice was that of a woman.

After brooding for a week over his humiliation by that snotty twist of a schoolmarm, Brandon Kelso saw the opportunity to gain his revenge. In the aftermath of the bandit raid on Muddy Gap, as more and more frontier trash moseyed into town, the thought came that he and his friends could get away with just about anything.

Sheriff Hutchins was dead, his deputies out on the trail of the gang that had robbed every store in town, and Marshal Larsen had taken to bed, complaining of a terrible gripe. His chance came unexpectedly on the day Smoke Jensen rode into town. It being a Saturday, Prissy Missy Parkins had no duties around the school. Instead, she had come out of her small house and walked to the center of town to purchase her needs for the week to come. She entered Blackmun's Ladies' Fashions first. Brandon quickly summoned his two willing accomplices.

They watched from the mouth of an alley as Virginia Parkins went from store to store. Her last stop, Harbinson's General Mercantile, coincided with the arrival of Smoke and his hands. Brandon Kelso paid scant attention to the strangers and the confrontation with the mayor. Intent on his prey, he had eyes only for Ginny Parkins.

When she came out of the general store, her

arms filled with packages, Brandon and his two loutish friends stepped out onto the boardwalk and formed a semicircle around her, Ginny looked up startled.

Braying in self-generated contempt, Brandon leaned close to her. "Sorry you tried to make a fool out of me now, you dried up sow?"

Although caught off guard, Ginny's quick wit came to her aid. "I never tried to make a fool of you, Brandon. You do quite well at that all by yourself. Now, please get out of my way."

Emboldened, Brandon reached out and gave her a shove. "You ain't goin' nowhere, you bitch. Not until we say you can. What a sorry waste of a woman you are." He cocked a sarcastic pose, one eyebrow elevated. "Never had a man, have you?"

"You vulgar gutter snipe, that is none of your business," Ginny answered hotly.

Brandon chortled, then spoke through a sneer. "Yup. You ain't never had a man. Bet you're a shriveled prune . . . know what I mean?"

"You filthy animal. Your father will hear of this." Ginny wished she had a free hand. She would slap the face of this impudent, odious, degenerate around on the other side of his head. Then, remembering the switch she had used on them at the school, her higher, moral self sternly chided her. *Bite your tongue, girl. Violence never really settled anything.* Ginny had only a second to rethink her outburst.

Stepping forward the three brutes snatched the packages and string net bag from her arms. Laughing nastily, they hurled the parcels into the street. Hooting in derision, they stepped off the boardwalk and began to kick and stomp her purchases. Paper bags burst, to spray flour and salt. Eggs splattered and ran yellow out into the dust to be absorbed. Three onions went flying.

Enjoying himself immensely, Brandon hauled back a booted foot and kicked a head of cabbage with such force it went flying through a second-floor window of the Wilber House Hotel across the street. Ginny Parkins gathered herself and put hands to the sides of her mouth.

"Stop that! Please stop. Someone help me. Please help me."

By that time, three drunken pieces of human debris had come out of the Sorry Place saloon to see what was going on. Brandon, carried away by his success so far, and seeking to impress the saddle tramps, spun back on one boot heel and snarled as he raised a hand as though to strike her. "Shut up, you bitch."

At that moment, Smoke Jensen stepped out onto the street. He instantly took in the tableau before him. His cold, gold-brown gaze fixed on Ginny as she cringed back and raised a hand defensively. Aroused by her helplessness, Brandon and his sidekicks took two quick steps toward her, the destruction of her groceries forgotten, and closed around her, their hands raised again. Laughing, the trio of worthless frontier rubbish joined them, and they began to push Ginny around the circle from one to another.

When she screamed again, Brandon brought up his ham hand to strike her in the face.

Suddenly an iron-hard grip encircled Brandon's wrist. His eyes bulged with the effort as he tried to move and found he could not.

It took Smoke Jensen only three long, swift strides to reach the scene of the shameful encounter. He lashed out with an arm and closed steely fingers around a thick wrist and squeezed. He encountered resistance and applied more pressure. At once, the hand of the punk he held in his grasp turned snowy, then began to swell and flush a dark red.

Let go! Leggo me!" Brandon Kelso wailed two octaves above his normal register.

Smoke Jensen yanked him around and drove a hard right fist into the pouting lips of Brandon Kelso. Blood flew and a tooth cracked. Kelso went slack in the knees. Smoke indifferently pushed him aside. Brandon sprawled face-first into the dirt. Smoke faced the three riffraff.

"Leave, if you don't want to hurt for a long time," he advised. "Leave town if you don't want to stay here forever, out on that hill above us."

Two of them still possessed enough sobriety to actually glance over their shoulders at the mounds of bare earth that covered seven graves. "Oh, yeah," the third, more inebriated one sneered. "Who do you think you are?"

Calmly, Smoke answered him. "Oh, I *know* who I am."

Jist who is that?"

With a nasty, deadly smile, Smoke answered him. "Folks call me Smoke Jensen. I'm the new sheriff in Muddy Gap."

"Oh, God," one of the less intoxicated blurted.

White-faced with sudden terror, his partner gasped and gulped and staggered to the edge of the boardwalk, where he bent over the tie rail and gave up his burden of beer. Gripped by the certain presence of sure, swift death, he bleated miserably to his companions.

"C'mon fellas, let's get out of here."

Quickly they stumbled away. Behind them, Brandon Kelso dragged himself to his boots. He looked confused at the departing backs of the saddle trash. He raised appealing hands to them.

"Come back. What's so important about who this peckerwood happens to be?"

Over his shoulder, one of them answered him. "Because he is Smoke Jensen, that's why."

Brandon looked down at his hands, then cut his eyes to Smoke. "That don't mean nothin' to me," he muttered and then charged.

Smoke Jensen squared off and met him with a solid left-right combination that rocked Brandon's head back, pink spittle flying from already split and bleeding lips. Brandon let go a wide, looping right, which Smoke blocked easily. Then the last mountain man stepped in and began a snare drum tattoo on the soft, pulpy belly of his opponent.

Brandon gulped and grunted. Eyes wild, pain flaming in them, he turned his head to appeal to his friends. "Wal, don't just stand there. Jump in an' help me."

Young Danny Collins held back, while Willie Finch, always in the sway of Brandon Kelso, and filled with false bravado, leaped forward to join the fray. Less than a second later, he began to regret it.

Smoke rapped Brandon in the mouth again and pivoted sideways to Willie, cocked back at the hips and drew up his right leg. When Willie Finch charged within range, Smoke unleashed that leg in a lightning strike. The flat of Smoke's boot sole caught Willie in the belly. Its force drove the boy back, doubled over, cheeks puffed out by the force of the wind knocked from him. Thin, green, bitter gorge rose up from his throat and spilled onto his shirt. Darkness danced before his eyes. Smoke turned back to young Kelso. Grinning, he made inviting gestures to draw the lout in closer.

"C'mon, you want more, don't you?"

"You bet your butt, mister. I ain't afraid of you."

"You ought to be," Smoke advised him.

"Oh, yeah? What for?"

Smoke shook his head sadly. "You just don't get it, do you? I've killed a hundred better men than you'll ever grow up to be. Now, get out of here, you little turd, before I break something serious."

"Like hell!"

By then, Willie Finch had recovered his courage and leaped on Smoke's back. Momentarily pinning Smoke's arms to his sides, he yelled in the gunfighter's ear. "I got him, Bran. I got him good."

Danny Collins found his nerve and waded in also. He landed two good blows to Smoke's side and belly; then Brandon was there. Before the leader of this collection of misfits could swing, he received one of Smoke's kicks. This one square in the crotch. With a shrug, Smoke broke Willie's hold and flung the thin boy away to slam into the front of the barbershop. With a soft groan, Willie slid down the clapboard wall of the tonsorial parlor.

Smoke turned at once to make a quick end of Danny Collins. He did it with a pair of swift, hard punches to the boy's face. Danny groaned and went down like he had been shot. Smoke gave his attention to Brandon Kelso.

Bent over, Brandon wheezed, gagged and moaned in blind agony. Knock-kneed with pain, he walked like a shackled duck toward escape across the far side of the street. Smoke Jensen stalked after him and closed in four swift strides. He put a hard hand on one shoulder and spun Brandon Kelso to face him.

Soft, deadly menace rang in Smoke's voice. "The lady is waiting for an apology."

"No—" sputter-wheeze—"way I'll do that."

"You want more, then?"

For the first time, Brandon's belligerence broke. He winced and cringed away from Smoke's intimidation. "No. No, man. But I ain't gonna apologize."

Smoke took Brandon's nose between his left index and middle finger and squeezed. With a good yank, he brought the lout along with him to where Virginia Parkins stood, hands over her eyes. Smoke tipped his hat and spoke politely.

"Ma'am, this pitiful piece of human garbage has something to say to you."

"No, I . . ." Smoke squeezed the nose.

"Eeeh—eeeh! Yes-yes. I'm sure sorry we busted up your stuff, Miz Parkins."

"And you will pay for their replacement, right?"

Another tweak of the nose. "Yes. Yes, I will."

"Dig it out, then."

Brandon Kelso fought back tears as he reached into his pocket. He brought out a fistful of coins. Smoke looked up at Virginia Parkins and then cut his eyes to her ruined purchases. "How much did this cost you, ma'am?"

She told him, and Smoke plucked the proper amount from Brandon's open hand. He handed it to Ginny, then turned Brandon by his nose and planted a boot across the junior thug's buttocks and sent him on his way. He returned to the boardwalk and looked up to see the mayor standing, openmouthed, staring at him. Smoke reached out his hand.

"Well, Mr. Mayor, I think I'll take that badge you offered. Looks like you have a need here, right enough."

"Thank you, Mr. Jensen, thank you from the bottom of my heart. But—what about your herd."

Smoke Jensen looked beyond the mayor to see his top hand standing there grinning. "Jerry, you take the herd on for a few days. I'll catch up before the end of the week."

"Right, boss. Say, you do good work, Smoke."

Mayor Norton led the way to the sheriff's office and jail. There he showed Smoke around and further explained the situation in Muddy

Gap. In particular he apprised Smoke of the names of the local boys he had taken down a notch minutes earlier. While they talked, Boyne Kelso stormed into the room. Fury exploded out of him.

"Mayor, I demand that the man who beat up my son and robbed him be arrested at once." He cut his eyes from Norton to Smoke, noted the badge and jabbed a long finger at him. "Well? What are you waiting for? If you're the new lawman I've heard about, you had better start earning your keep. I want that saddle bum arrested and jailed."

Smoke provided him a sarcastic grin. 'I'm afraid that is impossible. You see, I'm that 'saddle bum.' "

Kelso's jaw sagged a moment, then he regained his self-righteous outrage. "Lester, I can't believe you've hired a thief to replace Sheriff Hutchins."

"I haven't," Mayor Norton told him blandly. "This is Smoke Jensen. He is a former deputy U.S. marshal. And your boy was tormenting Miss Ginny."

"I don't believe it. Brandon is a good boy. He would never do such a thing."

Smoke took it up. "You had better believe it, Mr. Kelso. He and two other oafs assaulted the schoolteacher, took her packages from her and destroyed the contents. When your brat made to strike her, I intervened. The money I took was to replace what they had destroyed."

Indignation filled Kelso. "You can't do this. I'm Boyne Kelso. And, my son is . . . my son."

Smoke's eyes narrowed dangerously. "Are you

implying that you, too, assault women and ravage their property?"

Astounded, Kelso's mouth worked for a second before he could find words. "What impudence. I'm warning you . . ."

Smoke moved like a striking rattler. He crossed the short space between himself and Kelso with two strides and took the outraged man by the front of his shirt. With seemingly no effort, he shoved the portly body back against the closed door with enough force to knock the air from the blustering Kelso.

No, Mr. Kelso, I'm warning you. If that misbegotten piece of garbage you call your son so much as spits on the boardwalk, I'll coldcock him with my Colt and drag him to jail. From here on, he—and you—will be on the best possible behavior. Now get out of here and let me do my job."

Once Smoke saw the horses on their way, he waded into cleaning up Muddy Gap. His first target was the saloon out of which the drunken trash had come to join in tormenting the attractive young schoolteacher. Word had preceded him, Smoke discovered the moment he entered the barroom.

"Well, what do we got here?" a truculent voice demanded as Smoke strode through the batwings.

"Looks like somebody who don't have any business here," a tall, burly saddle tramp gritted. "Why don't you jist turn around and git the hell out?"

Smoke centered on him. His left arm extended, he shot an accusatory finger at the pugnacious thug. "I want your name. Now!"

Grinning in anticipation of a good brawl, the lout answered. "Rafer Diggins. I'm the meanest, toughest, woolliest he-coon in these parts."

Blandly, Smoke told him, "I doubt that."

With that in the mix, Rafer Diggins let out a roar and charged Smoke Jensen.

Five

Rafer Diggins saw himself as larger than life. A brawler since his early teens, he had never been bested since the day he walloped his brutal, drunken father and ran away from home. A man who stood a good three inches shorter and at least thirty pounds lighter would be an easy mark. Or so thought Rafer Diggins when he launched himself away from the bar.

A laughing companion shouted encouragement. "Go git him, Rafe."

Rafe puffed himself up on fighting rage and deep breaths as he closed on Smoke. The brawny barroom tough cocked a ham fist back by his ear, prepared to knock the lights out of this lawdog. Grinning, Smoke Jensen waited for it.

When the punch came, Smoke did not move his body. He jinked his head to the side, and the fist whistled past. Then he unloaded with a low, right uppercut. It buried to the wrist in the beer gut that leaned vulnerably toward him.

Diggins had time for one groan as his eyes bulged and the air gusted out of his lungs. Then Smoke laid a hard left to the side of the bigger man's jaw. Stars exploded before Rafe Diggins' eyes as his feet went out from under him and he landed on his axe-handle broad rear. He did not stay there long.

With a diminished roar, he sprang to his boots and waded in again. Methodically, Smoke worked at cleaning his clock. A right-left combination halted Rafe's advance. His arms groped ineffectually to get his opponent in a bear hug. Failing that, Rafe threw wide, looping punches that Smoke slipped on the points of his shoulders.

Staggered, Rafe tried a kick. Smoke caught his boot and raised it while he twisted. Pain shot up Rafe's leg, he went off balance and toppled backward. His head made a loud noise as it struck the edge of the bar. Sighing softly, he slumped to the floor and lay with his cheek resting on the lip of a brass spittoon. Confident that it was over, Smoke turned to address the cluster of the remaining trash.

"I want the rest of you out of here and out of town. You have ten minutes."

Before Smoke could continue, Rafe Diggins recovered faster than expected. He bounded off the floor with an enraged bellow; a glint came off a knife he held low in his right hand. Smoke saw it at once and pivoted to evade a straight thrust. Diggins had every intention to gut him like a deer.

Trying a back slash, Diggins bore in with his deadly blade. Smoke considered the alternatives for a moment, then acted as common sense dictated. Quickly he scooped up the leg of a chair broken in the fight. When Diggins lunged again, Smoke brought it down on his right forearm. Bones cracked and Diggins howled in pain. The knife fell from his grasp. At once the experienced brawler went for his six-gun left-handed.

He barely had the barrel clear of leather when Smoke Jensen shot him in the shoulder. Jolted back, Diggins rammed his back into the bar. He stiffened, then sagged in defeat. Smoke reached him in four quick strides. Roughly he slammed the man around and searched him for more hide-out weapons. Then he began to frog-march Diggins out the door and off to jail.

Grumbling, the other frontier debris followed after. Out in the street, Rafe Diggins roused enough to overcome his pain and make one more try. From a leather pouch suspended by a cord down his back, he snatched a straight razor and snapped it open as he made a vicious slash at Smoke Jensen's throat.

Smoke did not even hesitate. The big .45 Colt Peacemaker filled his right hand, and his fingertip lightly tripped the trigger. Rafe Diggins jolted to a stop and looked down disbelievingly at the black hole in the center of his chest that began to leak red. His uninjured arm dropped to his side, and the razor fell from his numb grasp. His face went slack. Slowly he canted forward and began to fall. He landed on his face with a thud, in a viscous puddle of mud. Smoke Jensen stepped over and looked down coldly at the dead man, whose head was a welter of shattered gore. Then he turned his attention to the thoroughly cowed collection of rogues.

"Like I said, I'm posting you out of town. After ten minutes, if any of you are still here, I'll come after you. And, I'm warning you, I will shoot to kill."

In a mad scramble, they left in all directions, like a flock of pigeons with a fox in the barn.

Word of Smoke's accomplishment spread rapidly around town. Aaron Tucker, the owner and daytime bartender at the Sorry Place saloon rushed outside when Smoke passed by to wring his hand and offer praise.

"Let me tell you, Sheriff Jensen, you're doin' a marvelous job. There was some shanty trash hanging around my place. Nothing I did could get rid of them. When they heard of what happened at the Gold Boot, they cleared out without a word."

"Well—ah—thank you."

"I'm Aaron Tucker. I own this place. Anything you want, any time you come in, it's on the house."

"That's not necessary, Mr. Tucker."

"No. I know that. That's why I'm offering it."

"Thank you again."

When he completed his rounds, Smoke returned to the office to find another form of gratitude. A small rectangle of cream-colored note paper lay on his desk. He opened it and read the contents.

"Dear Sheriff Jensen," it read. "I fear that I failed terribly in expressing my gratitude for my rescue at your hand. Violence upsets me, and I had recently been subjected to such shocking indignities, that I quite forgot myself. Please let me make it up to you with an invitation to a late supper this evening. I will expect you at eight o'clock, if that is suitable." The invitation had been signed simply, "Virginia Parkins."

Smoke Jensen puckered his lips as he put the note aside. It would appear the schoolteacher knew her manners after all. What's more, he had always been a sucker for a home-cooked meal. Especially one prepared by such an attractive young woman. Yes, he would enjoy their supper. Images of his Sally, so far away, clouded his anticipation. Smoke looked up to see a small, freckle-faced boy standing expectantly in the open doorway.

His name, Smoke had learned, was Jimmy. He had come by earlier and informed Smoke that he had done odd jobs for the late sheriff. "Like sweep up when the deputies were out on a posse," he had illustrated. Smoke decided to make use of his services now.

"Just a minute, Jimmy. I have something for you to do." Smoke found paper and a worn, steel nib pen in the top drawer. Carefully he drew the letters of his acceptance in a fine copper plate script. He blotted it, folded the sheet in half and extended it to the boy.

"Take this to Miss Parkins, please."

Jimmy's eyes went wide. "Our teacher? What's it about?"

Smoke gave him a brief frown. "That's not for you to know. Here's a dime for your trouble."

He handed a silver coin to the lad, who scampered off on bare feet, puffs of dust left behind by his heels. Then Smoke leaned back to reflect on his progress. Considering he had seven in jail, at least fifteen run out of town, and another on his way to Boot Hill, plus an invitation to supper, Smoke thought he had made a good start at getting a handle on the undesirable element in Muddy Gap. He might be able to rejoin the herd within three days.

"Mr. Jensen, you saved my life, my job and my reputation. I can't thank you enough." Virginia Parkins blushed lightly as she spoke. "Only one thing . . ."

"Yes? And, please, call me Smoke."

"Very well, Smoke. My friends call me Ginny." She took a deep breath and launched into her favorite theme. "I suppose that, all considered, there was no other way of handling that awful situation this morning. It's just that I have devoted my life to ending the violence with which we, as a people, seem obsessed."

Smoke Jensen sat, somewhat ill at ease, on a delicate, velvet-upholstered chair in the parlor of Virginia's tiny house. The rich aroma of a roasting cut of beef came from the cast-iron cookstove in the kitchen. Mingled with it was the unmistakable aroma of a peach pie. Their supper might be late, but far from light. Conscious of the need not to offend her, he carefully weighed his reply.

"You are right about the first part, Ginny. Under the circumstances, the only thing those craven louts would properly respond to was superior force. Bullies like Brandon Kelso take any show of politeness or mild-mannered behavior as a sign of weakness. That's exactly what they feed upon. So, in order to get them to behave in a proper manner, I first had to get their attention."

A slight frown divided the space between her eyebrows vertically. "You certainly did that. What if . . . what if one of them had produced a weapon?"

Smoke shrugged, trying to ease the bluntness his words described. "Then I would have had to shoot that one."

Ginny shivered. "May we speak of something else?"

"Certainly. Muddy Gap is a raw, new town. How many students does that afford you?"

"I have sixteen. From first to eighth grade."

"That's quite a few for a place on the edge of nowhere. My wife was a schoolteacher when I met her."

Again that small grimace of irritation. "Is that so? I'm surprised at her attraction to a lawman."

Smoke chuckled softly. "So was she."

That lightened Ginny's mood. "And were you?"

"Oh, no. I think I fell in love the first time I met Sally. She was, and is, so different than any other woman I had ever encountered. And beautiful, too."

"You are a lucky man, Smoke. To have wooed and won someone whom you feel so strongly about." She rose onto her high-button shoes. "I am sure that roast is ready now. Go on in to the table, I'll have everything on in a minute. All I need do is fix the gravy."

Smoke pulled a teasing expression of being highly impressed. "All that and gravy, too. I feel like a regular guest of honor. Don't tell me you have home-baked bread to sop with."

Ginny suppressed a giggle. "I certainly do."

"Then, let us begin."

Aaron Tucker was unaccustomed to being called back to the Sorry Place at night. His summons came from the night bartender, delivered by the old fellow who worked as a swamper. He showed up on the front porch of the Tucker house at eight-thirty that night.

"Fred says there's trouble brewin', Mr. Tucker. Some of those gunhawks are gettin' drunk and makin' talk about ambushing the new sheriff."

Aaron pursed his lips. "They might find that harder to do than they expect." He sighed heavily. "All right, I'll come."

When they reached the saloon, Aaron Tucker found the situation worse than he had expected. Five surly men lined the bar. Four more sat around a table, cards spread before them for a game of five-card stud. Behind the mahogany, Fred Barnes wore a worried expression. The only friendly face in the saloon was that of Mayor Lester Norton. He nodded a curt greeting to Aaron and cut his eyes around the room.

Aaron saw what he meant. The usual local clientele had been run out, or had not come in at all. Aaron walked up to him. "What brings you out tonight, Les?"

Norton rolled his eyes. "My mother-in-law is visiting. 'Nuf said?"

With his establishment filled with heavily

armed hard cases, Tucker had to force a chuckle. "How long is she going to be here?"

"A week. Or more. There's no telling with her, Aaron." Again he sighed. Then he broached the subject both of them feared. "I thought the new sheriff was working at clearing out this riffraff?"

"He is. Has to rest some time. And eat a meal." Aaron Tucker's admiration for Smoke Jensen had not diminished. "I hear the school-marm invited him to supper."

A chair went back with a loud bang when the back struck the floor. "Barkeep, these cards are greasy. You been storin' 'em with the free lunch?" growled one of the hard cases. "Bring us a new deck."

Fred Barnes shrugged and made a helpless gesture. "That is a new deck."

Aaron gave a nervous glance. "I think we need Sheriff Jensen. Les, will you—ah—will you go prevail upon him to come down here?"

Mayor Norton pushed away from the far end of the bar. "Sure, Aaron. The sooner we rid our town of this sort, the better. It won't take long to get him."

Smoke Jensen and Virginia Parkins sat in her parlor, sipping coffee and letting their meal set-tle. Smoke felt a minor discomfort at her prox-imity. He should have brought someone along, maybe the mayor. Or, Ginny should have pro-vided a third party. He felt a twinge of relief, then, when a knock sounded at the door. Ginny excused herself to answer. She came back with the mayor in tow.

Lester Norton did not waste a moment. "Mr. Jensen, it is certain that trouble is brewing at the Sorry Place. There are a number of ruffians gathered there. They've made talk of bushwhacking you."

Frowning, Smoke Jensen came to his boots. "They just lost their chance. Excuse me, Miss Ginny, it appears I have more to do before I can settle down at the jail."

Virginia came to him, put an admonitory hand on his forearm. "Be careful, Smoke. Surely they will be reasonable. Like those others who left town on their own?"

"I wouldn't . . . ," Mayor Norton started to blurt, only to stop at the hard look on Smoke's face.

Smoke filled the gap. "What the mayor means is that he wouldn't worry if he were you." Then to Norton, "Shall we go? This shouldn't take long."

Virginia still looked concerned and unconvinced. "Please—let me know how it comes out."

Smoke smiled. "I'll stop by before making my last rounds." He started for the door.

"We'll have pie," Ginny called after him.

It had all been worked out while the mayor had been absent from the saloon. The four men who had been playing cards now stood at the rear of the room, their backs to the wall. The five hard cases who lined the bar had spread out. They eyed the batwing doors intently, marking the time. Aaron Turner had gone behind the bar. One hand hovered over a hefty bung starter.

Mayor Norton entered the saloon first, nearly precipitating a fusillade. Two of the gunmen at the rear actually unlimbered their six-guns. Smoke Jensen came in a moment behind the mayor, his .45 Colt leading the way. He shot first one, then the other man who had drawn their weapons. Deliberately aimed high, the heavy slugs slammed into their shoulders. Two Colt Frontier models thudded in the sawdust on the rough-hewn floor.

In the next second, Smoke Jensen roughly shoved Lester Norton to the floor, and the air rocked to the roar of eight blazing six-guns. Smoke shot one of the trash at the bar and dived into a roll that took him halfway across the room. He came up with bullets cutting the air to both sides and over his head. Another quick shot and a would-be ambusher went down screaming, his kneecap shattered. Smoke raised his six-gun and fired again.

A fifth saddle tramp groaned and left the fight, shot through the right side an inch above his hip bone. Smoke dived behind an over-turned table and expended his last two rounds. Another man in the back of the room sprang backward and collided discordantly with the up-right piano. Smoke's final slug destroyed half of the top octave. The strings pinged musically as the lead snapped them.

Smoke holstered his right-hand revolver and reached for his second Peacemaker, worn high on his left side, butt forward and slanted across his hard, flat stomach. A slug from one of the hard cases at the bar clipped the hat from his head. He returned the favor with a bullet that struck the face of the cylinder in the offending six-gun.

Hot needles of pain shot through the shooter's hand, and he let go of his damaged weapon. Another tried to work his way around to Smoke's blind side. He made three side steps along the bar and stopped suddenly when Aaron Turner rapped him smartly on the top of his head with a bung starter. The gunhawk crashed to the floor with a meteor shower behind his eyes.

Alone in a reign of such fury, the remaining hard case chose wisdom over pain. He reversed the revolver and offered it to Smoke butt first. Far too wise in the ways of gunhandling, Smoke did not fall for that one. Instead he gestured toward the green baize top of a poker table.

"Lay it down there. Do it or I'll shoot you anyway." Smoke turned to where the mayor remained sprawled on the floor. "Now, Mr. Mayor, if you'd be so kind as to help me take this garbage out of here and lock them up."

"What's the charge?" complained the one with the red, swollen, throbbing hand.

"Assaulting a peace officer, for a start. Maybe the territorial attorney can make attempted murder stick."

Fear loosened the brigand's tongue. "No, man, I swear, no. We didn't intend to kill you, just bust you up a little and run you out of town. Nobody said a thing about killing. I swear it."

Coolly, Aaron Turner put in his contribution.

"He lies." He nodded to the one Smoke had killed. "That one stood right here and said they would bury you come tomorrow. They all thought it a good idea. The mouthy one there said something about drilling you tonight and planting you in the morning."

Smoke Jensen stopped in his roundup of the casualties. "Say, I wanted to thank you for your timely assistance. You're pretty handy with that thing."

Turner looked down at the bung starter in his hand and back at Smoke. He smiled shyly, and his ears colored. "Oh, this. I get a lot of practice."

Smoke nodded. "Might be you won't have near as much for some while." With that he and the mayor started off with their prisoners.

Before making his last rounds of the business district of Muddy Gap, Smoke Jensen returned to the small house owned by Ginny Parkins. He found it dark. *Odd,* he thought. *She said we'd have pie when I returned.* He raised one hand and rapped knuckles lightly on the front door. Silence answered him. He knocked again, a bit louder.

A floor board creaked behind the closed portal and Smoke heard a rustling. "Ginny, is that you? Did I disturb you?"

"Go away."

"What? I thought . . ."

"I heard the gunshots. I heard it all. I know what that means for you to be here now. Someone else didn't survive. I'm sorry, Smoke. But violence, and those who cause it, are not a part of my life. Now, goodbye."

"Uh—yeah. I—ah—goodbye, Ginny. Thank you for a delicious supper."

Smoke trudged away, thinking gloomy thoughts about schoolteachers. His own dear Sally had had similar opinions when first they had met. At least this time, he had no one to woo and win.

Six

Reno Jim Yurian and his gang sat around a large table in the office of what had once been a prosperous, if short-lived mine. A good twenty years earlier, Arapaho warriors, angered at seeing the belly of their Earth Mother plundered, had attacked and killed the six men working the claim. Because the mine shaft was accessed from a small shed attached to the office, the Indians did not burn it down out of religious awe. Now a new wealth visited the abandoned structure. Each of the outlaws had a stack of coins and currency in front of him.

To the casual observer, they could have been preparing for a poker game. In fact, Reno Jim had only seconds before finished the distribution of each man's share of their most recent forays into the criminal life. It came to quite a tidy amount. As one, they began to count the total. Reno Jim waited until they had finished and he had their full attention.

"That's only a start, boys. We'll move the cattle and horses at the same time."

"Won't that cost a lot to feed the cattle so long, boss?" Prine Gephart asked.

Reno Jim bit the tip from a skinny, black cigar

and lighted it before answering. "Not really. They're on graze and there's plenty of it. When we have the horses, we'll move them at once. First, though, there is the problem of this fast gun running the horse herd. If he wasn't bullin' Colin here." He clapped the wounded brigand on the shoulder, and Colin Fike winced. "We have a serious obstacle in our way. And his name is Smoke Jensen."

Early the next morning, Smoke Jensen left the sheriff's office and paid a brief breakfast call on the town marshal. Inside the Iron Kettle, Grover Larsen glared across the red-checked tablecloth at the badge adorning Smoke Jensen's chest. Somehow he could not manage to meet the amber-flecked eyes. His voice was surly, uncertain.

"What did you drag me down here for?"

"I need your cooperation, Marshal Larsen."

Suspicion and unease briefly lighted Larsen's flat, gray eyes. " 'Cooperation'? What kind?"

"The Harbinsons have a printing press over at the general store, don't they?"

"Yes, they do. Why?"

"I want you to come over there with me. I intend to post guns out of town. It would help if I had your name and signature on the flyers also."

Grover Larsen considered this while he chewed a bite of ham. "That doesn't sound like too much to ask."

"Then you'll do it?" Smoke watched as Larsen shrugged slightly and speared another piece of ham.

Another shrug and the jaws worked methodically. Grover Larsen swallowed and spoke softly. "You bought me breakfast. I suppose it's the least I can do. Besides, it's my duty. Mind, though, I'm opposed to interfering with a man's right to carry a gun."

Smoke smiled, satisfied that there might be some grit left in the man after all. "So am I. I intend only to post against nonresidents. The citizens of Muddy Gap, and those known to be local folks, will not be affected by it." Then Smoke dropped the other boot that Larsen had been waiting for. "That's why I need your help in enforcing it. You know who belongs and who don't. Will you do it, Marshal?"

Larsen's worried frown turned to a deep scowl. "I didn't count on that. There's some rough characters out there."

"That's why I'll see you have someone to back your play. While you relieve any strangers of their guns, they can cover them."

Cocking his head to one side, Larsen mopped at an egg yolk with a fluffy biscuit. "Might work after all. Yep. Let's finish up and we'll go see young Eb Harbinson."

A black mourning band showed prominently on the sleeve of Eb Harbinson's shirt. He seemed reluctant to dig into the cast type and dirty the press to print so small a run. He listened to what Smoke wanted, nodded to show the ability of his equipment to do the job, and rubbed the palms of his hands on his trouser legs.

"We planned to start a newspaper. But there aren't enough people in town yet to justify the expense." He came to his feet from the chair in front of a rolltop desk. "I suppose printing these flyers is a better use of the press than gathering dust. But, if you want signatures, you'll either have to sign each one separately, or I'll have you do it on a blank plate and etch around them."

"How long will that take?" Smoke asked.

Eb rolled his eyes to the ceiling. "I'd say you could have them late tomorrow.

"Not soon enough. We'll sign them."

"How many do you want, Sheriff?"

Smoke calculated aloud. "I want one in each business in town, on the church and school, also. And two for each end of town. A few spares in case someone takes exception to them. Say twenty-five, thirty."

Eb nodded his understanding. "Fine, I can have them ready by ten o'clock this morning."

After leaving the general mercantile, Smoke Jensen started his rounds of the saloons, to hustle the unwanted element out of town. The first of the unsavory milieu he encountered were Bert Toller, Quint Cress, and Big Sam Peiper. The trio of fair-to-middling gunfighters stood at the bar in the Golden Boot tormenting the swamper. The gray-haired, older man toiled to put down fresh sawdust after the previous night's cleanup and moping.

"Hey, *boy*, yer hand's shakin' so much you got sawdust on my boots," Quint Cress complained.

"What you need is a drink, old-timer," Big Sam told him through a nasty chuckle.

Harvey Gates looked up with the eyes of a cornered animal. "No, sir. I done gave up drinkin'."

Cress twisted his face into a mean sneer. "Oh, yeah? When? After they invented the funnel?"

"Please, fellers, I've—I've got work to do."

Quint Cress crossed to the cowed man and yanked the bucket of sawdust from his grasp. "You get sawdust on my boots again an' they'll be plantin' you before sundown."

A steel-hard voice came from the doorway. "That's the last time you do that."

Cress whirled, a shower of yellowish wood chips flying from the rim of the bucket. "Oh, yeah? Who says so?"

"I do. Sheriff Jensen. Now, return the bucket to the man and let him get on with his work."

From farther down the bar, Big Sam spoke hesitantly. "Uh—Quint, I think that might be a good idea. This be Smoke Jensen."

A crazed glint shone in the eyes of Quint Cress. "You think I don't know? I don't care a damn, either. I say he's not as hot as he's put up to be." He dropped the bucket to the floor and started for the door. "I'll be waitin' for you outside, Jensen."

Smoke let him go. He turned to the remaining pair and addressed Big Sam. "You seem to have more sense than your friend. This town is off limits to you and your kind. So, I'll ask you politely. Gather up whatever you brought with you, mount up and ride out. You have fifteen minutes."

Big Sam Peiper made a show of considering that for a moment; then his voice rang with new strength. "I don't mind you raggin' Quint some. He needs tooken down a notch. But, you jist asked something we can't do. Why, we'd be the laughing stock of the whole territory. No, sir, we ain't gonna go."

With that, he and Bert Toller, who had said nothing so far, dropped hands to the grips of their six-guns. Smoke let Sam Peiper, whom he figured more for a mouth than a shootist, get his long-barreled .44 Colt clear of leather, choosing instead to take on Toller first.

A good choice, he soon discovered as Toller moved with a blur, his six-gun snaked out and on the rise by the time Smoke snapped his elbow to his right side and leveled the .45 Peacemaker in his fist. The hammer fell, and a puff of cloth and dust flew from the front of Toller's shirt. A dark hole appeared some three inches above the belt Toller wore. A second hole popped into place directly above it a fraction of a second later, to form a perfect figure eight.

Immediately, Smoke swung the smoking barrel of his Colt to Big Sam Peiper. Big Sam stared at his partner and watched him die. Bert Toller had barely hit the floor when Sam let out a despairing shout and bolted for the door.

"No!" he screamed. "I ain't gonna die." Wildly he threw a shot at Smoke over his shoulder.

Smoke had dropped to a crouch when Big Sam started his direction, so the shot went high, to spang off the stovepipe and crack the plaster behind. Smoke fired his third round as Big Sam hit the batwing doors. Sam Peiper crashed through the swinging partitions and onto the boardwalk, as blood streamed down his thigh. Smoke Jensen came right behind him.

Limping, Big Sam Peiper headed toward Quint Cress. "Ga'damn, he shot me, Quint. It hurts real bad."

Cress looked surprised. "You ain't never been shot before? What kinda gunfighter are you?"

"Naw. Ain't been shot. I always was faster."

Quint Cress shook his head. "Sam, Sam, get out of the way, let me finish this amateur."

Big Sam staggered in a tight circle, raising his Smith American. "No. I'm gonna do it. Nobody puts a hole in Big Sam Peiper."

He faced Smoke Jensen now, who much to the consternation of Big Sam had an amused expression on his face. With careful deliberation, his own visage screwed into a grimace of pain, Big Sam raised his revolver. To his dying instant, he knew he had never seen Smoke Jensen draw his Colt. Yet, all of a sudden he saw the yellow-orange bloom and a thin trail of smoke start from its muzzle.

Then a bright white light dazzled him, and immense pain erupted inside his head. All feeling left his hands and feet. The alabaster radiance swelled and enveloped him. For a fraction of a second, Big Sam Peiper saw a tiny black dot form at the center of the sphere. Unfeeling, he toppled to the ground, the back of his head blown away, and in a twinkling, the blackness overwhelmed him.

Quint Cress stared in horror. No one could be that fast. Hell, Big Sam already had his six-gun cocked before this Smoke Jensen drew. For the first time, the bravado deserted Quint. Yet, he knew inexorably that the hand had to be played out to the end. He swallowed hard to remove the lump in his throat and dropped his hand to the grips of his Colt. Jensen, his head wreathed in powder smoke, could not possibly see him draw.

Wrong. Quint Cress had his Frontier Colt free of leather and on the way up when an invisible fist slammed into his stomach. He started to double over in reflex, only to be straightened up by another enormous pain in his chest. He wound up on his back, staring up at Smoke Jensen, who held his Peacemaker in a steady, level grasp.

Quint Cress used the last of his dying breath to ask his most pressing questions. "Wh-what are you, Jensen? Who are you?"

A tiny mocking smile lifted the corners of Smoke Jensen's mouth. "Some people have called me the gunfighters' gunfighter."

And then, Quint Cress heard and saw only blackness.

Early that same morning Reno Jim Yurian and three of his men sat astride their mounts overlooking a long, narrow depression in the prairie, too shallow to be called a valley. A wide, deep ravine defined the western margin, with a large, round knob bordering the east. In its center ran the trail north through the Bighorn Mountains, and on toward Buffalo, Wyoming. From there, it led north into Montana and the Crow Reservation. Reno Jim tilted back the brim of his black, flat-crown Stetson and waved a gloved hand at the peaceful spread of terrain.

"There it is, boys. The perfect place to take that herd. I reckon it will be here in no more than a day, two at the most. Hub, I want you to set the boys up to preparing an ambush. Take your time and make it look natural. The last thing we want is them to get wise too soon. Also, make sure there's enough mounted men on both sides, beyond the rise, to take quick control of the herd.

"Right, boss. You gonna be here with us?"

Reno Jim produced a thin-lipped smile. "I wouldn't miss that for anything. For now, me and Smiling Dave are going to set up camp so you boys can have something hot to eat after you get done."

What he meant, of course, was that Smiling Dave Winters would do the work while he sat under a tree and practiced his card-dealing tricks. Naturally, no one mentioned it to Reno Jim. Under Hub Volker's direction, the men spread out to locate a good spot to establish a roadblock-style ambush. It took only a short while to accomplish that.

Garth Evans rode back from around a slight bend in the trail with a cheery smile. "Hey, Hub, I've got the ideal place. That bend there"—he pointed behind him—"will mask it, an' there's some cottonwoods to form a barricade."

"Good work, Garth."

At once, Hub put men on cutting down the trees. Using hand axes was a sure invitation to blisters and sore hands, yet the outlaws set at it with a will. The sound of their chopping rang across the prairie. One by one the thigh-thick cottonwood trees tottered and fell with a crash. Dragged into place by horses, the logs were trimmed and made ready. Sets of post augers appeared from a chuck wagon, and the outlaw rabble groaned.

Hairy Joe cut his eyes to Prine Gephart as he plied a clamshell post-hole digger. "Doin' that corral for the cattle was bad enough. Now we gotta build a damn fort wall." He slammed the device into the hard ground again.

Prine cranked the long handle on his screw-type digger. "It ain't a fort, Joe. It's a sorta fence, like we're makin' the whole valley into a corral."

Hairy Joe groaned. "This is gonna take a week to close across the whole valley. From what I hear, we ain't got that much time."

"We'll get it done," Gephart assured him. "If Hub has to make us work all night."

"Oh, great. I can hardly wait."

Progress went quicker than Hairy Joe thought. By nightfall, all but a hundred yards at each side of the valley had been closed off. Tired far beyond their usual limits, they gathered quietly to eat plates of carne con chili Colorado, bowls of beans and corn bread with which to sop up both of them. Only four of them pulled bottles of whiskey from saddlebags to take long pulls before settling down like the rest into deep slumber.

Meanwhile, Smoke Jensen set about a quick, harsh cleanup of Muddy Gap. He picked up the posters at ten-fifteen. After putting one on the bulletin board outside the general store, he gave half to Marshal Larsen, and they set about posting the entire town. Their actions generated immediate reaction. Several merchants came onto the boardwalk to voice protest. It never failed to draw a crowd.

"Now, see here," the butcher, Tiemeier, declared in a loud bray. "You can't do this. I've got a right to carry a gun."

"You are not affected, Mr. Tiemeier," Smoke explained patiently. "Read it carefully. Only non-residents are required to surrender their arms."

"Even so, you have no right to do this on your own."

"I'm not. You can see the city marshal's signature right there beside mine. And, this morning the mayor and city council met and passed the ordinance."

For half an hour, Smoke busied himself tacking up the edicts, ending with the two at the north end of town. He had finished the final nail when five specimens of range trash drifted up. Hats pulled down low on brows, they walked their mounts to the gate post where Smoke had affixed one of the flyers and read it with obvious difficulty. At last one of them turned to glower at Smoke.

"Who are you to try to make us do that?"

Smoke tapped the badge pinned to his vest with the hammer. "I'm the law."

Leaning forward, the mouthy one jabbed a thick forefinger at Smoke. "You're a fool if you think we're gonna give up our guns."

Smoke stepped closer to him. "You do or you don't cross the town line."

This time the belligerent one reached even farther and poked Smoke in the chest and emphasized each insult with a thrust. "You'll play hell stopping us, you two-bit, tin-star, yellow-belly—Yeeeiii!"

His scream came when Smoke dropped the hammer and reached up swiftly to snatch the offending finger and bend it backward until the bone snapped loudly. At once, Smoke let go and grabbed the front of the man's shirt. With a solid yank, he jerked him clear of the saddle. Pivoting, Smoke slammed him to the ground hard enough to drive the air from his lungs.

He dropped on one knee to the loudmouth's belly and delivered a left-right-left combination to his face that left the man dizzy and gurgling. Immediately, the others went for their guns. Smoke came to his boots in an instant and hauled his Colt Peacemaker clear in a blur. The four thugs gaped at him.

"Now put your guns on the gate over there or pick up your friend here and get the hell out of town."

Cutting their eyes from one to another, the four stared in wonder. Not a one had half-drawn his revolver. One of them looked at their companion groaning on the ground. "Just who the devil are you, mister?"

"Smoke Jensen."

For all his misery, the one at Smoke's feet got up quickly and mounted his horse. All of them tried not to meet the hot eyes of Smoke Jensen, which bored into them. With submissive touches of their hands to the brims of their hats, they turned their horses and rode away.

Little Jimmy showed up at noon with a plate for Smoke from the Iron Kettle. It held fried chicken, gravy with boiled potatoes, and hominy. He also had an encouraging message.

Freckled face writhing with the energy of his delivery, Jimmy informed Smoke, "Fred Chase, one of your deputies, is back in town. He says he'll come out and relieve you after dinner," he squeaked. "Said he should be here about one-fifteen this afternoon."

"Thank you, Jimmy." Smoke dug in his pocket for a coin. Jimmy looked at him expectantly.

"Can I stay here until you finish? I'll take yer plate back. Okay?"

"It's may I, Jimmy," Smoke corrected, the image of Sally hovering in his mind. "And, yes, you may."

Jimmy's eyes glowed. "Oh, boy, maybe I'll get to see you wallop a few bad men."

Smoke frowned. "You had better hope you don't. Which reminds me. If anything turns rough out here while you are around, duck. I mean, crawl underground."

"Yesss, sir," the little lad replied in disappointment.

When Fred showed up and introduced himself, Smoke explained what was expected of him and what to watch out for. Then he walked back into the center of town with Jimmy at his side. He gave the boy another dime and sent him off to the Iron Kettle with the empty plate. Then he started for the first of two saloons he had on his list to clean out this afternoon.

When he shoved his way through the bat-wings, Smoke walked smack into a fist in the mouth.

Seven

Smoke Jensen rocked back on his boot heels, then lowered his head and drove into the man who had hit him. Off balance, the tough back-pedaled until he struck a poker table and sprawled across it, scattering coins and chips.

"Hey, get off the table," one of the irate players complained.

From the bar, another added, "Yeah, Red, I thought you were gonna really fix the new sheriff. Looks like he's done fixed you."

Goaded by the taunt, Red Cramer sprang to his feat and made a dive for Smoke Jensen. Smoke waited for his charge. At the last second, he side-stepped and clipped Red behind the ear. Red flew sideways and crashed into yet another table. Beer gushed upward in amber geysers as schooners broke in showers of glass, and the table's occupants sprawled in disarray. Red wound up face-first across the collapsed table. Slower this time, he came to his boots.

Smoke stood there ready to meet him. Only this time, Red decided he had enough of bare-hand grappling. He dropped a hand to his holster and hauled on his hogleg. He should have known better.

Although superior to most of the thugs Smoke had faced since coming to Muddy Gap, Red Cramer managed to bring only the muzzle of his Colt to the top of the pocket before Smoke shot him in the chest.

Red's expression of surprise spoke volumes. For a moment he could simply not believe that he had been beaten. Especially by some nobody from Colorado. Then came the rush of certain knowledge. How could this be happening to him? Red Cramer went limp, and his Colt thudded on the floor. His eyes rolled up, and he sighed as though in regret for his short life and many sins. Then he died.

Smoke faced the remaining occupants of the Red Rooster saloon. "You men were already in town when I posted it. Though by this time, you have to have seen one or more notices on your way in here. So, I'll give you exactly thirty seconds to rid yourselves of every firearm you are carrying, and any knife with more than a three-inch blade. There are no exceptions," Smoke added as one of the toughs started to voice a protest. "Failure to comply will result in being escorted out of town, by way of a visit to the justice of the peace and a stay in jail."

A long, silent fifteen seconds clicked away on the octagonal face of the oak-cased Regulator wall clock above the piano. Then, grumbling lowly among one another, three of the riffraff began to deposit weapons on the bar. When the slender, black hand reached twenty seconds, four more began to divest themselves of six-guns and knives. The thirty-second deadline arrived in the Red Rooster, and Smoke Jensen cut his eyes from one to another of the three holdouts, then down at the corpse cooling on the floor.

"If you don't want to join him, I'd suggest you join your friends over there at the bar."

Two of them looked at Smoke as though he had spoken in tongues. The third scuttled to the bar and began to unburden his person of all arms. The pendulum of the Regulator ticked again, and the second hand advanced. One of the holdouts began to sweat profusely. His hand trembled visibly as he raised a finger to point at Smoke.

"I've heard of you, Jensen. They say you're fast."

Smoke nodded. "D'you reckon to be faster?"

"N-no—ah—no." His gaze fixed on his boot toes, his bravado deflated as he shuffled to join the others who had given up their weapons.

With a flicker of a smile, Smoke addressed the thoroughly cowed brigands. "Thank you, boys. When you are ready to leave town, you can pick those up at the sheriff's office." Then, to the bartender, "Herb, put the hardware behind the bar. Someone will be by to pick up all of it later." With that, he turned on his heel and left.

Shortly after noon, Smoke Jensen left the task of collecting firearms to his deputy, Fred Chase, and headed for the Sorry Place. There he ordered a schooner of beer and helped himself to the free lunch counter. He stood at the bar, munching on a sandwich he had made of ham, rare roast beef, and two cheeses, when four of the local merchants entered and walked purposefully toward him.

"Sheriff, we have to talk," Eb Harbinson, their spokesman, declared.

Smoke laid down his sandwich, took a bite of hard boiled egg and faced them calmly. "What's on your minds?"

"This scheme of yours might work well for you, Sheriff, but we believe you have gone too far."

"How is that? There are less hard cases in town, isn't that right?"

Momentarily at a loss for words, Eb Harbinson watched as Smoke bit into a fat dill pickle and chewed thoughtfully. Eb took a deep breath and went on. "What you say is true. Only there may be too few of them around."

Smoke remained terse. "Meaning what?"

Eb felt his surety draining from him. "Well, we've talked it over and we all agree. This posting has been bad for business. Sales are down all over town. You have to stop turning people away."

Shaking his head, Smoke tried to reason with them. "I am not turning people away. They have a choice. Surrender their guns or they don't come into town."

Eb looked pained. He started to speak, only to be interrupted by Tiemeier, the butcher. "The way we see this, it's the same thing. A lot of local ranchers have heard about it, and they're not coming in for their supplies. That hurts business all around."

Smoke looked hard at Tiemeier's blood-stained, leather apron. "Don't you think they butcher their own stock?"

Red-faced, Tiemeier snapped back. "Of course they do. If I don't sell them beef and pork, there's still hams and bacon. Folks don't build smokehouses around here, wrong kind of wood. Then, there's my friends here, the other merchants in town. They are really suffering. You have to let people come into town."

Smoke studied the protesters awhile, noted the expressions of urgency they all wore, then tore off a mouthful of sandwich and munched it. A flash of anger crossed Tiemeier's face at this. That was what Smoke had been waiting for. His eyes narrowed, and he swallowed to clear his mouth before speaking.

"What you are asking is not possible. The mayor prevailed on me to help rid your town of the trash. I'm doing exactly that. I do not need the people I'm supposed to be protecting to come whining about slow business. The last time I looked, there is not a cradle-to-grave assurance of being taken care of in this country. A man's got to carry his own weight here.

"It's not the job of government, whether city, territory or the stripe-pants boys in Washington, to guarantee you anything, let alone a right to success. That's up to you to do the very best you can. If you don't participate, and wait for someone else to do it all for you, you deserve to fail. I'd suggest you all give Eb here a little more business for that printing press. Do up some flyers of your own, explaining that not one local will be turned away, and you might even list a few specials in your shops. Then see that they are circulated among those living outside town. Now, I'd like to finish my—"

Tiemeier interrupted him. "By God, man, you can't be serious."

Smoke grew a scowl. "If you are going to bring God into this, Preacher always taught me that He helps those who help themselves. I'd suggest, gentlemen, that you abide by that rule." Smoke started to add more advice, only to be interrupted by a loud disturbance out in the street.

A pair of gunshots racketed off the building fronts. Glass tinkled in their wake. Raucous voices raised in curses mingled with laughter. Another window went in a shower of silver shards. A bullet cracked into the clapboard front of the Red Rooster saloon. The protesting merchants had grown quiet and now ducked with alacrity as another slug bit a gouge of splinters off the front of the liquor emporium.

"Hey, Drew, that's purty good shootin'. See if you can hit that lamp."

"Easy, Grant, Watch me."

Hot lead spanged off metal, followed by the tinkle of broken glass. The odor of kerosene reached Smoke Jensen's nostrils. He looked around to find himself the only one standing. Quickly he strode out onto the boardwalk.

Two gangling, young louts stood unsteadily in the street, reeling from the effect of too much liquor. Their dirty-blond hair hung in long, greasy hanks that swayed with each drunken step they took. They could have been twins, except that one stood a good four inches shorter than the other and looked as though his face had yet to need a razor. The older wore a scraggly wisp of yellow hair on his chin. He also held Marshal Grover Larsen by the shirt collar. He spoke as Smoke came into the light.

"You done that right nice, Drew. But you got a ways to go to be good as me. Watch me shoot the 'o' outta the word 'Groceries' on that winder." Grant raised his six-gun and fired.

To the right of the door to the general store, the window collapsed in a cascade of shards. From beyond his back, Smoke heard a groan. He shot a hard glance over his shoulder to Eb Harbinson.

"Would you like to see your other window go? Or do you want me to do the job I was hired for?"

"Go. Go on," Eb moaned.

Smoke Jensen stepped off the boardwalk and took a stance in the dirt street. "That's enough, boys. Let Marshal Larsen go and give me those guns."

Grant Eckers and his younger brother Drew had ridden into Muddy Gap to get supplies for their father's ranch. They also intended on having a few drinks and maybe sporting some with the girls in the Gold Boot. Although only sixteen, Drew had been assured by his older brother that he would have no trouble getting whiskey.

"After all," Grant had assured Drew, "Paw darn near owns this town. Ain't nobody gonna refuse us."

They had ridden up to where Marshal Grover

Larsen stood watch. Being locals, the lawman had passed them on through. Unfortunately for him, the brothers had been sucking on the dregs of a bottle supplied by Grant, and their liquor-fogged brains made them take exception to the prohibition signs. After reading the notice, Grant had grabbed the marshal by the scruff of his collar and forced him to run alongside the boy's horse as they trotted into town.

When they dismounted, Marshal Larsen tried to make good an escape. Grant proved too fast for him. In two strides the strong youth caught up and yanked Larsen back. He held the lawman by one arm while he and Drew pulled their six-guns and began to bang away at the building fronts.

"Serve them right, getting uppity like that," Grant pronounced sentence.

The whiskey had started to wear off when Grant heard the cold voice behind them, demanding they give up their guns. He turned with his captive, a laugh on his lips, expecting to see another worn-out old man like the marshal. Instead, he saw the hard, rangy body of Smoke Jensen and the icy light in those strangely colored eyes. Beside him, Drew stumbled around also, his six-gun pointed at the ground, and sobered abruptly.

"What th' hell? Who you, mister?"

"I'm the new sheriff. I'll thank you to turn the marshal loose now."

His eyes narrowed, belligerence flared in Grant's voice. "And what if we won't?"

Smoke spoke matter-of-factly. "Then one or both of you will be seriously hurt."

"We'll see about that, Sheriff." Grant swung his Colt up in line with the side of Grover Larsen's head and eared back the hammer. "You try anything an' we'll splatter the marshal's brains all over the street."

Smoke Jensen gave a slight shrug. "Go ahead, he doesn't mean anything to me anyway."

Confused by this unexpected attitude, Grant hesitated a moment. In that instant, Smoke pulled his Peacemaker with blinding speed and shot Grant in the right shoulder. The impact of the bullet knocked Grant's Colt off target and caused it to discharge harmlessly down the street. Grant dropped his revolver as though it had turned red hot. An astounding transformation passed over him.

Face red and puckered, he began to whimper and moan like a frightened infant. He let go of Grover Larsen and curled his body downward. A large, wet stain appeared in the crotch of his trousers. Drew gaped at his older brother and kept his weapon pointed carefully skyward. Forty-five still in hand, Smoke Jensen pointed at Grant.

"Marshal, take this whining baby to jail and get him patched up." Then to Drew, "You have two choices: give up or get a bullet like he did."

For a brief moment, Drew tried to tough it out. "That's my brother. You shot him, you son of a bitch."

"And you're next if you don't do what I say. Lay down that gun and come along peacefully."

Sullenly, Drew did as he had been told. Smoke Jensen spun the boy and gave him a quick pat-down. Then he roughly shoved Drew in the direction of the jail.

An hour later, Harmon Eckers stormed into the small room that fronted the jail and served both sheriff and marshal as an office. His ordinarily ruddy features had been made even more scarlet by the anger that boiled under the surface. He cut accusing eyes from Marshal Larsen to Smoke Jensen in turn. His voice came out harsh and demanding.

"What's this about my sons being arrested?"

Marshal Larsen nodded and released a long sigh. "That's true, Harmon. They're both back there in a cell."

Eckers raised a hand in a threatening gesture and spoke through a thunderous outrage. "Then don't just sit there, Grover, get them out here."

Smoke leaned forward, heat radiating from his eyes. "Sorry. That won't be possible."

"Why not? And who the hell are you?"

Speaking softly, although bridling his rising temper, Smoke replied, "Because they broke the law. And I'm the new sheriff."

"You won't be long, by God, not unless you release my boys. I've broken tin-star punks like you a dozen times. If you don't have my boys out here within two minutes, I'll snatch you out of that chair and snap your miserable back over my knee."

That proved an instant mistake. Smoke Jensen came out of his chair like a lightning bolt, the barrel of his Colt Peacemaker a blur as it sped from the holster. He raised his arm in a swift blur and swung like a batter in Abner Doubleday's new game of Bases. The barrel collided with the side of Harmon Eckers' head above his ear with a loud *clonk!*

He fell like a heart-shot deer. Not even a moan escaped his lips. Smoke looked from him to Marshal Larsen. He hooked a thumb over his shoulder. "Drag this piece of garbage out of here and put him in a cell."

They had to do something. Della Olsen realized that after the shock of her husband's murder began to wear off. For days she could not count, she had sat in a daze, seeing nothing, hearing nothing, not even caring. She dimly recalled that Tommy had cooked for his sisters, cared for her, saw that she kept her hands and face clean.

Through the miasma of her grief she recalled Tommy sweating as he dug the graves for Sven and the boy they had taken in, Elmer Godwin. Tommy's hands had been blistered and raw when he completed the sorrowful task. That had caused him to delay the burial until the next day, his throbbing hands smeared with salve and bandaged. Now, as she stirred herself to organize thoughts for their future, she heard in memory his sweet, child's voice singing Sven's favorite hymn.

"Rock of ages, cleft for me/Let me hide myself in thee." Now she sang aloud in the gentle morning sun as she turned her eyes to the dark mounds that rested under the spreading boughs of an

ancient spruce. Tears sprang to her eyes, which she hastily brushed away.

"Come on, children, we have to collect everything we can find. They are—our memories."

Tommy had been a real man, someone to lean on in the time of her darkness. She looked now and saw the wagon he had repaired. How hard he had worked, sweating as he labored. With his shirt off, she could see his immature muscles strain and tremble with the effort to work the jack and raise the wagon bed. Sven had taught him well, she thought, as she dimly recalled him replacing two spokes and sweating the steel tire onto the damaged wheel.

It had taken all his strength to lift the heavy object into place. Then he had tightened the hub nut and freed the jack. The beaming pride that had shone on his face made her heart lurch even now. Della heard the sound of a horse's hooves and looked up in surprise. Her satisfaction in her son soared as she saw him leading their old plow horse up toward the barnyard.

"Look what I found, Maw," he called out cheerfully. "We can use the wagon now."

"That's fine. That's wonderful, Tommy. Put him in the corral and come help us collect what belongings we can find. Maybe we can leave yet today."

Tommy took his role of man of the house seriously. "In that case, I'll jist hitch up now."

With their scant possessions loaded, Della handed the girls up into the wagon box and took her place on the driver's seat an hour later. Tommy took the reins and slapped the rump of the swayback, old gelding, and they rolled down the lane. With only a brief, backward glance at the graves, the Olsen family left the ruins of their ranch.

Smoke Jensen had finished a cup of coffee and made ready to return to a stint of duty on the deadline when Boyne Kelso stormed into the office, Mayor Norton in tow. The officious Kelso wasted no time on amenities.

"Sheriff, you have to release Harmon Eckers and his sons. Right now if not sooner."

Smoke appraised him coolly. "Why is that?"

"You have no idea what you have here," Kelso blurted.

"What I have here, Mr. Kelso, are two wet-be-hind-the-ears squirts, drunk as skunks, and shooting up the town. And their father threatening to break my back like a twig."

"That's not important." Kelso ignored Smoke's mood. "Harmon Eckers is the most influential rancher in the area. He runs eight hundred head of cattle, and employs three dozen hands. And he has friends," Kelso concluded ominously.

"Then it's likely he'll not be seeing them soon," Smoke told him. "He threatened a peace officer, and his sons broke the no-guns law and shot up the property of other people. Now, you'll have to excuse me. I have a saloon to clean out of drifters and trash, then I'm due on the posting line."

Eight

Smoke Jensen entered the Trailside saloon and came face-to-face with an even dozen angry hands from the Eckers' ranch. A bull of a man Smoke figured to be the foreman took a step away from the bar and faced him.

"We're gonna mosey over to that jail of yours and take out our boss and his sons. An' there ain't a damn thing you can do about it."

Laughing, Smoke raised his gloved left hand in a stopping motion. "I beg to differ with that."

Two more who rode for the Eckers brand joined the first, which made him even more vocal. "There ain't no way we're gonna allow any two-bit, tin-horn lawman to stand in our way."

He completed the last of that boast well within reach of Smoke Jensen. Setting himself— a subtle change of position missed by the pugnacious ranch hands—Smoke took advantage of that. His right fist, encased in a thin, black leather glove, shot out and caught the Eckers foreman a fraction behind the point of his chin. Smoke put shoulders and hips into it, and the blow lifted the surprised cowman's boots off the floor.

His eyes showed whites before he hit the boards. Smoke followed up immediately while momentary surprise froze the two range hands. He chose the one on his right first and delivered a one-two punch to chest and jaw that put out the man's lights in a blink. By then the other cowboy was moving.

He made a grab for Smoke Jensen's left arm, only to close his fingers on air. Smoke turned so quickly the hapless youth did not even see the fist coming that knocked him back against the bar. Dazed, he shook his head in an effort to clear his vision, wiped blood from his split lip, then launched himself at Smoke again.

Smoke waited him out. He blocked the first wild blow, caught the other on a shoulder point, then snapped a short, hard right to the cowhand's face. Blood spurted from a mashed nose, and the icy blue eyes crossed for a moment. Smoke followed up with a tattoo of rights and lefts to chest and belly. His knees sagging, the young cowboy gave up any attempt to cover himself and fell forward into the arms of Smoke Jensen.

Smoke swung him to the left and dropped the groggy youth into a chair. At once the battered man slumped over and laid his head on the green baize table. Four more of Eckers' hands decided to enter the fray. They started toward Smoke, one of them drawing a knife from his boot top.

They stopped as quickly at the loud, double click of shotgun hammers. "That's far enough, boys," Marshal Grover Larsen said from the open rear doorway. He held a ten gauge Greener, the muzzles lined up with their bellies. Slowly they eased back against the bar. Smoke Jensen looked them over thoughtfully.

"Not a one of you went for a gun, which speaks well for you. I can understand hotheadedness. What I can't abide is a cowardly act." With that he walked over to the one who had pulled his knife.

Smoke reached out and plucked the blade from a numb hand. He raised it before the man's eyes and took the tip between thumb and two fingers. Slowly Smoke bent the steel until it snapped in front of the hilt. A fleeting smile played across his lips as he dropped the broken knife to the floor. He pointed a finger at the man's suddenly ashen face.

"This one goes to jail. The rest of you drag these two out of here and get out of town."

Abruptly, Smoke turned his back on them and walked to the door. Meekly, the knife artist followed him.

Night caught up to Della Olsen and her children before she wanted it. She estimated that they had barely made twenty miles from their burned-out ranch in the past two days. The tired old horse Tommy had rounded up had to stop and rest far too often. An hour ago they had made camp.

Sarah-Jane had gamely gathered wood and buffalo chips for the cookfire. The eleven-year-old had taken her father's death harder than the other children, though Della had to admit that her daughter's spirits had lifted since starting for Buffalo, the nearest town. Sarah-Jane looked on the journey as an adventure.

While Sarah-Jane brought fuel, Tommy unhitched the horse and slipped a feed bag over the nag's nose. Then he unloaded the wagon and made a ring of stones to contain their fire. Della busied herself slicing bacon on the lowered tailgate of the wagon, paring potatoes and cutting onions. It would be a spare meal; Tommy had not found any game to shoot.

"Maw, what are we going to do when we get to Buffalo?"

Della looked into her son's clear blue eyes. "I don't know, Tommy. I'll find us a place to stay, take work somewhere. You and the girls will attend school."

Tommy made instant protest. "Awh, Maw, do we have to?"

"Yes, son. Lord knows I've done the best I can teaching you at home. At least you all can read and write and do your sums. But that's not enough. There's a whole world of things to learn out there."

Tommy swelled his chest. "I should get work, too, Maw. I'm too old to go to school."

"Buffalo has a four-year upper school now. I'm sure they will welcome you."

Thunderstruck, Tommy gaped at his mother. "You mean people go to school even after they are too old for the eighth grade?"

"Of course. Some people, like doctors and lawyers, even go on to college."

Tommy's fair, freckled brow furrowed. "That don't sound like something I'd like to do."

"It isn't likely you will get the chance." Della

cast a regretful glance in the direction of the ranch. "Although your father and I had our dreams."

After the meal, a sky full of stars brought back painful memories to the children of their father. Della busied herself with the cleanup, her concentration broken when she heard the sniffles and muffled sobs of little Gertrude. She turned to find Tommy seated between the girls, an arm around the shoulder of each.

"I know it hurts. I . . ." Tommy's voice broke. "I miss Paw, too. And Elmer. There's this great big empty place inside me. But we have to go on, you know. We have to look out for Maw."

Tears welled in Della's eyes, which she hastily wiped away. How strong her boy was. A thrill of pride ran through her.

"But, Tommy, we're . . . jist so little," Gertrude complained in a tiny voice.

Tommy's shoulders heaved as he drew a deep breath. "We're big enough. We have to be. Look, you two, dry your tears. We'll go roll up in our blankets. We can watch the stars cross the sky."

"What will it be like when we get to Buffalo, Tommy?" Sarah-Jane asked, rising.

Tommy paused a moment, sorting his thoughts. "There'll be wonderful things. Horehound drops and rock candy an' . . . an' real ice cream."

Right then, a coyote yowled mournfully. The girls squealed in sudden fright. Even Tommy shivered. Della knew, at that moment, that everything would work out all right. This man/boy of hers, only turned fourteen this summer, would see to that. While the girls scampered off to the wagon, Della walked over to her son and put her arms around his shoulders, hugging him tightly.

"Thank you, son. Thank you for helping with the girls. They need the comforting . . . and so do you."

"Me, Maw? Shucks, I'm okay. An' so are you, right?"

Della smiled to herself and tousled his hair with her chin. "Yes, son, I really am."

Once more the coyote howled as the family took to their bedrolls in the wagon box. Slowly the coals ebbed until only the frosty light of the stars shone down upon them.

Early morning brought more frontier trash to be expelled from town. Roused from only four hours' sleep, Smoke Jensen thought his head might be stuffed with wool as he hurriedly shrugged into trousers and boots. He pulled a shirt over his head and tucked it behind his belt. A wild yell and a gunshot reached his ears through the thin walls of his room at the Wilber House Hotel as he buckled his cartridge belt in place. The twin Peacemakers rode his frame like old companions. Smoke clamped his hat on his head and started for the door.

Out on the street, small knots of curious townspeople gathered to watch the unfolding of what was fast becoming a regular event. Down at the end of the block, Deputy Fred Chase faced six proddy saddle bums, a hand on the butt of his Colt. Smoke lengthened his stride.

He came up on the quarrelsome thugs from an angle that left them unaware of his presence. One, slightly in front of the other five, gestured angrily and bellowed in a rusty voice. It served well to hold the attention of Fred Chase. A mistake that Smoke noted at once. He would have to talk to Fred later. For now, his attention riveted on another lout who sought to take advantage of the deputy's distraction.

Smoke stepped up soundlessly behind him as the young punk drew his six-gun. Smoke's arms darted out, and he grabbed the back of the man's shirt and vest. Unceremoniously, Smoke dragged him from the saddle. In a flash, Smoke had his .45 Colt in his hand and slammed the barrel across the head of the would-be sneakshot.

Immediately, the others became aware of Smoke's presence. His eyes cut from one to the other, clearly defying them to make a move. None of them did. Quickly, Smoke waded in, yanked another from his seat and disarmed him. While he worked his way through them, Smoke wondered, not for the first time, if it was all worth it. From his right, Smoke heard a solid clunk and looked to see a grinning Fred standing over the supine figure of the self-appointed leader of the collection of garbage.

Smoke nodded his approval. "Send them on their way, Fred. I'm going to go see who is in for an early drink."

On his way to the Sorry Place saloon, Smoke came upon a quartet of surly, low-browed louts milling in the street outside the general mercantile. They turned sour looks in his direction. One of them, a lank shock of dirty blond hair hanging down over his nearly nonexistent forehead, poked a thick, stubby finger at Smoke.

"Who says we can't wear guns in town? The man in there"—he hooked a thumb at the general store—"said we had to give up our guns or get out of town."

"He's right. By my orders."

Another of the thugs pushed his way forward. "There's four of us and jist one of you. How'er you gonna make us?"

With the skill of a conjurer, a .45 Colt Peacemaker appeared in Smoke Jensen's hand before the others could close fingers around the butt-grips of their weapons. "With this, if necessary."

The first mouthy one cocked his head to one side. "Who the hell might you be?"

"I'm the sheriff. T'name's Jensen. Folks call me Smoke."

Four faces drained of blood. "Awh, hell, we done got the wrong town," declared the second piece of trash.

"That you do," Smoke told him blandly.

A third one spoke up "Damn, those people down in Colorado don't talk about nothin' but how good you are with a gun, Mr. Jensen—uh—Sheriff. We'll leave, an' we won't make no trouble, honest."

"I believe that. Now have a nice ride out of town."

Smoke watched them depart, then turned to observe that the shot-out window of Harbinson's Mercantile had been boarded up. While he idly inspected it, Eb Harbinson stepped out onto the boardwalk. He rubbed his hands industriously on his apron tail and produced a smile.

"Sheriff Jensen, I want to tell you that I was sure wrong about you and your posting law. Yessir, wrong as can be. You know, my business has actually picked up. Those advertising flyers you suggested have been a godsend. You're doing a good job. An excellent job, in fact. I want you to know that all the good people of town are behind you a hunnard percent."

Smoke gave him a quizzical expression. "If they are, how come none of them are rushing over to volunteer to be deputies, Mr. Harbinson? Tell me that."

Early in the afternoon, Smoke Jensen worked at his teeth with a whittled stick as he stepped out of the Sorry Place. The pig's feet had been tasty and tender, with just the right amount of vinegar pickle to them. He ambled along the boardwalk and noted with satisfaction the lack of hard cases and drifter trash. He had nearly reached the front of the Trailside when three shots blasted out of the interior.

Smoke reached the batwings in three long strides. Over the curved top of the louvered doors he saw a bulldog-faced hard case standing over the body of a local rancher, a smoking six-gun in one hand. Smoke stepped through the swinging doors, Peacemaker in hand.

"Put it down and raise your hands," he commanded.

Unwilling to comply, the gunman shouted his

defiance as he tried to turn and fire at the same time. "Like hell I—" he got out before Smoke Jensen shot him through the heart.

Two other gunslicks, friends of the dead thug, took exception to Smoke's treatment of their companion and went for their guns. A bullet from Smoke's .45 crashed into the bar beside one of them; then the pair fired as one.

Smoke Jensen had already moved, spoiling their best chance. His third round found meat low in the belly of one shootist," which slammed the man back against the bar and turned him part way around. Dimly he saw the reflection of Smoke in the mirror behind the row of bottles on the back bar. He tried to hold himself up with his left arm while he struggled to raise his six-gun and get off a shot.

Meanwhile, Smoke had moved again. He traded shots with the third gunman and dived low behind a faro table. A slug from the rogue's Colt scattered chips on the layout. On his knees, Smoke shot back.

A thin, high scream came from the bewhisk-ered gunman, who dropped his weapon and staggered three steps toward the door. All at once he began to tremble. His body went rigid, and he crashed into the sawdust. Beyond him, the wounded brigand at last had his revolver in position. Cursing Smoke, he fired.

Though not before Smoke Jensen had ducked low and rolled across an open section of floor. The bullet went wild, shattered a coal oil lamp and lodged in the wall. Smoke had far better aim with his second Colt.

Splinters flew from the rough pine planks of

the bar when Smoke's bullet exited the chest of the stubborn gunhand. He looked down in surprise and blinked once, slowly, before his eyes rolled up and he teetered over the brink into eternity. Smoke came to his boots and looked around for further resistance.

He had none, he soon saw. Then he took in the gawkers, who peered into the saloon from the windows and over the double batwing doors, drawn by the sounds of the brief, deadly shootout. One of them he soon recognized as Mayor Norton, when that worthy entered, face beaming with relief and pleasure.

"You've done it, Sheriff Jensen. That's the last of them. There's not a piece of riffraff left in town. I never believed anyone could do it so fast."

"I had some help, Mayor."

"You're too modest. You're the one who put the backbone back in Grover Larsen. Fred Chase was only doing his job. The credit is all yours."

Smoke Jensen cut his eyes to the three cooling corpses. "There's a lot of it I would rather not have had to do."

Corpses did not enhance a politician's popularity, so Mayor Norton hastened to close the discussion of the killings. "Of course, of course. I understand."

That, of all the things that had been said since he had come to town, rubbed Smoke the rawest. "No, Mayor Norton, I don't think you could possibly know how I feel." Smoke reached for his badge and pulled it from his vest front. "I'm through here. My job is finished. I have a herd to catch up to."

* * *

Twenty minutes later, Smoke Jensen had all of his possessions loaded into saddlebags and placed in the pouches of a packsaddle rig. After a few pointers to Fred Chase, he left the sheriff's job in his capable hands, mounted Cougar and rode out of town with a rented packhorse on lead. To his surprise, nearly the whole population turned out to see him off. But not all of the residents of Muddy Gap gathered to wish their recent sheriff a fond farewell.

Seated behind his desk, Boyne Kelso turned a hard glower to the second-floor window, from which he could see the tall, lean figure of Smoke Jensen riding out of town. He wet full lips and tossed down a shot of bourbon. In the chair opposite him, his son, Brandon, sipped at a beer.

"You'll get yours, you bastard," Boyne Kelso growled as Smoke went out of sight.

"What do you mean, Paw? He ain't gonna be around here no more."

"Never mind, son. Where he's going, he is about to step into a hornet's nest."

Which brought Boyne's thoughts to the immediate. He had to get a message to Reno Jim Yurian to inform him that the owner of the herd of horses they intended to rustle was the notorious gunfighter, Smoke Jensen. His next thought brought Boyne a great deal of comfort. He had every confidence that Reno would know exactly what to do.

Nine

Smoke Jensen rode hard for two days. Unencumbered by a slow chuck wagon and the remounts, he covered considerable northward distance. When he topped a long swell in the high plains early the morning of the third day, he saw in the distance what appeared to be a wagon with a woman and three children on board. Smoke held back and looked around carefully for any sign of the woman's husband, or any other man accompanying them. When he saw none, he urged Cougar on at a faster gait.

Riding undetected to within twenty yards, Smoke reined in and hailed them, standing in his stirrups. He noted the cringe and frightened reaction. Something was decidedly wrong here. He called out again. "Hello, you folks in the wagon. I mean you no harm. May I ride up?"

A quick conference between the woman and a gangling boy, who might be sixteen, resulted in a hesitant invitation. Smoke rode in, careful to keep his hands clear of his guns. Two small girls looked at him with wide-eyed, solemn faces. The boy wore a frown, although more of puzzlement than anger. In his hands he competently held a .32-20 Marlin rifle.

"Howdy, folks. M'name's Jensen. I own that horse herd whose sign you've been markin' along the trail. I'm on my way to catch up to them."

"What got you behind in the first place?" demanded the auburn-haired, freckle-faced boy.

Under any other circumstances, Smoke would have found such impudence an affront. Considering that they were obviously alone, and frightened of something, he let it go.

"I got mousetrapped into cleaning out the scoundrels and saddle trash from the town of Muddy Gap."

"You are a lawman?" the woman asked suspiciously.

"I am. Deputy U.S. marshal. Though I'm not on government business at present," Smoke added.

"I see," Della responded, though she did not in the least. "Your horses are ahead of us, then?"

"Yes. Will you pardon me if I ask a blunt, personal question? Are you on your way to meet your husband?"

Della paled. "My husband—my husband is dead. He was murdered by outlaws who stole our cattle and burned our ranch."

Right on top of her words the boy spoke. "Why weren't you there to stop it, Marshal?"

Smoke curbed a flare of impatience. "As I said, I am not here on official business. I am sorry to hear that, Mrs.—?"

"Olsen. Della Olsen, Marshal Jensen. This is my son, Tommy, and my daughters, Sarah-Jane and Gertrude."

Smoke touched his hat in acknowledgment and made an instant decision. It was not safe for such vulnerable people to be out here alone. "Pleased to meet you. I'd appreciate it if you would tell me where you are headed."

Della considered a moment. "To Buffalo. It's not far actually. We should be there in two or three days."

"More like six, I'd say," Smoke countered. "I don't wish to be pushy, Mrs. Olsen, but do you mind if I accompany you? At least until we catch up to my horses?"

Relief blossomed on Della Olsen's face. "We would be grateful, Marshal Jensen. And, please, call me Della."

"Thank you, Della. Folks generally call me Smoke."

Tommy's eyes grew wide and bright. "Oh-my-gosh! The gunfighter and lawman? I read about you in a dime novel."

Smoke seemed uncomfortable. "All greatly exaggerated, believe me. Truth is, I've been both, son. Right now I'm raising blooded horses and selling what I can of them." To Della, he went on to say, "This really is rough country for you to be traveling alone. I hope that revealing my identity does not change your opinion too much."

Della took a deep breath and settled her disquiet. "Not at all, Smoke Jensen. As a matter of fact, right now I can't think of anyone more welcome to accompany us."

Tommy fairly bubbled. "Good for you, Maw."

* * *

Rapid as his travel had been for the previous two days, Smoke now found his pace diminished to the painfully slow crawl of the aged plowhorse that drew the Olsen wagon. At the nooning, which Smoke would have ordinarily taken afoot, walking Cougar while he munched a strip of jerky and one of a dozen biscuits he had purchased at the Iron Kettle, Smoke made a suggestion.

"Della, what say we swap my packhorse for your critter for the time being. We could make a good twenty, twenty-five miles a day that way."

Still defensive around this living legend, Della chose to take offense. "If we're holding you up, Mr. Jensen, you can ride on alone."

"Now, that's just what I didn't want to happen. Don't take me wrong. I'm sure you are eager to get to Buffalo and settle in. I'm only trying to help."

Suddenly contrite, Della reached out impulsively and laid a hand on Smoke's forearm. "I'm sorry. All that has happened has . . . unnerved me. Yes, that is a good and practical idea. Generous, too. Thank you." She raised her voice. "Tommy, see to unhitching Barney and exchanging him for Smoke's packhorse."

With that accomplished, their pace picked up considerably during the afternoon. When Smoke indicated the place they would camp for the night, Tommy came to him. The lad had an eager expression that foretold his expectations.

"Mr. Jensen, my paw told me I'm a fair shot. What say I go out and find us some rabbits for supper?"

Smoke grinned broadly. "Fine with me. You have a shotgun along?"

"No, sir. Only my thirty-two-twenty rifle." Then Tommy added proudly, "I only make head shots."

"Then go ahead." Smoke reserved his praise for when the results came in.

Which, half an hour later, surprised and pleased him. He had heard only four shots, and Tommy came back with as many plump rabbits. Deftly, the boy skinned and dressed them, laid aside the livers for the frying pan, and laced the carcasses on green willow twigs, which he inclined over a bed of coals. After the meal, Smoke took Tommy aside.

"Out here, Tommy, it's important a man is able to fend for himself. I see you can provide for the table. Now, I want to give you something to help in protecting your family. I took these off a hard case who won't be needing them any longer," he explained as he opened one envelope of his pack rig and took out a .44 Colt Lightning, double-action revolver and a .44 Winchester.

"I can see no better use for them than that you have them," Smoke went on.

Tommy's eyes grew large and round. "I ain't got money to pay for them, Mr. Jensen."

"They're a gift, Tommy. Only one thing; always use them properly.

"Yes, sir. I promise. Is there cartridges for them?"

"What you see in the belt and another twenty rounds. It's not much, but a good shot like you can surely make them count."

Tommy's chest swelled, and he gulped as he accepted the weapons. "I'll . . . never do wrong with them, Mr. Jensen."

"I'll take your word for that, Tommy. By the way, how old are you?"

"F-fourteen."

For a moment, Smoke regretted his impulsive gesture, then considered the boy's size and sturdiness. He'd do. He remained satisfied with his decision until Della came to sit beside him later, after the children had gone to sleep.

"That was a generous thing you did for Tommy, Smoke. Though I must admit it worries me some. A boy his age with such powerful weapons."

Here it comes, Smoke thought to himself. But Della's next words surprised him. "Though if he is to be the man of the house, he must take upon himself manly things. It's decided, then. Tommy will keep the rifle and the revolver. And, thank you. I feel safer just knowing that someone as considerate as you is around."

Smoke poured them both coffee. "Your loss is so recent, I don't suppose you feel like talking about it," Smoke prompted.

"As a matter of fact, I don't. But I must face it. It was a gang, a big one. They came riding in like a band of wild Indians. Their leader was a fancy dresser, like a gambler, with a red silk lining in his black coat. My Sven was killed early on. It took a while to get poor Elmer."

"Your older son?"

"No. Elmer Godwin. He worked for us. Although we treated him like one of the family, goodness knows. An orphan boy."

"Do you know what caused the attack?"

"Not really. They were after the cattle, I suppose. They drove them off when they left. The children and I were in the root cellar. Tommy had his little rifle, but I don't think it would have done much against those monsters. They burned our house and the barn."

"Then you are wiped out?"

"Yes, Smoke. All we have are the clothes on our backs, a few sheets and blankets, that old wagon and a broken-down horse."

"And a mighty tough spirit, Della. When we reach Buffalo with the herd, I'll do whatever I can to help you get settled."

"You're a kind man, Smoke Jensen."

Smoke flushed slightly. "No. Only practical. There are a lot who would take advantage of a woman in your distress. They might find it more difficult cheating me."

Della studied him awhile in silence. "You are a most unusual man, Smoke."

They talked on until the moon rose. Then Smoke put out the fire with the coffee dregs and rolled up in his soogan, his head on his saddle.

Jerry Harkness had been uneasy since the previous afternoon. He did not doubt his ability to ramrod the drive. Yet, the responsibility of doing it had begun to weigh on him. At midmorning, with the sun warm on his right cheek, his discomfiture intensified to a full-blown premonition.

He did not like the looks of the treacherous

ravine on the left, nor the steep hill to the right
that forced the trail into a blind curve. Anything
could be lying in wait ahead. Jerry pulled a long
face and dropped back to alert the men. That
left a young wrangler named Brad in the lead
position. Jerry quietly informed the other hands.
As usual, the eternal optimist, Utah Jack, made
light of it.

"You goin' old maidish on us, Jerry? Hell,
there ain't nobody out here but us."

"And a couple of thousand Cheyenne," Jerry
reminded him. "Jist keep your eyes sharp. Don't
overlook anything."

By then, the head of the herd had walked out
of sight around the bend. Utah Jack, who rode
drag, whistled to the stragglers to hurry them on.
Jerry Harkness had just started forward when the
first shots sounded.

Yancy Osburn bossed the left flank of the
Yurian gang ambush. He spied the approach of
the horses and felt a surge of elation. Here they
came, by God. If only the fellers in the center
held off long enough, the whole herd could be
contained right there. The lone rider in the
header position looked up right then and saw
the barricade built the previous day. His startled
expression faintly reached Yancy where he
waited.

"What the devil is this?" Brad turned in the
saddle to call back to the swing riders. "Hold up
the herd. There's some kind of roadblock."

At once, the two swing riders nearest the head
of the string of horses began to squeeze in, to

stop forward motion. From his vantage point, Yancy Osburn saw two white puffs of powder smoke bloom behind the obstructing abatis.

A second later, the drover, whose name he did not know, threw his hands in the air and sagged crookedly in the saddle. His mount trotted nervously a few paces, then turned and looked about in confusion. Three more shots cracked from the palisade, and another wrangler went down. The remounts began to whinny and mill about.

That served as a signal for Yancy Osburn, on the left, and Smiling Dave Winters, who commanded the right flank. They jumped their horses into motion, followed by the ten men each commanded. Yancy in the lead, his flankers swarmed around the breastlike swell of the hill, intent on closing on the herd and preventing a stampede.

Smiling Dave did the same, leading his men up out of the ravine and directly against the middle swing rider. Two six-guns blazed, and another Sugarloaf hand went down. The loose remounts went straight-legged in shock, then bolted inward, against the pressure of mounted horsemen. The outlaws whistled softly and uttered soothing words in an attempt to prevent the explosive moment in which the animals bolted in all directions. Two hundred horses at forty dollars a head represented a good lot of money. On the far side, Smiling Dave watched as Yancy killed yet another of the drovers. So far, Dave considered, it had gone well.

* * *

Luke Britton came face-to-face with one of the rustlers. He fired instinctively and felt a jolt of satisfaction when he saw the front of the outlaw's vest jump and a black hole appear close to the heart. Moments earlier, Jerry Harkness had disappeared in a cloud of dust and powder smoke. Luke looked for his friend, avoiding death by a narrow margin when he jumped his mount forward unexpectedly. At once he swung on the bandit and fired his six-gun.

"Gotcha, you varmint," he shouted in satisfaction as the gunman fell from his saddle.

To Luke's right, another Sugarloaf rider cried out and fell across the neck of his touchy roan. This was quickly going from bad to worse, Luke decided as he ducked low and kneed his mount in the direction where he had last seen Jerry.

Seconds later, the two friends found one another in a wild melee. A red stain washed along Jerry's right side, from a bullet gouge along his ribs. Having exhausted their cartridges, three rustlers swung their six-guns by the barrels in an attempt to club Jerry from his horse.

At once, Luke shot one of the bandits, and the other pair pulled off to reconsider. Jerry took the time to shuck the expended cartridges from his Colt and reload three rounds before the murderous trash sprang forward again. He and Luke fired as one and drilled the nearer robber through one lung and his liver. He would not live to ride clear of the fight.

"There's too many of them," Jerry opined. "We've got to pull back."

Luke protested immediately. "But the horses. We'll lose the herd."

Frowning, Jerry revealed his hasty plan and the reason for his decision. "We're gonna lose them anyway. Alive, we can trail them. If we stand our ground, there won't be a one of us left. Go tell the others."

Caleb Noonan had his horse shot out from under him. He went down with a wide roll away from the heavy creature as it fell. Quickly he scrambled back and used the dead beast as cover. From that vantage, Caleb took aim and blew a rustler out of the saddle. He fired again; then a hot line burned painfully along his left side. The offending slug smacked into the belly of his mount a split second later. Caleb rolled and snapped off another round.

He heard a cry in the midst of the roiling billow that blanketed the majority of the riders and the horses. Noonan took time for a fleeting smile and looked for another target. Be damned if he'd let these yahoos take the herd.

Pop walker had come up with a sprained ankle and had been relegated to the chuck wagon and the duties of a cook. He grumbled about it, but secretly prided himself in the grub he turned out. To the chagrin of the regular trail cook, many of the men complimented Pop on his culinary endeavors. When the ambush erupted in their faces, he had been behind Brad Plummer when the young drover had been shot through the breast. Pop Walker hauled on the reins and tried to turn the wagon, while he shouted a belated warning.

Immediately, bullets began to crack into the side of the converted buckboard. Pop set the brake, dropped low under the driver's bench and unlimbered his six-gun. The old Remington conversion fired well enough, but the barrel locking pin had been weakened by the hotter, cased ammunition loads. That caused the barrel to wobble on discharge, which played hob with his accuracy.

He took careful aim and fired at the face of a shouting rustler. The bullet went low and smacked the outlaw's horse between the eyes. The animal reared and threw its rider, then dropped in place. The gunman swung free of his saddle and threw a hasty shot in the direction of Pop Walker. Splinters burst in a shower at the top of the highest board, and Pop felt their sting, like so many bees, on his face. He raised up to fire again, and pain exploded in his right shoulder. Heat and numbness quickly followed. Awh, hell, he thought in a dizzy moment, how would he cook now?

"We've got 'em on the run," a jubilant Prine Gephart shouted through the dust.

"What says?" came a defiant question.

"They ain't standin' their ground anymore. We've got the horses free an' clear."

Reno Jim Yurian answered him. "Not so free. We've lost five good men so far. Tighten up those horses, don't let 'em run."

Suddenly, the fiercely fought ambush turned to equally desperate herd management. More dust rose to blind the Yurian gang and the Sugarloaf hands alike. An occasional shot blasted into the stillness of milling horses. An annoyed whinny usually answered it. Gradually the confusion diminished. A stiff breeze blew up from the southwest and carried away the brown cloud that had shrouded everything.

A moment after Pop Walker had shouted his warning, bullets flew all around Ahab Trask. Being saddled with the handle of the hated King of Judah gave him reason enough to use only his surname, he decided long ago. He ducked low and skinned his Smith American from its holster. From the volume of gunfire, Trask knew that this was no highway shakedown for tribute to use the trail.

These men had to be after the herd. The realization gave Trask renewed determination. He sought a target and at last sighted in on a pale face seen through a gap in the logs piled across the trail. He fired, and the face disappeared in a haze of red liquid. Once more he searched for an outlaw.

He did not have to look far. Brigands swarmed from around the side of the hill on his right, while more poured up over the lip of a draw on the left. Working drag, along with Utah Jack, Trask had the advantage of distance. He fired again, and one of the outlaws left his saddle. Then Trask looked at Utah Jack.

"We've gotta get these horses out of here."

Utah Jack spoke with authority. "No, Trask, we've got to hold them. If they stampede, we'll never find 'em all, an' the rustlers will have their pickin's."

Right then, a slug fired from the six-gun of Smiling Dave Winters cut a deep gouge along Trask's thigh and diverted upward to smash it-self against the thick leather of his cartridge belt. It drove partway through the buckle and embedded there. Stunned and winded, Trask saw blackness swim up to engulf him.

Dapper as always, although his fancy clothes bore a patina of gray-brown dust, Reno Jim Yurian stood in his stirrups and surveyed the scene of carnage.

Not a sign of the wranglers with the herd. An old man lay slumped against the dashboard of a chuck wagon. He bled from his shoulder. Quickly Reno Jim counted the fallen opponents. Eight of them. There had been a dozen. Some-how, four had gotten away. No matter, he de-cided. He waved an arm at the milling horses.

"You boys get them lined out and headed for the canyon." Reno Jim eased back into the sad-dle.

"What about them that got away?" asked Yancy Osburn.

"Not our problem. No doubt they were wounded. Bound to die before they can get to any help. Same for that one in the wagon."

Yancy Osburn sent men to clear the obstruc-tion across the trail. They worked quickly and efficiently. Pop Walker lay still and watched

them through slitted, pain-misted eyes. If what
their leaders—a man Pop saw as dressed in
fancy gambler's clothes—had said was true, he
would be a gonner soon. Damn, that rankled.
He did not want to die out here all alone.
Slowly, the herd came under control and moved
on up the trail. Before the severity of his wound
knocked him out, Pop heard one of the outlaws
mention him.

"I still say we ought to finish that old-timer."

"No," the fancy-dressed leader responded.
"Leave him for the coyotes."

Ten

Two days went by with the stolen herd getting farther away by the time Smoke Jensen and the Olsens arrived at the scene of the rustling. He hove into view a few minutes before eleven o'clock in the morning. Jerry Harkness saw him first. Although his ribs ached and burned from the infection that had invaded his wound, he raised his arm and waved eagerly to make certain Smoke knew someone had survived. Smoke turned to young Tommy when he saw signs of life.

"Bring the wagon along quick as you can. Those are my men down there."

Smoke cantered along the curve to within ten feet of the chuck wagon. There he reined in and dismounted, ground hitching Cougar. He made a quick count of heads while he strode toward Jerry. Five men. Only five left who were not seriously injured. At least they had managed to keep their horses. For a moment, Smoke tasted the bitter flavor of defeat.

"They ain't in any hurry, Smoke," Ahab Trask hastened up to inform Smoke. "An' they ain't hidin' their trail. We can catch them easy."

Silent, Smoke took in the injuries of his

hands. He doubted that these men would be catching up to anyone soon. He spoke beyond the haggard group to Luke Britton. "Luke, I want you to take the most seriously wounded and strike out to the east for the nearest town. If you come upon a big ranch, that might serve. Get the injured taken care of and gather someone to help get that herd back. The trail leads along the south fork of the Powder River, through the Bighorn Mountains, and into Buffalo. Join us there."

Luke looked around in surprise. "Who is 'us,' Smoke?"

Smoke nodded toward Tommy Olsen as the wagon rolled up. "Me, Utah Jack and him. That's Tommy Olsen, he's a good shot and level-headed. He'll have to do."

I'm going with you, Smoke," announced Jerry Harkness.

"No, you are not."

"Yes, I am." Jerry sat up abruptly and winced at the agony that shot through his chest. "I was only restin'. See? I can sit a saddle."

Smoke raised a gloved hand and pointed at Jerry. "You're not in that condition."

"It don't hurt that much, Smoke. It's getting better, really it is."

"Let me have a look."

Jerry knew better than to refuse, or even try to. He shrugged, pinched his features again and gave in with a sigh. Smoke climbed into the wagon and pulled Jerry's shirt away. The gouge cut by the bullet was scabbed, with oozing yellow pus escaping, bright red flesh all around. Long, scarlet lines, like the tentacles of an octopus, radiated out in two directions.

"I'm going to have to clean this, drain it and put a poultice on, Jerry. It's going to hurt like hell. But the only condition under which you are going along is that we get that infection whipped."

Eyes bright with a mixture of hope and sickness, Jerry looked intently at Smoke. "Go ahead. Whatever you do won't be any worse than what I've gone through so far."

"Don't be too sure of that. Luke, go to the nearest trees. Find some with moss. Then gather the yellow and gray parts. A whole lot of it. Also find some yarrow, if there is any, and bring the whole blossom. A double handful if you can get that much. Tommy, you go over to the creek and cut me an armload of red willow branches. Bring them back and we'll peel them."

Tommy looked at Smoke quizzically. "What's that for?"

"Red willow makes a good pain killer. We'll boil the scrapings from the bark and make a tea. I'll pour a lot down Jerry before I soak off that scab. He'll need it. Now, there's where you come in, Della. Find me some clean cloth, all you can spare, and tear it into strips. Those we'll boil to clean and bandage the wound."

In ten minutes, Smoke had a fire going. He examined all the wounded and treated the lightest injuries with liniment, bandaging them tightly when the boiled strips of a bed sheet had dried sufficiently. After half an hour, Tommy returned with a huge armload of willow branches. Smoke set him and his sisters to stripping the leaves, while he peeled and scraped the bark. He used a coffeepot from the chuck wagon, over mock protests from Pop Walker, who wasn't injured as badly as he thought, to begin to steep willow bark tea. When the boy finished cleaning the twigs, Smoke showed him how to peel and scrape the bark.

While they worked, Utah Jack Grubbs watched intently. At last he spoke. "That's Injun medicine you're cookin' up, ain't it?"

"Sure is, Utah. I learned it from Preacher when I was not much older than Tommy here."

"From a preacher, eh?"

"No, Utah. From the mountain man named Preacher. His given name was Arthur, but I don't think I ever heard his family name spoken."

Tommy looked up shyly from under long, auburn lashes. "He's the one you were tellin' me about the other night, sir—er—Smoke?"

"The same. He was quite a man. A real living legend."

"I've heard of him," Utah Jack pushed back into the conversation. "Wasn't he a bloody-handed murderer? They say he back shot more men than he faced down. Ambushed and kilt a whole passel of fellers."

"I don't know where you got such fool notions," Smoke replied lightly, attempting to disarm this scurrilous accusation. "I know better, because I was there most of the time. Preacher was no more a back shooter or a bushwhacker than I am. I learned my gun manners from him."

"Sorry, didn't mean to run down an old friend."

Smoke gave the equivocating horseman a frown. "There's not many men, living or dead, who could run down Preacher." Abruptly he came to his boots, poured a cup of yellow-red broth from the coffeepot and walked to where Jerry Harkness lay in the wagon.

"Here, Jerry, drink some of this."

"Do I gotta? That stuff tastes bitter."

Smoke shrugged. "Better bitter than not drink it and put up with what I'm going to do to you."

Jerry Harkness made a face and reached for the tin cup. He swallowed rapidly to get the liquid out of his mouth as quickly as possible. When he finished, he made to put it aside. Smoke reached out and took the container from him, filling it again.

"More?"

Smoke suppressed a grin. "More."

After the third cup, Jerry had about reached the gag limit. He licked his lips and made another sour face. By then, the medicinals Smoke required had been gathered and brought to the rough camp. Smoke rummaged in the chuck wagon again and came up with a wire basket popcorn popper. This he filled with the fungus and put it to dry over a low bed of coals.

With that in progress, he located a smooth, flat rock and piled the yarrow blossoms on it. He looked around and could not find what he wanted. He gestured to Tommy Olsen, who came to see what Smoke Jensen needed.

Pointing to the distant, tree-lined water course, Smoke made his request. "Tommy, go back to the creek and find me a fist-sized, water-smoothed rock. Wash it clean and bring it to me."

"Sure, Smoke," Tommy chirped. A mischievous, sly light came to the boy's eyes. "If I'm gonna get a good one, I bet I'll have to get in the water."

Having raised two sons and in the process of raising a third, Bobby, Smoke was wise in the ways of boys. "If you do, don't take more than ten minutes, and dry off good before putting your clothes back on."

Face alight with expectation, Tommy sped off after thanking Smoke for nothing more than acquiescing to the obvious. Smoke chuckled softly behind him. After all, he was not so old as to have forgotten his own boyhood.

Tommy returned with the rock twenty minutes later, his auburn hair a darker color, still dripping drops of water. His fair complexion, under the freckles, flushed a pink glow from the chill water of the creek. Proudly he handed Smoke a perfect stone.

Smoke thanked him and set immediately to crushing the yarrow flowers. He added more of the red willow scrapings and a bit of water to form a paste. This he covered with a strip of cloth from those drying on a thin line strung from the back of the Olsen wagon. During the process, he frequently checked the drying fungus.

When it reached the desired consistency, he added half to the poultice he had prepared and put the rest to soak in an especially strong liquor of willow bark. He looked up to see Luke Britton standing over him.

"I'll start off now with the wounded, if it's all right with you, Smoke."

"Do that. They're patched up as good as I can do. Take the best of your horses. We have two wagons. Pop Walker can drive one, Utah Jack the other. Tommy and I have horses. We'll get on the trail by mid-afternoon, and stick to the sign left by the herd. Join back up as soon as you can. And . . . good luck."

"It's you who's gonna need the luck, Smoke."

Smoke agreed readily. "Don't I know it."

Taking up his medicines, Smoke walked to where Jerry awaited his fate. With Della's help, he administered more of the potent tea and then took hot water and cloth strips and, using his sheath knife, began to scrape away the crust of dried blood that had scabbed over the wound channel. Jerry bit his lip and suppressed a cry of pain.

Smoke Jensen worked deftly and quickly, to peel open the long gouge along the ribs. While he progressed, at his direction, Della Olsen mopped up the yellowish matter that had collected under the surface. In a brief two minutes, which seemed like hours to Jerry, the whole raw wound had been exposed. With hands surprisingly gentle for their size and muscularity, Smoke bathed the savaged muscle tissue. Then he packed the groove with the poultice he had concocted.

Wonder registered on the face of Jerry Harkness. "It feels so cool. Like you'd rubbed ice on me, Smoke."

In the distance everyone heard two quick shots from the light .32-30 rifle carried by

Tommy Olsen. "We'll change that in a couple of hours and then try to get some broth down you."

Pop Walker grumped his opinion. "What are you gonna make it outta? Most of our grub got flogged by those rustlers. We've been makin' do with corn bread and beans."

Smoke showed him an amused smile. "If I'm not mistaken, we'll have rabbit, or maybe some prairie chickens, might even be deer meat on the menu."

Pop looked surprised. "Y'mean that li'l tad of a boy's gonna fetch us our dinner?"

Smoke nodded. "Just so. I told you he is a crack shot. He never fires if he can't hit what he's shooting at. So, if I were you, Pop, I'd get to whipping up some of that corn bread. And see if you can't round up some onions, wild or otherwise. Anything to flavor a stew."

"Well, I'll be gol-derned." Pop Walker brightened. "I'll do that right away."

After they had eaten their fill, with Smoke Jensen urging everyone to stuff themselves and put aside what would keep, because it would be a cold camp that night, he changed the poultice and bandages on Jerry Harkness.

Smoke beamed down at his trustworthy ranch hand. "You may not feel like it, but you're looking a lot better. The poultice is drawing, and the infection is not headed for your armpit anymore. Another day or so and you can ride."

"That's good news. Say, the kid did a right smart job of gettin' that antelope. When do I get off this baby's broth and sink my teeth into some real meat?"

"By tonight, I'd say. I set the ribs to smoking over the coals. They should be ready by the time we break camp."

Jerry looked admiringly upon Smoke. "Do you ever not think of everything, Smoke?"

Smoke produced a wry smile. "Not since Preacher boxed my ears for leaving a perfectly good fireside trestle behind. He got right exercised by that."

Thirty minutes later, the refugees of the ambush started off after the herd. Most rode in silence. Tommy, atop the swayback plow horse, trotted up to ride beside Smoke Jensen. Smoke noted the boy had his Winchester along.

"What do we do when we catch up to your horses, Smoke?"

Smoke did not even have to think. "You fall back and protect your mother and sisters. That Model Seventy-three has range enough to make certain none of them get close. It'll be like shooting game. Make sure of your shot, never miss, and go for the head shots when you can."

Tommy went suddenly pale. "But, I . . . ain't never shot at a man before." His voice croaked from just beyond the threshold of puberty.

Smoke's reply, although candid enough, spared Tommy the more gruesome aspects of the reality. "It's not nice, ever. And you never get over it. But a man has to do what he has to do. I'm not worried, Tommy. You'll be all right when the time comes."

Much relieved, Tommy heaved a sigh. "If you say so, sir. I'll try to do my best, Smoke."

Jerry Harkness had been sitting upright the last several miles, leaning over the left sideboard of the Olsen wagon, his eyes on the multitude of hoof prints. He called out to Smoke now, his eyes alight with confidence.

"It's them, all right. Unshod hooves an' all." An amusing thought suddenly occurred to him. "Say, those army farriers are gonna play merry hell with these critters when we finally get them there."

Merriment twinkled in Smoke's eyes, and he pulled a wry expression. "It's all part of the plan. At least that's my understanding from what Colonel Albright said in his letter. The shoeing of these horses is to be part of what the army calls On the Job Training. He's been burdened with green farriers. They need breaking in as fast as these mounts."

That brought a laugh from Jerry Harkness, which caused him to wince. Smoke trotted over to the wagon and climbed into the bed. He tied Cougar to the tailgate and went to his Cheyenne medicine supplies. Quickly he tended to the wound on Jerry's side and repacked it with fresh poultice. When the task had been completed, he cut his eyes to those of his ranch hand.

"You're doing better, faster than I thought. The red rays of infection have shrunk by half." He pointed to the formerly alabaster skin over Jerry's rib cage. "And you are taking on a more natural, pinkish coloring. For sure, by tomorrow you'll be driving that wagon, instead of riding in it."

"That's good news. Now, what's the bad news?"

Smoke sobered at once. "You won't be up to fighting form for at least three more days."

Jerry looked jolted. "Then you were right all along. I'm being a burden on all of you. I should have gone with Luke. A gimped-up man ain't no good in a fight."

Smoke sighed explosively. "If I had thought you were seriously wounded, outside of the infection, I would have made you go. Now stop feeling sorry for yourself and heal so you can carry your load in a fight." The last of that he said with a gruffness from the affection he held for this courageous young ranch hand.

That night, the small party settled into what would be the first of many cold camps. The generous portion of leftover antelope ribs, served out by Pop Walker, along with the remaining corn bread, biscuits and a pot of cold beans, left everyone with full bellies. While they ate, Tommy hunkered right up close beside him, and Smoke became aware of something that for the moment perplexed him.

Throughout the afternoon, Tommy had ridden resolutely at Smoke's side. In camp, the boy had stuck close to him; wherever he went, Tommy came along. No matter what chore he was given, Tommy went about it cheerfully and with an eagerness that belied the usual surly mood of teenaged children. While he conducted his labors, the lad constantly cut his eyes to Smoke to see if his efforts were being noticed. When his gaze locked with Smoke's, Tommy flushed furiously and looked away, suddenly burdened with ten thumbs. So frequently separated from his own brood, it took Smoke some time to figure it out.

No doubt about it, he allowed in late evening when the boy trudged along beside Smoke for a final check of the horses on the picket line. Tommy had transferred his need for a father figure to Smoke. *Damn!* Smoke thought. That was going to get the boy's feelings bad hurt before this was over. Somehow, that didn't seem right. For his part, rather than do the popularly accepted thing of spurning the youngster's devotion, Smoke responded by roughly teasing the boy. To Smoke's surprise, it seemed to strengthen the bond the lad sought to forge between them.

"Hey, Tommy, are you sure that water wasn't too cold this morning?"

A puzzled frown formed on Tommy's forehead. The water had felt wonderful. "Why's that, Smoke?"

"Your voice is a full octave higher than before."

Blushing, Tommy made feeble protest. "Awh, it is not. It's jist . . . sometimes it breaks, goes back to bein' a little kid again."

Smoke reached out and ruffled the youngster's tousled auburn hair. "Growing up is hell, ain't it?"

"Yessir, it purely is," Tommy agreed from the depths of his adolescent misery.

Early the next morning, Smoke's party lost the trail of the herd on a wide stretch of hard shale outcroppings. The wagons pressed on while

Smoke and Utah Jack fanned out to search. Shortly before noon, Utah Jack cut their sign. He swung back to the wagons and fired three shots to alert Smoke. When the last mountain man arrived, Grubbs gave him the good news.

"I found them. They're headed for Powder River Pass up yonder in the Bighorns. The tracks look a whole lot fresher. They must be havin' trouble with the remounts."

Smoke considered that a moment. "That means they are straying away from our intended route. If that's the case, they have a place close by to hold the horses until a buyer can be found. That makes our job easy."

Utah Jack challenged this at once. "How do you figger that? There ain't but three of us fit to do any fightin'."

"Jerry can hold his own in that wagon. And as I said before, Tommy's a fine shot." Smoke looked up to find the boy at his side, eagerly soaking up every word.

"Yeah, but are you gonna take a little boy of fourteen into a fight with more'n twenty hard cases?"

He hadn't been any older when Preacher got him into a shoot-out with some angry Pawnee. Smoke almost spoke his thoughts aloud, though he refrained because he did not want to give Tommy any encouragement. Instead, he flavored his response with a frown. "I'm not going to get Tommy into any fight if I can avoid it."

"Awh, Smoke," Tommy protested. "You jist said I was a good shot. The sooner we get your horses back, the sooner you can get us on to Buffalo."

Momentarily stymied, Smoke pushed back the brim of his Stetson. "The kid's got a point, you have to admit.'

Prine Gephart leaned over and tapped Garth Evans on one shoulder. With a grunt, Garth ended his mid-afternoon snooze and shoved his hat up off his face. "Huh? What is it."

"Lookie over there. That's them comin'. You can bet on it, believe me."

Garth Evans rubbed sleep from his eyes and focused on the distant ridge. Two wagons labored down the facing slope. Three riders, one of them looking to be no more than a boy, formed a wedge in front of them. Dust boiled up from the wheels.

"Hummm. You might be right, Prine. If so, what do we do now?"

Gephart snapped testily. "What we was put here for. We're supposed to be lookouts, right? What we had best do is that you light a shuck outta here and catch up to the gang. I'll keep ahead of them and guide the boys in when they come. Now, best make tracks."

Garth Evans started to swing into his saddle. Prine Gephart roused himself to sit upright. "No, dummy. Walk your horse at least a mile before you mount up. You want them hearing you?"

"Uh! Never thought of that."

In minutes he had walked out of sight of the pile of carelessly strewn boulders. Prine Gephart went next, also walking his horse until well ahead of the slow-moving caravan. Then he took to the saddle and ambled along the wide path left by the horses. His confidence soared. He had counted heads. This little annoyance would be easy to get rid of.

Another cold camp. From a close examination of the hoof prints, Smoke determined that they had quickly closed the gap. The width of the trail indicated that the rustlers were indeed having trouble with the herd. Obviously not experienced wranglers, they let the horses spread out too far, making control difficult. Their nearness continued to gnaw on Smoke.

There would be no chance to retake the herd with so few able-bodied men. The best he could hope for would be to continue to keep watch and wait for reinforcements. After a supper of antelope ham and cold biscuits, Smoke felt it necessary to reassure Della. He took her aside.

"I don't want you worrying about Tommy, or yourself and the girls. I have no intention of going after those horses without a lot more gunhands than I have. We'll trail along, keep out of sight and wait."

"I'm so relieved." Della waved a hand in a half-circle gesture that encompassed the terrain and their condition as well. "All of this. It's . . . it's so bizarre. Outlaws stealing horses, raiding our ranch and burning it. Now chasing after these evil men. It was not like that back east. Not at all. We were—always so safe."

"Yes, but didn't you notice how much freedom you had to give up to be that safe?"

Della considered that as though a novel idea.

"I never thought of that. A policeman on every corner. He knew everyone by face and name."

"He also knew everything everyone knew, said, or thought, right?"

Again a frown of concentration. "Yes. You're right. Any miscreant was soon hauled off the streets and questioned until he confessed."

Gently, Smoke probed farther. "Do you have any idea how those confessions were acquired?"

"N-no. Now that you mention it."

"Usually with boots, fists, and night sticks. Not that lawmen out here have found that method unworkable. It's effective; yet to me, it seems to take something fundamental out of the one beaten and the one doing the beating."

With an uneasy trill of laughter, Della dismissed the grim images. "That did not apply to our life. Sven had a good position at a large steel mill in Pennsylvania. He was an accountant, before becoming a pioneer."

"Your children were born there?"

"Tommy and Sarah-Jane. Gertrude came along after we moved west. First, it was Kansas. That's where Sven learned how little he knew about farming. Especially dry farming like they have to do there." She cheered slightly. "But he found he had a knack with livestock. Cattle in particular. We nearly lost the farm. Sven had a lucky streak when he found a buyer. We bought seed stock and started west. We ended up here in the territory."

Smoke listened sympathetically to her narration for the better part of an hour. When Della got to a recounting of her husband's death, she broke down and began to sob softly, hands clamped to her mouth. Solicitously, Smoke comforted her while she cried on his shoulder. The moon had set by the time she retired to the wagon, and smoke rolled up in his blankets to sleep.

Shortly before dawn, five members of the Yurian gang ghosted into camp and fired shots in the direction of the sleeping forms on the ground. A second later, Smoke Jensen replied in kind, and all hell broke loose.

Eleven

Sadly lacking in frontier skills, the Yurian gang had been heard crashing through the brush by Smoke Jensen several minutes before their attack. It had given Smoke time to prepare a nasty surprise. As the gang poured into camp, and fired at the dark forms rolled into blankets, they only served to pinpoint their locations. Answering shots came immediately, and from outside camp.

"Them ain't people," blurted Ainsley Burk.

Colin Fike added to their confusion. "They were layin' for us outside camp."

Thirty feet away from him, Jerry Harkness triggered a round from his six-gun. The man beside Colin Fike grunted and went down. Then a voice heavy with authority broke through the confusion.

Hub Volker barked his brief orders. "Forget them. Get that woman and the brats and let's get out of here."

At once the outlaws concentrated their attention on the wagon on the far side of the camp. Jerry Harkness dropped another thug, then gave covering fire to Smoke Jensen, who darted at an oblique angle toward the Olsen wagon. Three outlaws fired at his movement. Their slugs cut the air behind Smoke. Hub Volker and Smiling Dave Winters reached the wagon first. Hairy Joe tripped over a saddle, robbed of his night vision by muzzle bloom, and stumbled up next.

He reached the vehicle in time to take a round full in his face from the Winchester in the hands of Tommy Olsen. Reflex and impact flipped Hairy Joe backward, to land with his head in the softly glowing coals of the fire pit. The long, greasy strands of his black hair ignited instantly and formed a ghastly halo. Already dead, the now Hairless Joe did not feel a thing.

Smiling Dave lashed out and yanked the rifle from the grasp of the boy, who stared in disbelief at the destruction he had wrought. Sarah-Jane and Gertrude began to scream as the men climbed into the wagon box. Della fought with clawed fingers; her sturdy nails raked deep furrows along the cheeks of Garth Evans, who recoiled in astonishment. At once, Della snatched up the Colt Lightning Smoke had given her son and squeezed the trigger.

A .44 slug burned a hot, painful trail through the left shoulder of an incredulous Garth Evans, who howled and fell out of the wagon. Della looked around desperately to locate help. She saw Smoke's path blocked by two hard cases. Both had revolvers in their hands and raised them toward the last mountain man as she cried a warning.

Smoke's six-gun came up before either outlaw could fire a shot. The nearer one jolted backward and bent double as a .45 caliber bullet shattered the tip of his sternum. Without delay, Smoke triggered another cartridge. A thin, wavering cry came from the second thug as, gut-shot, he went to his knees. He dropped his weapon and began to try to stuff a bulge of intestine back inside his belly.

Behind him, Smoke Jensen heard a brief cry of pain as Jerry Harkness took another wound, this time a through-and-through hole where his neck met his shoulder. Smoke took a step forward only to see an obscure blur directly before his eyes. In the split second before the rifle butt crashed into his forehead, Smoke saw the grinning face of Smiling Dave Winters looming over him. Lights exploded in his head, and darkness swept over Smoke Jensen.

Something cold touched the throbbing core of the pain in Smoke Jensen's head. Light flickered against his closed eyelids. His dazed senses registered wetness next. Cautiously he tried opening one eye.

Tall grass and a muzzy blue sky swam above Smoke. With a soft groan, he opened the other eye. The spinning slowed, then ceased. A startled grunt came, and Smoke vaguely realized that he had made it. Suddenly a blurry face appeared to fill the entire span of Smoke's vision.

"Man, am I glad you're back. I was afraid we'd lose you, Smoke." Jerry Harkness, his shoulder crudely bandaged, hovered over Smoke Jensen for a moment, then raised back to where he came into focus.

Smoke opened his mouth to a taste like an overused outhouse. His words came out in a croak. "Jerry . . . is—are the—the Olsens all right?"

Jerry's grim expression forewarned Smoke. "They're gone, Smoke. Those bastids took them, their wagon, everything. We're afoot, no chuck wagon nor a horse in sight."

Smarting at his failure to protect the vulnerable family, and shamed by his weakness, Smoke extended a shaky hand for Jerry's help in rising. "What about Pop Walker and Utah Jack?"

Sadness touched Jerry's features. "Pop's over there. They killed him, Smoke. I don't know about Utah. I can't find him anywhere. They may have taken him and killed him somewhere else."

Tentatively, Smoke touched his face. He found blood still crusted in his eyebrows and along his jaw line. "I've got to clean up. Then we'll bury Pop Walker and figure out what we do next. Is there any doubt that they were from the gang who rustled the horses?"

"None. But, Smoke, what can we do?"

"We can take stock and decide that later, Jerry."

With the help of his top hand, Smoke Jensen washed the blood away in a dented metal basin. Then he touched the bandage Jerry had put on his split forehead. A wave of nausea rose in Smoke's throat. He fought it back.

"We have to get something to eat."

"I'll dig a hole for Pop, Smoke. Are you up to a walk to the creek? Maybe you can catch us some fish."

Smoke nodded grimly. "Yeah. I follow that.

We can't afford to waste ammunition on rabbits."

"You've got the right of it. I took stock while
you were still out. You have your Colts and a
Winchester. I've got my six-gun. Together we
have about a hundred fifty rounds. You've got
forty for the rifle, sixty-three for your revolvers. I
have the rest."

"Sounds better than I expected." Smoke
headed to where his saddlebags lay, their contents scattered on the ground. A small square of
folded buckskin produced a coil of braided-
twine fishing line and four hooks. Reclosing the
container, he pocketed it and sought out a thin
branch from a cottonwood nearby. He used it as
a staff to aid his progress toward the stream.
Behind him, he heard the steady chunk-chunk
as Jerry Harkness drove a shovel into the turf. It
could be worse, Smoke thought to himself.
Though somehow he could not picture exactly
how.

By the time Smoke had devoured three pan-
sized bullhead catfish, his head had stopped
swimming. It only throbbed slightly. He availed
himself of some red willow bark and scraped a
small pile of powder, which he washed down
with water from the creek. Then he turned to
the matter that had absorbed him since recovering.

"Jerry, I have to keep after the herd."

"Don't you mean we, Smoke?"

"No. You've been wounded twice so far. What

I want you to do is set out down the trail and find help. Bring as many men as you can."

Harkness had plenty of protest left. "You already sent someone east for help. I say we can do better if we stick together."

"I don't think so. The riders I sent are going to be waiting for us north of Sheridan. The herd won't be moving too fast. And with the Olsens, it will slow the rustlers even more.

"What I can't figure, Smoke, is why they took them in the first place?"

"As insurance. Whoever is running that gang figures we will not try to take back the herd with a woman and children along. That's just their latest mistake."

"What was their first one?"

Smoke's hickory eyes narrowed. "Taking my horses in the first place."

While Smoke prepared to set out on foot, they talked of how he would leave sign if the herd changed directions. He would take his saddle and saddlebags along. Jerry would gather up anything useful when he returned with a posse. When everything had been decided, Harkness still had an objection.

"What if that head wound is worse than we think? I should stay with you in case you pass out again."

"That makes sense, but there are only the two of us. I have to keep after the rustlers. Now, get goin'. And, good luck."

Reno Jim Yurian found himself plagued by second thoughts. Burdened by the slow-moving horses, and the wagon with the hostages, the gang's progress had been slowed to a walk. Perhaps he should not have told Hub to grab the woman and her kids. Though they might make a good bargaining point. Another reflection gave him a sudden chill along his spine.

This Smoke Jensen had proven more stubborn than he had expected. Reno knew the name, of course. Jensen had himself quite the reputation. A gunfighter of the first order, who was supposed to have been raised by some mythical mountain man named Preacher, Jensen was reported to have killed his first man when barely fifteen. Or was it sixteen?

That detail didn't matter to Jim Yurian. Smoke Jensen was supposed to be so fast with a gun that only five men had ever cleared leather ahead of his draw. *That* worried Reno Jim more than he was willing to admit. If Smiling Dave had failed to bash in the man's skull, then as sure as the sun would rise tomorrow, Jensen would be coming after them. Reno didn't believe for a moment he would come alone.

Seeking distraction from such gloomy thoughts, Reno Jim turned his horse aside and waited while the lead gather of remounts walked past. The Olsen wagon came next, between the divided herd. As it rolled even, he touched the brim of his black hat with a gloved hand. A thin, teasing smile flickered.

"I trust you are comfortable, Miz Olsen?"

Della warred with herself over outrage at their capture and their apparent continued safety. She loathed this jaunty outlaw in his impeccable black suit and rakish tilt of hat. The pencil-line mustache on his upper lip seemed to mock her. Grudgingly she had to admit he was a superb horseman. He sat his mount well and flowed with its movements whether at a walk or a canter. The nickle-plated, pearl-handled revolvers he wore reminded her that although a dandy, he was a dangerous one. She did not want to answer him, but found that she must.

"So far we have not been treated too badly. Though I would like to give your underling, who slapped around my son, a lasting headache."

To her surprise the outlaw leader laughed. "I can understand your feelings, madam. Although you must admit that your boy did kill one of my men, as did you, I do believe."

He remained amused when Della started a hot retort. "I only wish—" Aghast at her temerity, she stopped.

"That it could have been more?" Reno Jim concluded for her, rightly gauging her intent. "Fortunately for you it was not. My men are fiercely loyal to one another. Had you been successful, they might have done . . . some violence to you all."

Shrewdly, Della checked him. "You would not have allowed that, now would you?"

Reno Jim made a show of being resigned. "You have me, madam. Truly you are my hole card. But, be assured, I will play you however it appears to my best advantage."

Della displayed her knowledge of card language. "You will forgive me if I say that I sincerely hope you lose the hand? Because, believe me, you are bucking four aces if you go against Smoke Jensen."

There was that cursed name again! Coming from this woman of considerable fortitude almost had him believing it. Perhaps if her faith became shaken, it would deflect from his own cold premonition. Maybe he should relax his prohibition somewhat and let the boys enjoy a trailside reward.

After plates of sow-belly and beans, flavored with hot peppers and vinegar, and skillet bread, several of the outlaws broke out bottles of whiskey.

When the liquor had made several rounds, one of the trail scum, fired by the raw rotgut, piped up to his companions. "What say we cut high card for who gets to do them gals tonight? First ace for the littlest, first king for the older one, and the first queen for the woman."

"What? Jist one each tonight?" complained Prine Gephart. "I'll bet the ol' woman an' the older girl can each take on at least four of us ev'ry night."

A snigger answered him. "Mighty likely they could, if we was all built like you, Prine."

Gephart took immediate exception. "Hey, you bassard, that ain't funny." The chorus of laughter that raised said otherwise. That set Prine off on a single-minded course. "That does it, you smart-asses. For that, I'm gonna go over there and plow all three of them fields, all by myself."

His challenge met immediate response. Yancy Osburn came to his boots, hand closed around the butt-grip of his Smith American. "Like hell you are. It's gonna be fair share. Everyone gets a chance."

Gephart put on a pouting expression. Only his eyes showed his combativeness. "You gonna pull that thing, Yance? Reno said we could ride those fillies an' the mare to our heart's content. I aim to do exactly that."

"Draw for high card, dammit," growled Colin Fike.

Not nearly far enough away, Della Olsen clearly heard their angry voices and knew only so well what it was they intended. Quickly she reached out and covered her younger daughter's ears. She noted to her satisfaction that Tommy did the same for Sarah-Jane. Then the boy spoke with heated sincerity.

"If any of them so much as touches one of you, I swear, Maw, I'll make the sons of bitches pay."

Fear for her son's life blotted out her shock at his language and spurred her to dissuade him. "No, son. They—they'd kill you this time."

Tommy Olsen slitted his eyes. "Not before I got a lot of them."

Still determined to press for his equal right to pester the woman and her girls, Colin Fike pushed his insistence. "Cut the cards, Prine, we got a right."

Enraged by this defiance of his authority, Prine Gephart snarled at his subordinate. "As long as you're a member of my crew, the only rights you have are those I give you. You'd best learn that well." His anger crackled as he loosened the Merwin and Hulbert in its holster. To his eventual regret, Colin Fike pushed once more, and too hard, for his rights. "I'm not your slave, by damn. Haul out that iron."

Brain fogged by whiskey, Gephart eagerly obliged him. Even drunk, Prine Gephart was faster than the befuddled Colin Fike. His Merwin and Hulbert .44 cleared leather in a blue-black streak, leveled, and the firing pin descended toward the waiting primer before a startled Colin even closed fingers around the butt-grip of his Smith American.

In the same instant, Yancy Osburn bellowed forcefully, "Nooooo!"

A gunshot blasted the night's silence. Prine Gephart's bullet struck true, burst the heart of Colin Fike and erupted through his back with a fist-sized hole. Instantly, the established herd leader let out a squeal of alarm, and whinnies of fright answered. Another bugle from the lead stallion, and the herd dissolved into a mindless, panicked mass of walleyed, terrorized animals. They jolted to the right, then back to the left, then in a second dashed away, tails high, in all directions.

"You idiots!" Hubble Volker bellowed over the noise of the stampede. "You goddamned idiots. Get to your horses, get after those critters. Move or I'll kill you myself."

And so it ended before it even started. Della stared in disbelief and relief as the outlaws raced for the picket line to throw saddles on their mounts and flog them after the splintered herd, all thought of rape driven from their minds.

Twelve

Crouched down on the parched ground, Smoke Jensen searched for a small, smooth pebble. With a fiercely hot summer sun burning down over the previous afternoon and through most of his second day in pursuit of the stolen herd, Smoke had exhausted the content of his single canteen. In the past he had gone without food many a time, and he knew that hunger was endurable. Now, plagued by thirst, Smoke stretched his perseverance to the limit by entertaining images of what he would like to do to the rustlers who had shot up every visible water container at his former campsite. He had to find an alternative or give up his quest. On his third try, he came up with a suitable, light brown stone.

Smoke used the last few drops of water from the canteen to wash the little rock, which he then popped in his mouth and worked under his tongue. At once, saliva began to flow. With his temporary measure in place, he began once more to trudge along the swath of disturbed turf that marked the passage of the stolen horses. So long as he found water by nightfall, he would be all right. Failing that, Smoke realized he could not survive.

Back in Muddy Gap, Ginny Parkins found herself restless and ill at ease as she tried to get a gaggle of ten-year-olds to understand the mysteries of long division. When a fit of giggling broke out among the fifth grade girls, she dismissed school early for the day. Her charges stormed the exit with squeals of jubilation. That still left Ginny with an empty feeling.

And, darn it, she knew the reason why. She had treated Sheriff Smoke Jensen most shabbily. No other word for it. He had only been doing his job. For a moment she wondered if he still enforced the law in Muddy Gap. The town had been so peaceful the past five days. Fortunately the riffraff had not returned after the final, brutal expulsion of the most unrepentant. No, Ginny chided herself, not brutal, rather *necessary*. Goaded by her conscience, Ginny Parkins left the former security of the schoolhouse on what she considered a delicate mission.

Her bustle swishing behind her, Ginny Parkins reached the downtown sector of Muddy Gap slightly out of breath. With a start, she realized she had been walking at twice her normal pace. Face set in a prim expression, she looked both ways before entering the office at the jail. To her surprise, she found Grover Larsen sitting behind his desk, and Deputy Chase in the sheriff's chair. She looked around a moment in consternation.

"Is Sheriff Jensen making his rounds?" she enquired.

Grover Larsen answered her. "He's not sheriff anymore, ma'am. He's moved on with his horse herd."

Ginny did not believe what she had heard. "What?"

Fred Chase offered assurance. "It's true, Miss Ginny. I've been appointed interim sheriff until the next election. Smoke left four days ago."

"I—I don't understand. I c-can't believe . . ."

That he would leave without telling you? After the way you treated him? her mind mocked her.

Grover Larsen undertook to enlighten her. "Smoke Jensen is a rancher. He raises blooded stock for the rich folks, and a large herd suitable as remounts for the army."

"But, I thought he was some sort of gunfighter. A living legend."

Larsen smiled softly. "He's both, Miss Ginny. Let me tell you a little about Smoke Jensen. No one out here, but him, knows where he was born. His family was movin' west, out to Oregon Territory, when he got separated from the wagon train. He was a little tad, no more'n eleven or so. He managed to survive a few days on his wits.

"Some say he traded what few possessions he had with Injuns for food. They wanted to keep him, adopt him into the tribe, but Smoke had it in his head he could catch up and find his folks. That didn't happen. The old mountain man, Preacher, found young Smoke first. He took him in and raised him up. There's some argue it was a bad upbringin', that Smoke learned to fight and to kill. Supposed to have killed his first man at the age of twelve.

"Well now," Larsen continued, warming to his subject, "that ain't true. Preacher was through here a number of years back, when Muddy Gap was nothing more than a wide place in the road. I was a youngster then, myself, not more'n seventeen. I heard Preacher talkin' about Smoke Jensen. Said he got his name and the start of his reputation at the same time, when he was sixteen. That came from the man who should know. And in these mountains, Preacher's known to have never told a lie." Larsen flushed and waved a hand in dismissal. "There I go, ramblin' like an old fool.

Ginny protested at once. "No, please go on. I'm fascinated. I . . . never got to know Sheri— Smoke well."

"Well, Smoke grew up, like folks are likely to do. He learned Injun things, and their talk, too. Likewise, Preacher taught him to read and write and do his sums. Taught him to trap, skin and cure beaver hides, though the trade was fast dwindlin'. Smoke learned about horses from Preacher, also a lot about other animals, an' how to respect them and give 'em all space to live and move about. They say he's whipped the daylights outta more than one man who has mistreated animals. Seems quirky in a man who became a gunfighter an' eventual' a lawman. Don't you think?"

"I see nothing odd about a person who is fond of animals. After all, they need our care and protection," Ginny went on, taken up in her zeal. "They can't speak or write, so they can't stand up for rights like humans can."

Young Fred Chase put in his outlook. "I can't agree with you more, Miss Ginny. The way I see it, animals don't have any rights because they can't nego—negotiate what they will do in order to get them. So a man who mistreats a horse or dog is the lowest form of inhuman trash." He looked defiantly at Grover Larsen. "An' that's a fact."

Larsen offered coffee, poured and they talked on for another half an hour about Smoke Jensen. Before Ginny departed, Marshal Larsen raised a staying hand. "Oh, before you go, Miss Ginny, there's something I have to give you. Smoke Jensen left this for you against the time when you might need it."

He reached into his top drawer and came out with a small .38 Smith and Wesson revolver. Ginny gaped, gulped, stammered and gingerly accepted the gift. "Thank you for giving me Smoke's present, although I'm certain I shall never have use of it."

Ginny left feeling somewhat better at having secured a promise that Marshal Larsen would send a telegram to the town nearest Smoke Jensen's ranch with her apology. Yet part of her felt worse, over becoming owner of a firearm. She would write Smoke, too, she pledged as she crossed the street to the general store. She would have to thank him for the gun, but also assure him that she would never use it. Idly she wondered if she would ever see Smoke Jensen again.

* * *

Sweat stained the armpits of the shirt worn by Smoke Jensen. The afternoon sun beat down relentlessly. It sapped him of the precious little moisture his body retained. For the past hour he had been watching the hazy, insubstantial outline of trees in the distance. Certain he had not circled and come back to the Powder River, Smoke fixed on the long file of greenery that indicated a watercourse.

Even the pebble failed to do its magic. The length of his stride had shortened, and his head throbbed. Slowly, the pale green leaves of cottonwoods began to swim into sharp focus. A creek all right. Smoke forced himself forward. Another fifty paces. His footsteps faltered.

Thirty paces now. Alarmingly, the sweat dried on his skin to a clammy coldness. His body had stopped producing moisture. Twenty paces now. The individual trunks of the trees could be seen. He could smell the water.

Stumbling like a drunken man, Smoke closed the last distance to the grassy bank that hung over a narrow streambed; below, the water peacefully glided past. Its surface reflected a cool, inviting green. With the last of his strength, Smoke eased over the bank and lowered himself to a sandy shelf. There he removed his boots and cartridge belt, then jumped into the water.

Its coolness embraced him. When his clothes had become thoroughly wet, he removed them and washed out the salt and dust. His thoughts snapped back to young Tommy Olsen doing exactly the same thing not so long ago. Wringing out his garments, he flung them up on the grassy bank. The cool water exhilarated him, and he noticed his skin had turned a rosy pink. Satisfied, he climbed out and let his effluvium drift away before filling the canteen.

Then he gained the embankment and spread his clothes on a hawthorn bush to sun dry. He would continue to use the pebble in order to preserve his water, he reminded himself. While he dried off, he drank deeply, but slowly, from the canteen. When his limbs stopped trembling, he returned to the creek to refill the canteen. He turned his clothes once and was soon dressed and ready.

Fastening his cartridge belt around his waist and easing his weapons into place, Smoke started off. He had a goodly ways to go before dark. Idly, he wondered what he might find to eat along the way.

Well over eight feet long, the sleek, fat diamondback lay torpid on a large, flat rock. Drowsed by the lowering sun, the serpent only vaguely felt pangs of hunger. It had killed and eaten a jackrabbit three days ago. Now the time had come to hunt and feed again. So innervated had the viper become from the late afternoon sun that it only sporadically employed its early warning system. After a long two minutes, the forked tongue flicked out, sensing the vibrations and flavors of its surroundings. Then it flicked out again, the creature suddenly alert.

So silently did Smoke Jensen move that the rattlesnake did not sense his approach until the man nearly came into sight. Lethargically, the viper roused itself and began to coil for a strike at what seemed a huge food source. Ancient instincts stirred, and it completed its spiral with renewed alacrity. The upper third of its body arched into the air; the snake swayed backward, prepared to strike.

That was when Smoke Jensen saw it. Despite the debilitating effects of no food and little water, a man of Smoke's prowess and speed had ample time to unlimber his right-hand Colt and blow the triangular head off the viper as it arched toward him. Deprived of command, the huge body writhed and twisted across the ground.

Instinct caused it to try to recoil, but the necessary command center no longer existed, and it all but tied itself in knots. Smoke stood well clear while the reptile's violent motions slowed, his .45 Peacemaker ready. He well knew that prairie rattlers like this one frequently traveled in mated pairs. A bull this size was sure to have a harem.

When the creature's spasms reduced to an occasional twitch, he grabbed the body below the rattles and held it at shoulder height while he walked quickly to a stunted oak that rode the top of a low knob. Using a fringe thong from his shirt, Smoke tied the snake upside down from a low limb. Expertly applying his Greenriver sheath knife, he slit the skin from neck to rattles, peeled it back, then opened the pinky white body from severed end to its bung. He used his boot heel to dig a small hole to dispose of the guts, then washed the meat with a little of his dwindling water supply. With that accomplished, he looked all around, scanning the horizon for any human presence besides himself.

Satisfied that he was alone, he made a fire ring, gathered dead fall from the oak and kindled it to life from a tinder box he habitually carried. When the blaze took, he fed it twigs until a decent bed of coals appeared. Nearly smokeless, the fire under the spreading limbs of the oak gave off no telltale column of smoke. After threading the snake on a green branch he had cut, Smoke Jensen placed it over the fire. He wished for salt, then banished the desire. While his meat cooked, he located a choke-cherry bush and stripped it of a handful of berries.

He would crush these and rub them into the meat while it roasted. The bitter-sweet tang of the fruit would make a fair substitute for salt. When all had been accomplished, he feasted ravenously of the whole body, buried his fire, and made ready to leave. He had a lot of distance to cover before dark.

Smoke Jensen's lean, muscular figure cast a long shadow to his right when he saw the dust cloud ahead. He had caught up to the herd. He grew more cautious. Deserting the trail, Smoke bent low and drifted through the tall buffalo grass, skirted sage and hawthorn, and advanced obliquely on the rustlers. When the drag riders came into view, Smoke sank down and disappeared in the waving sea of grass. A quarter hour had gone by when he heard a faint "halloo" from far ahead. Those in the lead were halting the herd for the night. Smoke would wait until dusk to move again.

When the last thin, orange crescent sank in the west and only the afterglow fought against the encroachment of night, Smoke Jensen left his hiding place and made a circuit of the herd. It took him five minutes shy of an hour to complete the journey. He made careful note of the location of herd guards and, most importantly, their degree of alertness. While he ghosted from rock to tree to underbrush, Smoke concentrated on what choices he had. Looming large in his considerations was his need to know exactly how many men occupied the night camp. He would have to pay them a visit soon, but in order for that to happen, these outer guards would have to be drowsy and distracted.

Once he knew what he stood against, Smoke had several alternatives. He could run the herd off and make a break for it, leaving the Olsens to their fate. Or he could run the herd off, along with all the outlaws's horses, and possibly get the Olsens out with him.

Better still, Smoke reckoned, the ideal would be to locate the Olsens, get them mounted, and drive off all the other horses, leaving the rustlers afoot. He would have the remounts to Buffalo and beyond before the bandits could reorganize. From there, he would force the herd to greater speed, say twenty or twenty-five miles a day. At that rate, he would deliver them to the fort after a hard, three-day drive. Not bad. Smoke confidently believed that the stranded rustlers could not possibly close with them before then. Patiently, Smoke bided his time until shortly after midnight. Then he set out for the camp.

He slid past the inattentive herd guards with ease. Not until he drew close to the restive outlaws around their fires did he have to exert his greatest skill. They had picked their site wisely, Smoke noted. Two trees stood at enough distance apart to run a picket line to accommodate all of the horses not in use by the perimeter sentries. Good. That made his job much easier. Near the inner edge of the herd, Smoke caught a flash of a gray-and-black-spotted rump and recognized Cougar. At least they would all be properly mounted when the time came to take the herd.

Tommy Olsen had worked out in his mind what he could do to protect his mother and sisters. That being the case, he went in search of firewood rather than send Sarah-Jane. In the small stand of alders to one side of the camp, he searched the ground in the dim light. He had about given up for this night when his eyes picked out a gleam of starshine from the smooth surface of a rock.

At once, Tommy set down his armload of deadfall branches and used nimble fingers to pry the stone from the grasp of the earth. It came away at last and turned out to be slightly larger than fist-sized.

"Perfect," Tommy whispered to himself.

Quickly he rubbed it free of dirt and tucked it away inside his shirt. Tommy figured rightly that if any of the outlaws tried something funny, the rock could get him a gun, and that could sure fix any of them with designs on his mother and sisters.

"Yes!" he said aloud. "Yessss!" Visions of the rock crashing against the skull of a lustful hard case excited the boy. Then he would take the thug's gun and there would be hell to pay. Tommy never considered the very real possibility that he would be shot full of holes. When one was fourteen and just sensing the ebb and flow of manly sap within, one thought oneself immortal.

Two hours before dawn, Smoke Jensen considered that the optimum time had come for his move to recover his horses and free the Olsens. All during the night, while he waited and mentally rehearsed his actions, the sky to the northwest had grown incredibly black, and huge columns rose to blot out the stars. Ominous rumbles rolled over the craggy country in the foothills of the Bighorn Mountains. Smoke cast his gaze that direction more often as the hours wore on. Conscious of the impending storm, Smoke made a quick revise in his plans. When the thunder grew even closer, he used it to muffle his movements as he closed in on the slumbering gang.

Thirteen

A searing flash of forked-tail white split the sky asunder as Smoke Jensen stepped into the clearing where the gang lay. An instant later, a ripe crackling rippled the air, followed by a ground-shaking boom. With the swiftness of a mountain lion's pounce, a torrential thunderstorm broke loose overhead.

Fat rain drops fell wetly upon everyone and everything in sight. The torrent descended at a rate of three inches per hour, too fast to allow much water to sink into the parched ground. Rather it ran off to form miniature streams that gushed and gurgled. Smoke turned his back on most of the outlaws and froze in place. Grumbling, the rustlers wisely moved away from any trees, natural targets for lightning strikes.

In so doing, they exposed themselves to even more danger. With a loud clatter, like the unshod hooves of the demons in hell, barter-sized hail slashed down to bruise and punish flesh, even that covered by thick woolen blankets. The outlaw trash complained loudly, though few raised their heads to see the cause. Quickly the ice balls covered the ground with a two-inch-thick carpet of white.

Grumbling at this unexpected misfortune, Smoke Jensen eased his way out of a camp that was quickly becoming aroused. Men had to be called out to help contain the herd, or the storm would scatter them. His plan would have to wait for a better time.

By dawn, the tempest was only a memory. After containing the livestock and waiting out the half hour of determined rain, the soaking wet rustlers could not get settled down in soggy blankets. Instead, they took dry wood from under the chuck wagon and the Olsen wagon and kindled a large, roaring fire, then stood close to dry themselves. From his hidden vantage point, Smoke Jensen observed the morning routine. When the first, faint streaks of gray bloomed in the east, outlaw voices could be clearly heard.

"Yer right. Not a sign of him."

"You're sure? No chance he's hidin'?"

"None at all."

"Turn out some of the men and widen the search."

From his observation place, Smoke Jensen studied the flamboyant figure of Reno Jim Yurian. Again he felt a flash of having seen the man somewhere in the past. Following the exchange, the camp began to fume with activity. Several men rushed about, peering behind bushes and into small ravines. Still others grabbed up their horses and set out in widening circles around the campsite. Curious as to the reason, Smoke left his concealed spot to move in on a pair of searchers, who sat their mounts and looked back along the trail they had covered the previous day.

One of them removed his hat and mopped his brow. High humidity, left by the rain, combined with a burning sun to make it feel much hotter than the regular temperature. The hatless one spoke with fire in his voice.

"Damn that little brat. I'll bet he hauled his butt along our back trail."

"Yeah, Darin, you might be right. He smacked Phipps over the head with somethin', took his gun and stole a horse. Damn, how I hate a horse thief."

That brought a round of chuckles from both thugs. And it set Smoke to thinking along the correct trail. They had to be talking about Tommy Olsen. The gutsy little guy must have clobbered one of them and made an escape. Smoke pondered that a moment. Why hadn't he taken his mother and the girls? He would have to find the boy to learn the answer, Smoke reasoned.

No time like now to start that, he acknowledged. It would make it easier if he no longer had to go afoot. To solve that immediate problem, he must seek out a lone searcher. Smoke found himself one twenty minutes later and three miles from the outlaw camp.

Oblivious to Smoke's presence, Ainsley Burk ambled his mount past where the last mountain man lay in the buffalo grass that grew belly-high to a horse. When Burk presented his back to Smoke, the lean, hard man came to his boots and uncoiled his powerful leg muscles.

He vaulted onto the rump of Ainsley Burk's

dapple gray, his Colt Peacemaker in hand and ready. It collided with the side of Burk's head and sent him off to sleepy times. Smoke shoved the unconscious Burk forward onto the neck of his horse, tied the outlaw's hands behind his back, and unceremoniously dumped Burk from the saddle.

With a horse under him again, Smoke felt much better. Even if it was a knot-headed gelding, it would make do. At once, Smoke Jensen set off in search of Tommy Olsen.

Tommy Olsen regretted his rash action when three of the outlaws struck his trail and came hard after him. He'd been riding all night, and his stolen horse was on its last legs. Still, Tommy ran him from gully to gully and over yet another ridge, in his effort to evade recapture. Inexorably the hard cases closed in on him.

In a last, desperate effort, Tommy began to take shots at them, although he felt sure they remained out of range. He had eared back the hammer once again when a fourth outlaw appeared behind the others, riding hard to close the gap.

His fourth bullet kicked up dust at the forehooves of the lead bandit's horse. The animal reared and whinnied in fright. Tommy cocked the Colt again. When he started to take sight, he saw a puff of smoke appear at the end of the trailing rider's arm. The thug nearest to the stranger arched his back and then flung forward off his mount to land face-first on the ground.

And then the stranger ceased to be an unknown for Tommy Olsen. It had to be Smoke Jensen! That left the remaining three who rode hard toward Tommy. He took more careful aim and clipped the hat from the head of one man, then prepared to fire his final round. The firing pin fell on an empty chamber. A moment later they closed on the boy and surrounded him.

Though not for long. Smoke Jensen shot one through the shoulder and swung a wide loop from the lariat that had been attached to his saddle skirt. It settled over the shoulders of another hard case at the same time Tommy used the Winchester he had brought along, carried over his legs on the bareback mount. Without time to aim or fire, he wielded the rifle like a club to knock the third rustler to the ground with the butt.

An instant later, Smoke yanked tight the rope and hauled his target out of the saddle. The thug landed with a bone-jarring thud. Tommy kneed his mount over close to Smoke. "Smoke! Am I glad to see you."

"I imagine so," Smoke replied drily. "They are bound to have heard those shots back in camp. Let's gather up the horses and hightail it out of here."

Tommy gave him a blank, incredulous stare. "You mean, we're gonna run?"

"Just so. I counted a tad over thirty men in that camp last night."

"More like forty-two, by my count," Tommy added. "Still, we gotta get Maw and my sisters out of there."

"We will. But not if forty-some hard cases fall on us like these did. We need to be well out of sight by the time they get here. And, these extra horses will help confuse them as to who we are and where we went. We'll tie bodies on each of them so they have the weight of a man."

"Why do we need to do that?"

"To confuse them, Tommy. Even outlaws have smarts enough to be able to tell if a horse is carrying a rider or not. We'll take them out a mile or two and then send them off in different directions. That'll make the rustlers think there is a whole lot of us and we split up."

Tommy looked on Smoke with new awe. "You're right smart, Smoke. Think it will work?"

"If it don't, we'll be up to our a—ears in outlaws before nightfall. Now, get goin'."

Twenty minutes later, they rode away, the outlaws, the living and the dead, slung over their individual saddles. A quick look downward gave Smoke Jensen the satisfaction of noting the authentic appearance of the tracks left behind. Frequent checks of their back trail showed no sign of close pursuit.

Sundown found Smoke Jensen and Tommy Olsen in a cold camp amid a heaped mound of boulders. They had with them three outlaw horses, which had not strayed far from their course during the day. They had left the wounded hard cases tied up on the ground before they abruptly changed directions and headed northward, back toward the camp. While they munched on biscuits and fatback taken from two pair of outlaw saddlebags, Smoke listened to Tommy's account of his escape.

"I had gotten this rock, see? It was to use if any of them decided to pester my maw or the girls. Oh, they'd talked about that before an' I knew what they meant. I figgered to clobber one and get his gun. So when that storm broke out, I wondered why not get a gun and a horse, and come find you? It worked, sort of."

Smoke snorted in reply; then Tommy went on. "Oh, one other thing. That feller with you, Utah Jack? Well, he's a turncoat. Seems he was workin' with the rustlers all along. I'd like to fix him good."

Smoke gave him a short nod. "His time will come, right enough. Now, let me tell you how I figure we're going about getting your mother and sisters out of there."

For the next twenty-five minutes, Smoke went over in detail what he had in mind. He emphasized what he expected of Tommy by two repetitions and concluded with a third. "You will take the three extra horses to the spot I determine to be best and hold them there for your family. You are to do nothing, absolutely nothing, else. Now, repeat that for me."

Tommy did and Smoke pressed him further. "Is that clear? No room open for second guessing what I expect of you, Tommy?"

"It's clear, sir. I'll do what you say."

"Good. We'll be ready to head out at one in the morning. Now roll up and get some sleep."

Far from the foothills of the Bighorn Mountains, Sally Jensen watched from her darkened living room while three scruffy men, who even in her most charitable of moods Sally would have to call saddle bums, walked their mounts to the tie rail outside the bunkhouse. They dismounted and threw their reins over the crossbar and looped them loosely. They started for the door in the yellow light of a kerosene lantern hung from a peg in the front wall. As they progressed, they eased their six-guns in their soft pouch holsters.

Their earlier furtive actions had already decided Sally Jensen, even if she had not seen this latest threatening move, and she had crossed the room to an oak, glass-fronted, upright chest. She opened the hinged face piece and reached inside. She selected a light-weight, 20 gauge Purdy shotgun and plucked six rounds of No. 4 buckshot from a box, then dropped them into a pocket of her skirt.

She opened the front door as one of the prowlers reached for the knob to enter the bunkhouse. "Odd hour to be looking for work, strangers," Sally announced from behind them. Startled by the unexpected voice, and a female one at that, they stiffened, then turned toward her as one.

They found themselves confronted by the twin black circles of the shotgun muzzle. Immediately, they spread apart, one holding the center while the other pair took small side steps to put distance between them. The piece of trash in the middle raised a gloved hand and pointed at Sally, his face screwed into an expression of mean humor.

"Now, missy, that little-bitty scattergun ain't gonna do us a whole lot of harm, don't ya know?"

"I figure I can take out two of you even before my hands get a shot at the last of you trash."

Rat-faced and unshaven, the talkative one hooked a thumb over his shoulder. "You mean the *hands* in there, missy?" he sneered. "Why, they ain't there, now are they? They all rode out early this afternoon. We watched them go. That's why we decided to pay the place a visit."

Determined to keep control of the situation, Sally spoke confidently. "Then tell me why you were headed for the bunkhouse?"

Nasty laughter answered her. "We jist wanted to make sure every one of them left. Since nothin's happened to us through all this palaver, I think we can be sure there ain't a soul at home."

"Yeah," the one on his right said through a giggle. "So we might as well get right down to the fun part. Be a good girl an' gather up all the hard money around the place. Bring it to us, along with any jewels you've got. After that, you can fix us up some grub. We're real hongry."

A sick giggle came from the other side. "He-he, tha's right, missy. We need to build our strength with some good vittles. 'Cause after that, we're gonna give you a whole lot of what you've been missin' for a while. He-he-he."

Sally had said her last word in argument. Instead, the Purdy spoke for her. A full load of No. 4 buck splashed into the chest and belly of the pig-faced satyr who had hinted at rape. He went down with a soft moan. A split-second later, Sally unloosed the other barrel on the dirty, rat-faced trash in the middle. As he bent double in shock, he saw a flicker of movement at one of the windows of the bunkhouse.

A boy's face, under a mop of white-blond hair, appeared in the open space, along with a rifle. It barked twice rapidly, and the leader saw his last man go down, shot through the belly and his left thigh. His vision dimmed while Sally pushed the locking lever and opened the breech of the shotgun. Calmly she extracted the spent brass casings and inserted two more. Then she walked across the yard to stand over him, a shy smile on her lips.

Gasping, he looked up with blurred, close-set eyes. "You're a . . . a hard woman, Missy. Who—who is it that killed me?"

"My name is Sally Jensen. This is the Sugarloaf, the ranch of my husband . . . Smoke Jensen."

Already pale from blood loss, the drifter turned alabaster white, his jaw sagging. "Oh, Lord. Oh, Lord, have mercy on me."

"He'll have to be the one. I have neither the time nor the inclination. And you won't live long enough for me to develop them."

"But . . . I don't . . . want to—die!"

Ignoring the thug's mortal protest, Bobby called out exuberantly, "We got 'em, Maw. We got 'em good."

"Yes we did, Bobby."

From beyond her boot tips came the appeal. "Who's that? We didn't see anyone else around."

"That's Bobby, our adopted son. He killed your sidekick over there."

"My God, a whole fambly of gunfighters. What did we walk into?"

"Your doom." Sally bent down and retrieved his weapons. He shivered violently and groaned. Then his death rattle rose eerily in his throat.

That night, Smoke Jensen escorted Tommy Olsen to a strategic spot near the outlaw camp. He spoke briefly of the importance of controlling the three spare horses they had brought along.

"Keep a tight rein on them, Tommy. When I scatter the remount herd, many of them will head this way."

Tommy nodded vigorously. "I'll do it, Smoke."

"Good. You won't have much doubt when things get started."

With that, Smoke faded into the blackness and headed for the new camp. Due to the search for Tommy and their missing men, the gang had moved the horses less than fifteen miles that day. His first task was the same as the previous night.

Smoke located two outriders easily. They sat their horses, faced inward to the remounts, oblivious to any threat from outside. One rolled a cigarette while they talked about inconsequentials. Smoke dismounted and approached stealthily through the tall grass. A softly soughing breeze masked his movements.

After lighting his quirley, one of the outlaws queried his companion. "Rafe, where we takin' these critters?"

"To bent Rock Canyon, Norm."

Norm drew in a deep draft of smoke. "Kinda a roundabout way, ain't it?"

Rafe nodded agreement. "Way I hear it, the boss wants to make the herd disappear somewhere over by Buffalo. Then we head south to the canyon."

"How do we make all these horses disappear?"

Norm did not get an answer. Smoke Jensen chose that moment to leap atop the rump of the horse Norm rode. Arms extended, he grabbed each outlaw by the side of his head and slammed them together with enough violence to insure they would stay unconscious for a long while. When Smoke released the hapless pair, they fell to the ground.

Smoke dropped into the saddle and calmed the horses. Then he dismounted and tied the insensible men hand and foot. He led the horses off a distance and tied them to a sage bush. That accomplished, he set off to find more of the herd guards.

Smiling Dave Winters had little use for night herd duty. He looked upon himself as a leader, not a flunky. At least three of the men in his section of the gang had caught this turn with him. He had not encountered any difficulty in ordering around the other five. Which allowed him to make a circuit of the entire herd in a casual, relaxed mood.

That was until he discovered two men missing. Neither of them patrolled the sector he had been assigned to. At first it did not cause him any concern. With the horses quieted, no doubt they had wandered off to jaw with another of the sentries. Then he recalled who this herd was supposed to belong to. If true, there could be something very wrong with these missing men.

He became convinced of that when he found a third of the herd tenders swinging from a tree limb, at the end of a rope tied around his ankles. Quickly Smiling Dave dismounted and hurried to the side of this apparition. Hank Benson had been gagged, and his hands bound behind him, although he remained conscious. The fury that burned in his eyes told a clear story to Smiling Dave.

A quick look around failed to reveal to Smiling Dave a darker, more substantial shadow among the many that surrounded him. With one hand on the butt of his six-gun, Smiling Dave reached for his sheath knife. With a hiss, the loop of a lariat settled over his shoulders. Before he could react, it yanked tight, pinning his arms at his sides. The bite end of the rope went over the same tree limb that suspended Hank Benson, and Smiling Dave Winters rose into the air. Top-heavy, he turned head down the moment his feet left the ground.

His hat went flying as his forehead struck the turf. He sensed light tugs that indicated the free end had been secured around the tree trunk. Then a human form, which appeared to be upside down to Smiling Dave, walked into view. The stranger deftly removed the weapons from the captive and studied his face closely.

Then Smoke Jensen spoke in a whisper. "You're the one who put a bullet in Jerry Harkness and killed one of my hands. Then you smacked me in the head with a rifle butt."

Although he didn't really need to ask, Smiling Dave blurted out, "Who—who are you?"

"I'm Smoke Jensen. And you are a dead man."

Smoke used Smiling Dave's knife to slit the outlaw's throat. Then he headed off to find the rest of the herd tenders.

Fourteen

Smoke Jensen had but a little distance to go in order to locate another sentry. He glided up behind him while the man stood on the ground, easing cramped leg muscles. With a single, swift blow, Smoke cracked him over the head with the butt of his Peacemaker. He tied the unconscious man and relieved him of his weapons. Then he glided off afoot to locate more.

By one-thirty in the morning, Smoke had located all but the final sentry. The outlaw sat his mount, one leg cocked up around the pommel of his saddle, rolling a quirley. Smoke eased in close and spoke in a low, though friendly, tone.

"Could you use a cup of coffee?"

"You bet. I'm obliged." He leaned forward as Smoke reached out with his left hand.

When the thug's head reached the proper level, Smoke swung his right arm and laid the barrel of his .45 Colt alongside the outlaw's cranium, a fraction above his left ear. The victim uttered a low grunt and continued earthward from his perch. Swiftly, Smoke Jensen secured him and started for the distant camp, his goal the picket line.

On the way, he worked through the remounts

until he found his 'Palouse stallion, Cougar. The spotted-rump horse followed Smoke without need of a halter or reins. At the picket line, Smoke went from one animal to another, undoing the ropes that held them to the tether. He left Cougar there with a borrowed bridle and skirted the camp beyond the orange glow cast by the bed of coals. He emerged from the darkness when he reached the Olsen wagon.

Smoke awakened Della first, with a hand over her mouth to prevent a cry of alarm. He whispered in her ear, and she tried to turn her head. Smoke eased his grip, and she glanced left to verify that it was indeed he.

In a soft breath, Smoke explained his presence. "I came to get you away from here. Wake the girls and meet me out there in the dark, just beyond your wagon."

Della started to protest that their meager possessions would be lost, only to have Smoke shake his head sternly. "Would you rather it be your lives?" he asked harshly.

Smoke remained behind to cover their escape. When the youngest Olsen girl disappeared into the darkness, Smoke withdrew from the edge of the camp. He found them huddled together at the base of a gnarled cottonwood and led them to the picket line, where he lifted the girls atop two of the outlaws' horses. They settled astraddle with accustomed ease. Then Smoke turned to assist Della.

"I've not ridden bareback since I was little," she told him with a toss of her silver-frosted, light brown locks.

"You'll remember how easy enough," Smoke

assured her as he made a step-up with cupped hands.

Della hoisted the hem of her night dress, placed a foot lightly in his grasp and grabbed a handhold in the mane of the horse. She swung aboard and settled in. Smoke vaulted to the back of Cougar and turned to take in the Olsens.

"Now what?" Della prompted.

Smoke waved a hand in the direction of the herd. "Now we stampede the herd."

He could not clearly see Della's reaction, but Smoke heard her gasp. Then she spoke in a reasonable tone. "Then we're going to need a way to guide these beasts." So saying, she bent forward and formed a reasonably good hackamore out of the tie rope. With a steady hand, she eased over to her daughters and did the same for them, then spoke softly.

"You girls stay close by me, hear?" They nodded, and Della turned to Smoke. "We're ready."

Smoke drew his right-hand .45 Colt and eared back the hammer. A chilling wolf howl quavered from his lips, and he fired three rapid shots. The horses bolted at once. With wild whinnies, they raced off in the direction Smoke intended that they would take.

Several of the rustlers yelled in alarm, and two screamed in agony as the remounts thundered through the camp. One of the screamers grew silent after a fifth set of hooves pounded into his chest and belly, pulped vital organs and shattered ribs. Taking care to keep the Olsens in sight, Smoke pushed the herd from behind. The terrain proved an ally, as the startled animals swerved to avoid rock outcrops and disastrous ravines.

Thus channeled, the horses streamed toward where Tommy waited with the saddled mounts. Behind them, Smoke could hear the curses and uproar created when the outlaws found their own mounts missing. So far, he thought, not a bad night's work.

Smoke Jensen wasted not a second longer than required to retrieve his saddle and re-mount the Olsens on saddled horses. Then he gave them hurried instructions on how to bring the stampeding horses under some form of control. Over the days they had been together, Smoke had come to accept the fact that Tommy Olsen was mature beyond his years. He entrusted the left flank to Tommy and his mother. He took the two girls with him on the right flank. With only swing riders it would be difficult, yet Smoke trusted that the terrain of the foothills, which now narrowed the trail, would be to their advantage.

Which set Smoke to thinking about another matter. If they continued to Powder River Pass, it stood to reason that the rustlers would jump them again. They could head due north, to Granite Pass, which would bypass Buffalo on the far side, where the Olsens wanted to go. Or they could turn west, which would take them far from the Crow Agency and Fort Custer. All three courses had advantages, but the disadvantages outweighed choosing the lower altitude Powder River Pass.

Silently, he pondered his choices through the night. When the faintest gray ribbon spanned the eastern horizon, Smoke called a halt on the bank of the north fork of the Powder River. By then the horses had lost their fright and settled down in loose bunches under the herd leader and his subordinates. Comfortingly, to Smoke's way of seeing it, the largest gather, some seventy animals, led the pack. The stop would do everyone good, even the critters.

At least, they did not need any supervision to walk mincingly into the shallows and drink from the river. In the cool, mountain breeze, their coats steamed and their breath fogged the air. Smoke shared out some cold, hard biscuits and strips of jerky. He and the Olsens munched them industriously while the herd drank. At last, Smoke spoke what was on his mind.

"We've covered what I'd reckon to be fifteen miles from where we left the rustlers. I think we should get some rest here, then move on. Sleep awhile if you can."

Della Olsen looked at the rugged Smoke Jensen with a radiant face. "Oh, I'm much too exhilarated to sleep. Goodness, getting rescued is certainly exciting."

Sarah-Jane and Gertrude nodded eager agreement. "And we get to ride astraddle, like Tommy," Sarah-Jane declared in delight.

Della's eyes narrowed for a short moment. "Not too much of that, young lady. It is not proper for a woman to ride that way."

"But Momma, you're doing it," Sarah-Jane protested.

"Yes, but I've had three chil—" Della broke

off abruptly and blushed furiously. "Oh! What am I saying? You must think me terribly brazen, Mr. Jensen."

Smoke hastened to reassure her. "Not at all, and it's Smoke, remember, Della? My wife rode side-saddle until after our second child was born." He gave Della a mischievous grin. "Although I could never figure out why."

Her embarrassment vanished, Della produced a relieved smile. "Oh, we women have our reasons, Smoke. Now, have you figured out what we are going to do for food?"

Smoke scratched idly at his chin. "After everyone gets the hang of handling the herd on the move, Tommy can take off and hunt for game. There's wild bulbs and plants we can gather, also. No one has ever starved out here unless the weather was against them or they were just plain stupid."

"Did you ever eat pine nuts, Smoke?"

"Oh, yes, many a time."

"My hus—Sven was exceedingly fond of them."

"They're a good source of energy."

With that revelation, they continued to eat in silence until the first thin slice of orange slid above the eastern horizon. With that growing, Smoke roused a lightly slumbering Tommy Olsen and called the family together.

"We're going to do this a little differently today. Della, you and your youngest will take the right swing, Tommy the left with Sarah-Jane. I'll ride drag."

* * *

Furious over the loss of the herd and their own horses, Reno Jim Yurian stood in the orange light of the new sun and cursed Smoke Jensen with fervor. When he at last ran down, he pointed a finger at Yancy Osburn.

"Yancy, take five men and spread out until you find some horses. Head north. I think I heard a couple whinny right at sunrise. If you find them, keep going until you have more."

"Sure, boss. Do we take saddles with us?"

"No, just bridles. We need those horses fast." Reno Jim turned to the remaining gang members. "The rest of you, see what you can find to salvage in a camp that's been run through by two hundred forty-five horses."

With that, he kicked a crushed coffeepot and swore with renewed vehemence.

With only a boy, a woman and two small girls to control the herd, Smoke found little to celebrate, beyond the rescue of the Olsens. In daylight, with the horses refreshed and tested, difficulties began to crop up almost at once. First to impinge on Smoke's quiet reverie were the rebellious outlaw horses. A shout from Tommy alerted him to the problem.

"Hiii! Hiiii-yaah! Get back there. Get back," the boy yelled as he streaked along the left flank of the herd in pursuit of four fractious mounts with minds of their own.

Smoke veered to cut off the runaways. He and Tommy managed to contain three of them. The fourth put its tail in the air and streaked between them, back in the direction from which they had come. In disgust and defeat, Tommy spat a word that Smoke did not think the boy had in his vocabulary. He decided that a little fatherly advice was called for. He walked Cougar over and clapped a hand on the boy's thin shoulder.

"Better not let your mother hear you say that." At Tommy's grimace, Smoke went on. "We're going to lose more than one of those horses. They belong to the rustlers and will try to break away every chance they get."

Tommy made a face. "But they're worth some money."

Smoke shook his head. "They don't wear my brand, and I can't sell them to the army. The idea is to keep them out of the hands of the gang long enough for us to get clean away. And with this herd, that will be hard to do."

Pondering that a moment, Tommy spoke his inner expectation. "I thought maybe I could sell them and get a stake for Maw."

"A generous idea, though it would make you a horse thief."

Tommy cocked an eyebrow. "D'you think *those guys* paid for their nags?"

Smoke shrugged. "Probably. Out here they still hang a man for stealing horses."

A tinkle of laughter erased the frown on Tommy's forehead. "Imagine that, rustlers buying their mounts."

Smoke took a deep breath. "Now that is settled, I think we should cut out all of their animals and send them off at an odd direction."

"Why, Smoke?"

"Once the critters take it in mind to run off, the others will jump at the chance, too. We don't have the manpower to round up the entire herd if that happened."

That sounded reasonable to Tommy. "Sure, but how do we find the right ones?"

"My remounts haven't been shod. Look for the horses with shoes."

With that as a guide, Tommy soon cut out twenty-three broom tails and scattered them to the winds. Seven more refused to budge from the herd. Smoke appeared satisfied with that and rode on, wondering what would happen next.

Tommy Olsen discovered their next setback when they had advanced into the high, steep pass. Ahead of him, the leaders turned about and began to mill among the horses that came after them. He trotted forward, only to return at twice the speed, his eyes wide.

"Smoke, there's a big ol' tree up there, fallen across the trail."

"Does it look like someone cut it down?"

"No. It's dead. I think it just fell over."

Smoke looked at Tommy as they cantered forward. "We'll have a devil of a time getting it moved."

"Yeah. No saws or an axe."

After a moment's thought, Smoke offered a suggestion. "We do have ropes, and plenty of horses. If we fasten onto some larger limbs, we can maybe pull it away."

"Who'll watch the herd?"

"Your mother and the girls."

Tommy made a face. That brought a laugh from Smoke. But he wasn't laughing when he

got a look at the downed tree—a large, old
pine, which if it had not been dead a long time
would have weighed tons. Even in its present
condition, Smoke harbored a small doubt as to
whether they could move it. He had little
choice, so he set about it with a will.

Smoke put Della and the girls behind the herd,
to calm and hold them in place. Then he and
Tommy cut out three of the remounts and took
ropes from each saddle. At Smoke's direction,
Tommy fastened the ends of the lariats to stout
branches high up the trunk. Smoke fitted the
loop ends over the necks of the three horses,
then took a fourth and did a dally around his
saddle horn.

"Get your horse, Tommy, and dally off that
last rope. Then we do a little pulling."

From beyond the herd, Della's voice reached
Smoke's ears. "Smoke, they're trying to push past
us."

"Walk your horse into a few of them, shove
them back," Smoke suggested.

"I wish I had a buggy whip."

That gave Smoke an idea. "Break a leafy
branch off a tree. Don't hit any of the horses
with it, just swish it in front of their noses.
Should work."

After a longer delay, while Smoke and Tommy
readied the animals for their pull, Della called
again. "It's working, Smoke. They're turning
back."

Smoke gave Tommy a nod, and they slapped
the rumps of the three unsaddled horses with
their reins. All five creatures lunged into the effort. The lariats went taut, one vibrating with

enough force to give off a low hum. The braided hemp stretched at first; then ever so slowly the constant strain caused the top of the massive barrier to move. Snapped-off branches on the bottom side began to screech and groan as they gouged the ground.

Smoke dug his heels into the flanks of Cougar and spoke to Tommy. "Harder. Keep the pressure on the remounts."

Gradually the gap widened. Then the hooves of the horses began to lose purchase as the tree hung up on some unseen obstruction. Smoke got them stopped and dismounted.

"Tend to the horses, Tommy. I'll see what's gone wrong." When the ropes slacked off, Smoke went forward and bent to peer under the trunk.

At first, he could not see any obvious cause. Then he noticed a thin ridge of rock jutting above the ground. In moving the tree that far it had butted three broken branches against the stone. Smoke drew his Greenriver knife and attacked the first of these, whittling at it to form a notch. When he had cut better than halfway through, he sat on the ground and worked his booted foot into position. With all the effort he could exert in that position, he kicked the protruding partial branch.

Nothing happened. He tried again. Once more, no result. On his third kick, Smoke heard a satisfying crackling and the limb flew free. At once he started on the second. It would play hell with the edge on his blade, Smoke reckoned, and no way to hone it in the near future. This piece proved to be afflicted with dry rot and quickly yielded to the cutting edge of Smoke's knife.

When it fell away, Smoke went after the third. It proved to be stubborn, nearly as stringy as oak. Smoke remembered a lesson taught by Preacher about the growth of trees. "When a branch gets whipped and twisted a lot by wind, it gets springy. The fibers are long instead of close and compact. It gets so they are jist like hardwood."

Which might have been the case with this difficult stump. Heat radiated up smoke's arm as he cut at the defiant wood. He made little progress over several minutes; then the blade sank into the heartwood, and the rest became easy. In another two minutes he had cleared the final obstruction.

Back in the saddle, he nodded to Tommy, and they again set the horses in motion. The ropes stretched and sang, and the animals strained into their burden. Then, with a grinding crunch, the tip of the fallen pine lurched forward and opened a grudging space. Quickly the man and boy halted the remounts and their own horses. Fists on hips, Smoke inspected the opening.

It was disappointing at best. Barely three horses at a time could squeeze by the sheer wall of the pass and the obstruction of the tree. That would have to do, Smoke noted, because the thick trunk had jammed tightly against a boulder at the side of the trail. He looked back at Tommy.

"Let's get 'em headed up and moving through. We've lost more time than we can afford."

Fifteen

Glancing at the horizon, Reno Jim Yurian produced the first smile he had worn since the herd had been run off. Five men astride unsaddled horses trotted toward him. He estimated that the drove had a two-day lead on them, provided they could find the animals again. He had to admit, he had greatly underestimated this Smoke Jensen.

Reno Jim reviewed what he knew of the man. Few on the frontier, or back east for that matter, had not heard of him. Thanks to the proliferation of dime novels, Smoke Jensen had been a legendary figure long before he went on that lecture tour in New England and New York City. Not that his trip had lasted for long. Trouble had come looking for Smoke Jensen, and he had quickly obliged.

That much Yurian had read in the San Antonio newspaper. An account that lasted over several days. In an amused tone, its first installment recounted a chase through Central Park, with picnickers scattered and food crushed beneath the hooves of several horses. In his usual manner, the reporter had recounted, Smoke Jensen ended the altercation with a blazing six-gun.

Someone like that could be real trouble. Yet

Reno Jim had discounted it as sensationalism.
Well now, by dang, it seemed Smoke Jensen was
indeed larger than life. And mean as a wet bob-
cat. Reno Jim abandoned his dark reflections to
hail the approaching riders.

"You've done good, as far as it goes," he informed them when they halted before him.
"Any sign of more of our horses?"

"Yep," answered Yancy Osburn. "Seen a few,
but they shied. Thing is, boss, they ain't comin'
from Powder River Pass. They showed up north
of this trail."

"Well, then, saddle up and get out there and
round up as many as you can. We're going after
that herd. Smoke Jensen might be mean as hell,
but he's only one man."

By nightfall, Smoke Jensen and the herd had
nearly reached the 8,950 foot summit of Granite
Pass. Tommy had bagged four plump squirrels.
He grumbled ferociously over the difficulty of
removing their skins. At one point, he looked
up at Smoke Jensen, blood on both hands, one
cheek and his little square chin.

"Why do these squirrels have to have their
hides attached by so many of these darned
thongs?"

Smoke took pity on the boy. "They are not
'thongs,' Tommy. They are erectile tissue. Squirrels need them to bunch up their skin in cold
weather."

Eyes large with wonder, Tommy looked down
at the creature he was working on. "Gosh, how
did you learn all that stuff?"

"From Preacher. He knew all about animals. And at one time, there was a larger market for squirrel hides than beaver. Here, let me show you an easier way."

Smoke started at the back end of the animal and made a long cut from bung to neck, then worked the skinning knife in under one side. He cut through the elastic retractors down one side, reversed the blade and severed the opposite ones. He peeled back the hide and did the back.

"There. Think you can do it like that?"

Tommy thrust out his chest. "Sure. Let me at it."

"You've got to gut this one first; then I'll put it on the fire to roast."

Smoke took the carcass and doused it in the crystal stream that burbled over smooth stones alongside the trail. Then he began to thread it on a green stick. For a second, he flashed back four days to when he did the same with an eight-foot rattler. He had given the huge rattle—there were eleven buttons—to Tommy. The boy wrapped it in a strip of cloth and shoved it deep in one pocket of his overalls. A good thing, too, Smoke thought. Out in the open, it would have the horses spooked all the time. Della came over while Smoke propped the squirrel over the coals.

"Smoke, I wonder if there is anything we can do to get washed off. The girls and I, that is. We've been taking on a goodly lot of dust of late and . . . well, I feel grimy."

Smoke looked left and right, then nodded toward a bend in the trail below them. "You can go down there, around the bend, and wash to your heart's content."

"But who'll guard us from wild animals or—or men coming along?"

"Take Tommy's little rifle. You can stand watch while the girls bathe, then Sarah-Jane can be lookout for you."

Della still seemed unconvinced. "There doesn't seem to be much privacy that way."

Smoke stifled the chuckle he felt building. "It's the best we've got. After you finish, Tommy and I can take our turns."

Pulling a face, Della confided to Smoke, "If you knew that boy like I do, you'd be in there with him. It's near impossible to get him out of the water."

Smoke answered her drily. "Cold as this is, I doubt it will be a problem."

Squeals came from beyond the bend only a few minutes after Della and her daughters disappeared. Their cleanup lasted only a scant five minutes. The three came back with a rosy glow from the icy water. Smoke went next, and wisely stripped only to the waist to wash away the accumulated dust. The snowmelt stung his skin and sent shivers along his spine.

Tommy had finished the last squirrel when Smoke returned. Eagerly the boy headed for the bend. Della had been right about her son, Smoke noted when he clocked Tommy at a full fifteen minutes before he reappeared.

"I thought you'd frozen solid," Smoke remarked.

"Naw. It was jist right. Though it would have been better with the sun shining." A hiss and plume of steam rose from the fire as one of the squirrels dripped fat. Tommy sniffed the air and rubbed his belly. "I'm hungry."

Della turned the meat while she looked up at Smoke. "How much longer?"

"Three, maybe four more days. We'll be on the Crow reservation by then. Before midmorning we'll reach the summit. I want to take a half-day rest. It's all downhill from there."

"I thought we were going to Buffalo first."

"Can't risk it, Della. Reno Jim Yurian and his gang would be laying for us on that trail. Even if they don't recover any of their mounts, they know Buffalo is the closest place to get more. Then they will be after us."

Early the next morning the riders sent out by Reno Jim Yurian returned with a dozen more of their missing horses. At once, Reno Jim named off as many of his best men, including Utah Jack Grubbs. They quickly saddled the animals and stood waiting for instructions.

"I'm coming with you. That gives us seventeen men. We are going to track down Smoke Jensen and finish him off. If any man sees Jensen first, save him for me. I want to make him die slowly," Yurian told them ominously.

Hazy sunlight bathed the schoolhouse in Muddy Gap. Inside, classes went on as usual. Outside, Brandon Kelso presented a far different agenda to his companions, Willie Finch and Danny Collins. Only the day before he had been released from jail by Marshal Larsen. His father had promptly boxed his ears for allowing himself to be caught in such a stupid way. Now he planned to get revenge.

"Here's what we're gonna do. We're gonna go in there and run all the kids out. Then we take care of that smart-ass schoolmarm."

Not the brightest of youths, Danny Collins had to ask. "How we gonna do that?"

Brandon grabbed his crotch and grinned wickedly "You jist follow my lead."

With that he marched to the front steps and climbed to the stoop. Brandon's massive hand closed over the doorknob, and he slammed the portal inward with explosive force. Ginny Parkins looked up sharply to find her nemesis framed in the opening. She bit her lip in trepidation, then recalled the message that had accompanied her gift from Smoke Jensen.

"You can march yourself out of here this minute, Brandon Kelso."

"Naw. Ain't gonna do that." Brandon waved to the upturned faces and staring eyes of the students. "All you kids get out of here. This is a school holiday."

Willie Finch put in his bit. "Yeah, everybody out. Exceptin' you, Prissy Pants."

Brandon's face turned dark red with self-induced rage. "That's right! Scatter . . . all of you." His beady eyes narrowed and fixed on Ginny as he advanced on her. "Not you, though. We're gonna give you something you have obviously never had. But you'll surely appreciate it once we're through with you."

Backed against the blackboard, Virginia Parkins fought panic as she sought some means to defend herself. She grasped a piece of chalk and hurled it at the face of her tormentor. The white stick hit edge-on and cut a gouge below his right eye. Enraged, Brandon charged her.

Nimbly, Ginny slipped under his grasping arms and dashed for her desk. Fighting to control her movements, she yanked open the top drawer and whipped out the small .38 Smith and Wesson given her by Smoke Jensen. She turned to face Brandon, and being inexpert in the use of the weapon, she fired it low.

Her first bullet ripped into the floor. The second smashed into Brandon's right kneecap and shattered it. A bellow of agony burst from the lout's lips as he went down on his good knee. Ginny turned her wrath on the other two.

"Take this little monster and get out of my school," she demanded in a cold, even tone. "Do it now or I'll shoot you, too."

"That won't be necessary, Miss Ginny," Marshal Larsen said from the open door, his shotgun held purposefully in both hands. "I saw them headed this way, and I thought I should come along and see what they had in mind."

"I'm glad you did, Marshal. They had every intention of—of having their way with me."

Marshal Larsen's face portrayed his disgust and outrage. "They'll not be any problem to you ever again, Miss Ginny. I'll take them from here."

"Arrest her, Marshal," Brandon blubbered. "She shot me for no reason at all."

"Shut up, you little bastard, or I'll use this shotgun to remove some of your teeth." To Danny and Willie, he commanded sharply, "Carry this filth out of here. You're all goin' to jail."

Behind them, little Jimmy Finch piped shrilly, "Three cheers for Marshal Larsen. Hip—hip—hooray!"

Shortly after halting at the summit of Granite Pass, and running a single-strand rope fence around the remount herd, Smoke Jensen heard a distant rifle shot. Ten minutes later, a grinning Tommy Olsen walked out of the stand of aspen that graced one side slope of the passage through the Bighorn Mountains.

"I need a horse," the boy announced.

"What for?" Smoke challenged good-naturedly.

"I bagged us a deer."

Tipping back the brim of his hat, Smoke gave off a low whistle. "I should have seen to it we got here sooner. A rack of venison ribs sounds mighty good right now."

Eyes sparkling from this fulsome praise, Tommy asked, "Which horse should I take?"

"How big is the deer?"

Tommy described the creature with wide swings of his arms. Smoke nodded and pointed to one of the purloined outlaw horses. "Take that one. He's the calmest of the lot. I'll get your mother started on making preparations, then go hunt down some wild onions and turnips. We can make stew out of the tougher parts of the legs."

"Umm. Sounds good. I'm hungry now."

Smoke reached out and ruffled the boy's tousled auburn hair. "You are always hungry."

"Uh—Smoke? When we get to the reservation will we see some real wild Indians?"

Smiling, Smoke shook his head. "The Crow are

not all that wild. Never have been. They took a friendly outlook to us whites. They've provided scouts for the army for years." He laughed softly. "They can just about kill you with hospitality if you happen upon them during one of their social dances. They'll stuff you with food, heap tobacco on you, drag you into the dance circle, give you the place of honor to sleep in the lodge."

"Lots of whiskey, I bet," Tommy opined.

Smoke frowned. "Given their choice, most Injuns shun liquor. They don't have much tolerance for it."

"What's tolerance?"

"In this case it means bein' able to hold their whiskey. And many Injuns can't. To most it's like any of the other white man's diseases. In a way it's a good thing. Someone has to stay sober out here."

Tommy studied Smoke in silence while the boy slipped a bridle on the horse. "You don't seem to miss strong drink much, Smoke."

"Never developed a fondness for it. I drink a little whiskey, though not enough to make a saloon keeper a profit, and two or three beers is my limit."

A serious expression altered Tommy's face. "I don't think I'll ever drink."

"None of us knows for sure what we'll do later in life. But good for you if you stick to it. You know, the Germans call beer 'liquid bread.' They don't think of it as liquor."

Tommy furrowed his smooth brow. "Then maybe I'll have some liquid bread when I grow up."

They laughed together, and Tommy swung up

bareback on the horse. Smoke handed him his rifle. After the boy trotted away, Smoke realized exactly how good some roasted venison would taste.

Well fed on venison and with the humans and animals alike rested, Smoke Jensen sent his amateur drovers down the trail that descended the northeast slopes of the Bighorn Mountains. Spirits remained high. Confident in their improving ability to manage the horses, Smoke put Tommy on drag and rode on ahead to scout the terrain they had to cover.

He had gone some five miles from the herd when he came upon two rather large men who took their ease outside a stretched canvas lean-to. Both had rifles ready at hand and revolvers stuck into the waistband of their trousers. Smoke counted three on one of them. Smoke reined in and greeted them in a friendly manner.

"Howdy to you, too, mister," the smaller, as compared to his barn-sized companion, replied. "Sorta off the beaten track, ain'tcha?"

"Could say the same for you two, I suppose."

A scowl replaced the earlier smile of greeting. "This here's our land, mister. We got papers filed an all, over to Sheridan way."

Trying to keep it light, Smoke observed, "An ambitious undertaking. You waiting for the trees to grow to build a cabin?"

Rather than take it in good humor, the larger man glowered and roused himself, to reveal a Cheyenne backrest that had been hidden by his slab shoulders. "That ain't none of your business," he growled. "But it is ours, as to what you're doin' on our place."

"Didn't know anyone had homesteaded out this way. But as it happens, I'm driving a herd of remounts north to Fort Custer."

"And you think to bring them through here?" the smaller one remarked.

Smoke found his patience a tad strained. "That's what I had in mind."

A head taller and a shade wider than Smoke Jensen, the smaller opportunist announced their avaricious intentions. "Well, then, there'll be the matter of a little toll."

"Yeah," the huge one joined in. "Say . . . two bits a head."

Smoke Jensen cut them a flat, deadly gaze. "I think not. This trail is a public throughway."

"You sound like a lawyer."

"I don't need a lawyer for this. The trail has been used freely since the Indians first got horses. We go through and there's nothing you can do about it."

With a low growl, the man-mountain started for Smoke. "Then we shut down the trail and shoot yer horses."

He lunged at Smoke, who did not even wait to dismount. Instead, he pulled one boot free of the stirrup and kicked the huge lout flush in the face. Blood spurted from a mashed nose and split lip. His eyes crossed, but he did not go down. Instead, he looked to his partner.

"B'god, Jake, he hurt me."

Jake, who apparently did not have the same confidence in his size, made an even more costly mistake. He went for one of the revolvers at his waist. In half an eye-blink, he found himself staring at the black hole in the muzzle of the .45 Colt in Smoke Jensen's hand.

"I don't want to kill you, but I will. Ease that iron to the ground."

"And if I don't?"

Smoke shrugged. "Your friend here can bury you."

A glint of cunning entered Jake's eyes, and he tried a new tack. "A real gunfighter never pulls his piece unless he's gonna use it. I think you are all bluff."

"He means it, Jake," cautioned the bigger man.

Smoke remained motionless, one corner of his mouth lifted in a mirthless smile. Almost casually he twitched his right index finger. The shot sounded thunderous, and Jake's Merwin and Hulbert went flying when the bullet struck his shoulder. Groaning, Jake dropped to his knees.

"Your friend was right. I did mean it. Now, shall we settle the question of a toll? If you fence off the trail, or take even one shot at any of my horses, I'll kill you both. In fact, if I even see either of your faces while we're passing through, I'll kill you. Do we understand one another?"

Their shame-faced, silent nods answered Smoke. Cowed for the time being, they turned away while Smoke Jensen rode back in the direction from which he had come. Defeated for now, Smoke knew full well he would have to be watchful of them when the herd came through first thing in the morning.

Sixteen

Even the canvas lean-to had disappeared when Smoke Jensen and the Olsens brought the herd down out of the pass and through the land claimed by Jake and his huge friend. On a still slightly downhill grade, the wisdom of a half-day rest proved itself. By one o'clock that afternoon, Smoke estimated they had covered twenty-five miles. At that rate, they would reach the main trail north from Sheridan by evening. It couldn't be too soon, Smoke acknowledged.

He saw only one drawback to this increase in speed. The dust kicked up by the horses formed a gigantic cloud that raised skyward on a breeze from the southwest. That blocked his forward view, but it kept a lot of it off the drag rider, a position Smoke chose for himself when the gait picked up to a quick trot. Like old hands, the Olsens kept the herd in a long, narrow gather that only occasionally spilled over the edges of the traceway.

Shortly before four that afternoon, his expectation of a forty-mile day assured, Smoke looked beyond the herd to see three men riding toward them. He stood in his stirrups and called out to Tommy Olsen.

"Come back and take the drag. I'm going to go find out who those men are."

Tommy looked forward, then back at Smoke, face puzzled. *He* hadn't seen any riders. But, if Smoke said they were there, they must be. When he reached Smoke's side, he received a nod.

"Keep 'em moving." Then Smoke rode off.

Smoke reached the front of the herd with only thirty yards separating him from the mounted men. He had no problem with recognizing a smiling Ahab Trask in the lead. Trask snatched his hat from his head and gave an enthusiastic, friendly wave.

"What are you doin' comin' at us from this direction?" Trask asked when they came within hearing.

Grinning, Smoke jerked a thumb behind him. "A slight detour. I managed to steal back the herd."

Trask appeared quizzically amused to see a woman and two small girls riding swing. "So I see. Who are your new hands?"

"A family named Olsen. Their ranch was raided by the same gang that rustled the horses. Della, that's the woman's name, told me that she and her son, Tommy, recognized the leader the first time they saw him."

"Dang, if that don't beat all." Trask flashed a white smile in his sun-mahoganied face.

"Where are the rest, Trask?"

"Over on the Sheridan Trace. We saw your dust and came over from there. It's only a couple of miles ahead. I—uh . . ." Trask paused, uncomfortable with what he had to say. "We could only get seven men, Smoke. They're borrowed from a rancher south of Sheridan who thinks highly of you. He'd also heard about the troubles in Muddy Gap."

Smoke looked at it philosophically. "That gives me ten more than I've had for the last three days. Send Bolt back for them, and we'll get headed for Fort Custer before beddin' down for the night."

Trask looked along the herd's back trail. "Any chance of those rustlers comin' after you?"

Smoke shook his head. "Only if they found enough of their horses."

Once settled down in camp, with introductions made around, Smoke found he liked the cut of these hands. They had worked the herd expertly, relieving Della and the girls of the necessity of keeping fractious animals in line. Smoke particularly liked the line foreman, Harper Liddy. Harp usually supervised the fence-mending crews for his boss, Solomon Blaire, who owned the sprawling Leaning Tree ranch.

Smoke had heard of it. Blaire was experimenting with the new English breed of Herefords. Squat and compact, the wooly-headed red-and-white cattle produced more usable meat than bone and hide, and seemed to flourish on the high plains. Smoke had looked into raising them before changing to horses. All considered, he had no regret. If the Herefords, especially the males, were not docked—their horns removed—they tended to do considerable damage to one another, even if altered into steers. When the new men settled around the fire for coffee, Harp Liddy talked about the breed.

"Some say their blood strain runs back to Iberian cattle, brought to England by the Romans. That's what makes them so aggressive."

Smoke found that doubtful. "After nearly two thousand years, they would have surely had that characteristic bred out of them. And, I've seen Iberian stock in Mexico. Most were black, with only a few a light, orangish brown in color. Not at all like Herefords."

Smoke looked up to see Trask pour coffee and come over to join him. Accustomed to working long hours and days without seeing another human being, Trask, like most ranch hands, did not say a lot. Only now did he bring up the subject of the missing hands.

"There was five of you when I left to find help, Smoke. What happened?"

"We came upon the Olsens first. Then the rustlers found our camp. They killed all but Jerry Harkness and myself. Jerry was wounded and I sent him off to get help. They should be joining us soon. Oh, and Utah Jack, who turned out to be with the gang."

"That low-down snake. Did he . . . kill any of the boys?"

Smoke thought back to it. "I can't say for sure. I nearly got my brains knocked out."

"Smoke coulda got 'em all, but he was tryin' to protect my maw," Tommy Olsen came to the fire to say.

"Truth is there were too many for me." Smoke yawned and stretched. "We'll head out at first light. I'm gonna turn in."

After Smoke left the fire, the new hands drifted to their bed rolls or to herd watch duty. In less than a quarter hour, silence held throughout the camp.

Listening carefully to the words of the young warrior, Iron Claw's eyes glowed. The number of horses headed their way seemed impossible. And so few men driving them. The Cheyenne war chief clapped a hand on the bare shoulder of his scout and spoke thoughtfully.

"You have done well, Sees-the-Sky. This means there will be more soldiers on the high plains. There are too many already, pushing out onto our hunting grounds."

"We should not let them keep these horses," Sees-the-Sky suggested. "We could run them off, steal all we can."

"I have already thought of that. We could possibly get away with half of them. Think how that would swell our pony herd. And they would not be ridden against us that way."

He looked beyond the young warrior to where his large raiding party waited in patient silence. Iron Claw raised his voice so all could hear. "We will follow along out of their sight and see what good medicine the Great Spirit gives us."

Iron Claw swung atop his paint horse and raised a hand to signal his dog soldiers. Formed into a line three abreast, they silently rode parallel to the herd beyond a concealing ridge. Sees-the-Sky returned to keep the white men and their horses under watch.

* * *

Hubble Volker knew it would be the smart thing to do. When three more horses ambled back in their general direction, he had them gathered in and sent two men on through Powder River Pass to Buffalo. They were to use a bank draft Hub had forged with Reno Jim's signature to obtain horses for the rest of the gang and bring them back. He ordered the remaining men to walk through each day, bringing along their saddles and tack.

On the third day after the herd had been stolen, he saw his gamble pay off. Over a long swell in the prairie, the three he had sent on came fogging back with fifteen horses for the men afoot. Some good-natured cursing rose among the outlaws. They had visions of recovering their lost fortunes. Some of them complained, though, when Hub announced his decision not to pursue the herd.

"What do you mean we're not goin' after them?"

Hubble Volker kept a calm demeanor. "We are. Only we won't catch them by following the way they went. We know where they are going. The shortest route to get there is through the pass to Buffalo and north from there. You said, yourself, Fred, that there is no sign those horses went through ahead of you. So they used the other pass. We'll catch them, don't worry."

They hastened to saddle the new horses and gratefully mounted. Hub took his place at the lead, then started them off. He reckoned that Reno Jim would appreciate his efforts.

* * *

Trudy Olsen lay in the bed of the buckboard brought along for supplies by the Leaning Tree hands. She had already thrown up three times this morning, and had been unable to control her bowels. She also complained of terrible thirst. Della suspected she had somehow contracted dysentery. The trek had been hard on all of them.

More so on Gertrude. Della worried most about Trudy, the youngest of her children. A thin girl, small for her age, Trudy had inherited her father's blond hair and large, square hands. Her precarious health had come from somewhere else. Colicky as a baby, she frequently took fevers and seemed to constantly have the sniffles, although that had markedly dried up since leaving the ranch. Della had no idea why. She rode with her daughter now, a damp compress to the child's brow.

"Momma, I feel sick again," Gertrude said weakly.

Della helped her to sit up and held her while she hung over the side and vomited. Could it be the water? Della wondered. Tommy rode forward from his position on swing.

"What's wrong with Trudy, Maw?"

Shaking her head in exasperation, Della answered her son. "I don't know, Tommy."

"Maybe I should get Smoke."

"He's a lot of things, son, but he's not a doctor."

Tommy looked shocked. "Is it that bad? Does she need a doctor?"

Della answered honestly. "I don't know. I think maybe so, Tommy." She thought for a moment, then spoke, a note of stress in her voice. "Yes. Bring Smoke back here. I need to talk to him."

When Smoke arrived, Della described the condition of her younger daughter. She concluded with an urgent appeal. "Please, can you route the herd past somewhere with a doctor?"

"I regret it, but I cannot."

"But why?"

Smoke seemed reluctant to answer. "There is nowhere along this trail until we get to the Crow Agency. No settlement that I know of."

"Then can't we turn back to Sheridan? It can't be more than a day's ride."

Smoke sighed. "For someone on horseback, yes. But with the herd and this wagon . . ."

"Oh, please. Isn't there something you can do?"

Smoke did not answer. For most of the day he had been seeing signs of Indians close by. He had no desire to further alarm Della, so he did not mention that. For her part, Della would not let it go so easily.

"Can't I send Tommy back to Sheridan for the doctor."

Shaking his head Smoke replied, "I'm sorry, I can't even allow that."

Della put quick, hot words to the thought that formed in her head. "You are absolutely heartless."

Still, Smoke would not speak of the potential danger. Tight-lipped, he responded curtly. "Not the way I see it."

Less than a day behind the herd now, Reno Jim Yurian and his sixteen men came down out of Granite Pass at a fast canter. Some five miles out on the prairie, they came upon the lean-to that sheltered Jake and his partner. The pair greeted Reno Jim familiarly.

Reno Jim responded in style. "Jake, Lutie, I haven't seen you boys in a while."

Jake made a face. "We got outta the outlawin' business. Gettin' to be too many lawdogs out this way."

Reno Jim cocked an eyebrow. "You goin' soft?"

Jake denied it. "Naw. Nothin' like that. Jist figgered it was time to settle down. Why, we even filed a homestead on this place. Got us a whole quarter section."

Lutie added his opinion of that. "At least what of it the Injuns don't camp on from time to time."

Giving their surroundings a quick examination, Reno Jim made a proposition. "Would you fellers object to makin' some real cash money?"

Lutie cut his eyes to Jake. They both read the same hunger. "Who we have to kill for it?"

"There may not be any killing," replied Reno Jim. "D'you have horses?"

"Yup. Speakin' of horses, a whole damn herd went through here a couple of days back," Jake offered.

"Those are the source of the money I'm offering you. We're gonna steal them back."

"You mean they's your horses?" Lutie asked.

Reno Jim produced a wicked grin and shook his head. "Not really. We rustled them from the fellers who have them now; then they stole them back. Far as we know, there's only one grown man, a woman and three kids with the horses."

"That's all we saw with them," Lutie admitted.

"Well, do you think that nineteen of us can take the horses from them?"

Jake swelled his chest. "Don't see why not."

Lutie cut his eyes from Reno Jim to Jake and back. "Uh—tell Reno what the big feller did."

Reno Jim leaned forward. "What was that?"

"Nothin'. Nothin' at all," Jake hastened to add.

Lutie looked hard at his partner then turned back to Reno Jim. "He got the drop on us and runned us off."

Reno Jim nodded. "No surprise. That feller is none other than Smoke Jensen."

Both of the former outlaws turned pale. Jake spoke up hurriedly. "Well, then, Reno, you done lost you two extra guns. Ain't no way I'm goin' up again' Smoke Jensen."

"You astonish me, Jake. There's eighteen others of us. That's too many for even Smoke Jensen."

Jake canted his head to one side. "Oh, yeah? How is it, then, that he an' a woman an' some kids tooken that herd from you, Reno?"

That hit Reno Jim Yurian where it hurt. He glowered at the pair for a moment, then spat, "Then stay here and eat grass if you're so yellow. Come on, boys, we're wastin' daylight." With that, he turned his back on Lutie and Jake and trotted off.

"Wheew, I'm sure glad they're gone," Lutie stated in utter relief.

Jake had a different outlook. "I'm jist glad we didn't try to push it with Smoke Jensen."

Strain radiated from Della Olsen's face when she came to where Smoke Jensen squatted beside the cookfire. "Trudy is worse. And now Sarah-Jane is looking a little peaked. Have you no pity? We could have been in Buffalo by now and none of this would have happened."

Smoke looked at Della, completely at a loss for how to console the woman. In most situations, Smoke easily communicated with the ladies. But, someone recently bereft by the death of her husband, with two ailing children, presented an entirely different predicament. Smoke nearly relented his refusal to allow Tommy to go after a doctor, in spite of his suspicion that they had been shadowed by Indians. He was about to speak his thoughts when high, shrill yelps and hoots came from around the herd.

"Injuns!" Harper Liddy shouted from that direction.

From his vantage point in a stand of cottonwood, Iron Claw watched the last of his dog soldiers glide into position around the horse herd. He switched his gaze beyond them to the two figures at the fire. The woman's posture spoke of some worry. Perhaps over the girl Sees-the-Sky told him about. The one who got sick over the side of the rolling lodge. He sensed the moment of indecision in the man. The time could not be better.

Iron Claw raised his face to the sky and uttered a piercing signal. "Kiii-yip-yip-yip!"

Cheyenne dog soldiers designated to move the herd whooped and howled in reply and began to flap blankets at the horses. Startled, the animals bolted. Yet, the white men who watched them did not lack courage. Several acted at once to channel the creatures as they thundered across the ground. Others sought the cause.

When they found it, gunshots crackled in the night. The sudden discharge served to prompt half of the remaining warriors to charge the camp. That, Iron Claw reasoned, would turn the herdsmen back to defend their brothers.

The darkness filled with shrieking war cries, arrows began to moan and hum through the air into the camp. Iron Claw watched as the big man smoothly shoved the woman to the ground and drew a long-barreled revolver. The white man went to one knee and fired in the direction of an arrow's flight. A brave cried out and began to thrash in the sagebrush, his hip shattered by the bullet. Iron Claw revealed himself at the edge of the copse and raised his rifle to signal the rest to join the attack. They responded with enthusiasm.

In seconds, Cheyenne warriors swarmed into the camp.

Seventeen

Smoke Jensen cocked his .45 Colt after shooting the warrior in the bushes and looked for another target. "Stay down, Della," he commanded.

From the wagon, a shot blasted into the night. Smoke looked that way. "Make sure what you are shooting at, Tommy. There are some of ours out there, too."

"Sure, Smoke. I'll watch careful. Yike!" The last came when an arrow thudded into the thick side of the wagon only three inches from Tommy Olsen.

Smoke snapped a shot at the warrior who had launched the arrow at Tommy and saw the Cheyenne flop over backward to twitch in agony from the shoulder wound. A quick check showed Smoke that the Leaning Tree hands had managed to channel what looked to be a little more than half the remounts into a ravine, where they held them in a milling, confused mass. Then came another outburst of war whoops, and more Indians charged into the clearing.

Trask and Bolt stood back-to-back and laid down a withering fire that caused the Cheyennes opposite them to recoil and seek a softer spot. They found none as other off-duty hands doubled up to defend themselves. Men whirled around as frantically as the horses.

Not many of the hastily fired rounds found a home in flesh. Smoke watched as the Cheyennes rallied to charge again. It could only be a matter of time, he thought. There were far too many of them. They were about to be swallowed up in screaming Indians. From the slope to one side came a strident yell.

Suddenly, the attack broke off. Swiftly, the Cheyennes deserted the field. Smoke could only stand and wonder.

From his vantage point outside the cotton-woods, Iron Claw judged the progress of his warriors. More importantly, he gazed over the disappearing rumps of the horses that had been successfully driven off. He made a quick decision. Turning, he spoke to Spotted Feather, the dog soldier society leader.

"We have enough horses. To try for more will risk the lives of too many brave men. And it might be bad medicine to kill a white woman and those children."

Spotted Feather smiled grimly. "You are right as always."

"What is an older brother for, Spotted Feather?"

Iron Claw's younger sibling put humor into his smile. He spoke in the ritual manner of his warrior society. "You may stop them whenever you wish."

Iron Claw raised his voice in a sharp, barking hoot like a hungry coyote. At once the warriors ceased their fighting. Many withdrew beyond the limited light in the camp. Quietly they sat their ponies. Iron Claw stepped forward to where he could be plainly seen.

He raised his arm in the sign for a parlay. The big man at the fire pit repeated it and strode for a big 'Paloose horse. Iron Claw eased his excited, cavorting mount into a mincing circle as he watched the white man approach at an easy trot. When less than fifteen feet separated them, Iron Claw could not prevent the display of chagrin and embarrassment that washed over his face.

"I see you, Smoke Jensen."

"And I see you, Iron Claw. Why are you stealing my horses."

Iron Claw shrugged and lifted the corners of his mouth in a smile. "Because they are here. And . . . I did not know they were your horses. They will be returned, old friend."

"Thank you, Iron Claw."

"Have your winters been light?"

Smoke produced a grin and a frown at the same time. "Now you want to get sociable? Yes, my winters have not been a hardship."

"I think of you often and ask the Great Spirit to watch over you and that black-haired wife. Your children are all grown?"

Smoke nodded. "Yes. Except for a boy we adopted recently."

Iron Claw raised eyebrows in surprise. "You are getting to be more 'Injun' every time I see you. He is a good boy?"

"I think he is."

"Then take your horses to where you were going and return to him, Smoke Jensen. The Cheyenne will not harm you more."

They exchanged the sign for peace, and Iron Claw turned his mount. He raised his feather-and brass-tack-decorated rifle to signal the dog soldiers. Without a backward look, they all rode quietly away.

Riding a lathered horse, his face beet-hued, Boyne Kelso ran recklessly down the main street of Muddy Gap. Flustered women put gloved hands to their mouths to stifle yelps of surprise. Men and dogs fled from his hazardous path. Kelso reined so viciously to the left that it drew blood from the tender mouth of his mount. Then he yanked up short in front of the sheriff's office.

Muttering angrily under his breath, he stormed to the door and slammed through. "Where's that idiot Larsen?" he demanded of a surprised Fred Chase.

"He's at dinner. Over to the Iron Kettle. What's got you so riled?"

"You damned well ought to know. I want my boy out of jail this instant."

"That ain't gonna happen, Mr. Kelso. Not with the charges against him."

Kelso shoved his mottled face toward the deputy. "And what might those be?"

Fred Chase made it clear he enjoyed this. "We'll take the minor things first. Brandon is charged with trespass, forced entry of a building, first-degree assault, and worst of all, attempted rape."

"What utter nonsense. My boy is not a criminal, nor is he depraved. Now get him out here so I can hear the truth of this."

"He stays where he is. No exceptions."

Kelso started to protest, then turned for the door. "Tell Larsen I'll be back."

Boyne Kelso had been at the holding pens in Bent Rock Canyon, happily counting their growing profits, when one of the Yurian gang brought word about his son being shot by Virginia Parkins and taken to jail by Marshal Larsen. It had taken him three days to get back. He'd be damned if it would take one minute more to free the boy.

To do so, he would have to have help, he reasoned. With a darkening scowl, he recalled the impudent smirk on the face of Fred Chase. How dare that stupid clod defy him? He started at once to round up supporters. His first stop would be the mercantile.

"What can I do for you, Deacon Kelso?" asked Eb Harbinson.

"You can come along with me. That mad dog lawman, Larsen, has locked up my son for absolutely nothing. And he's left orders that the boy's not to be let out for any reason. It came to me that a little moral persuasion is needed here."

"But, I . . . have the store to run."

"You've got clerks. I need you to back me."

Boyne made his next stop at the house of Mrs. Agatha Witherspoon, president of the local chapter of the Ladies' Temperance League. She also held Bible studies for the church. Kelso had calmed somewhat when he presented his case to her. Although well aware of the actual situation, Kelso invented "facts" to support his position. Grover Larsen must have been successful in keeping the real events quiet, because Agatha Witherspoon reacted with genuine shock and indignation.

"That's simply horrible. Why in the world would he do such a terrible thing? Your boy is a little—ah—brash at times, but that's no excuse for someone to shoot him and put him in jail. Who is it that shot him?"

Kelso's face darkened again. "The brazen, damned, unmarried woman who flaunts herself in front of our children in that schoolhouse."

Agatha's hand flew to her mouth to cover a gasp. "Young Miss Parkins? I—I can't believe that. She is so gentle, so meek. She's at every Bible study bee. And I hear that the children adore her."

"I'll show you adore," roared Boyne Kelso. "She shot the kneecap off my son for no reason at all!"

"That—that's terrible. Oh, he must be in such pain. Has he seen a doctor?"

"He's in jail, Agatha. I don't know if the doctor has been to him or not. I'm not even allowed to visit him."

Agatha Witherspoon made up her mind with that revelation. "That will never do. Come along. We'll find Parson Frick. The marshal cannot deny him. He'll get a doctor for your boy."

Sweeping regally down the street, the Witherspoon woman led the way to the parsonage. From there they went to the home of Rachel Appleby, the choir director. Her husband, Tom, made an effort at objecting to precipitate action. He had heard a couple of rumors of late. And he had little use for that arrogant, pushy, spoiled brat, Brandon Kelso.

It did him little good. With Boyne Kelso's tale embroidered by Agatha Witherspoon, it galvanized Rachel Appleby into immediate partisanship. Parasol shading her from the broiling sun, she hoisted the hem of her ample skirts and joined the ranks.

With his entourage in tow, Boyne Kelso returned to the jail. He stomped through the door with the church elders and minister and confronted a surprised Grover Larsen.

"I demand that you release my son at once, Larsen."

Parson Frick added his two bits' worth. "Yes, this is quite distressing. Hardly the Christian thing to do, withholding medical treatment."

Brushing up against Smoke Jensen must have given Grover Larsen new backbone. Ignoring the minister, he balled his fist and extended a thick index finger, which he jabbed at Boyne Kelso. "That no-account, shiftless offspring of yours is in serious trouble."

"Nonsense!" Kelso thundered. "He may behave foolishly at times, but he's innocent of any real dishonesty."

"That's where you are wrong, Kelso. He's not innocent, and neither are the other two who are locked up with him. Now get out of here."

Kelso took on a shocked expression. "You have three boys locked up in there? This is an outrage."

"Not for what they're charged with."

"And what is that?"

"He, Willie Finch, and Danny Collins made

improper advances to Miss Ginny. Your son attacked her in an attempt to carry them out when she refused."

Kelso snapped hotly, "I don't believe that."

"Why else do you think she shot him? He went after her in front of all the kids."

Beyond control, Boyne Kelso screamed with enough force that spittle flew from his mouth in a frothy, white spray. "That's a goddamned lie! I'll have your badge for that within twenty-four hours. And I'm going to have the territorial attorney charge that schoolmarm slut with assault."

For the first few minutes, Reno Jim Yurian could not believe his turn of luck. Hailed from behind them on the trail, Reno Jim turned to see Hub Volker and the rest of the gang headed their way. How had they caught up so fast? It came to him in a rush. Yeah, the horses came back, or they went into Buffalo and got more.

That would have put them on the way to this point for almost as long as he and his sixteen men. Now he had no doubt as to the outcome of their efforts to take back the horses. It would be simple with thirty-three men. They would wash over Smoke Jensen and the family with him like an ocean wave.

Believing themselves safe now, Smoke Jensen and his small band of drovers pushed the herd on northward the next morning. Shortly before noon, the missing horses returned under the guidance of Cheyenne warriors. The animals rejoined the gather without complaint. Smoke spoke words of thanks in the Cheyenne tongue and wished them well.

Tommy turned a big-eyed look on Smoke. "You can talk that stuff?"

"Sure, learned it young. It's an easy language."

"Could ya . . . teach it to me?"

"We won't be together long enough for you to get it all." At the boy's visible disappointment, Smoke relented. "I can teach you a few words, some expressions. Would you like that?"

Tommy beamed. "Would I!" He swiveled in the saddle and shouted to his sister. "Hey, Sarah-Jane, I'm gonna talk Cheyenne."

Smoke's confidence increased when they made thirty-four miles for the day. He located some herbs and blended them with sage leaves. This he had given to Gertrude Olsen, over the objections of her mother. By the nooning, Trudy showed obvious signs of improvement. Smoke dosed her again.

By evening, she was sitting up and took some broth. She drank water thirstily to replace that lost to the diarrhea. Della restrained her in that endeavor and smiled for the first time since the child had taken sick. She even went so far as to apologize to Smoke.

"I think you have saved her life. I want to say that I am sorry for the way I snapped at you. It was grossly unfair. Why didn't you try the herbs earlier?"

Smoke gave her a knowing smile. "There weren't any of the right ones around. And, you weren't desperate enough to allow me to use them."

Della looked shocked. "Why, that's a terrible thing to say. I would do anything for my children."

"Even if the remedy came from an Indian medicine man?"

Della gaped at him. "I never thought of that."

"I did."

"Smoke, I feel foolish."

"Not at all. You're just a very protective mother. That's a good sign. Your children know it and appreciate what you do for them. Now, I think Trudy needs more rest."

"Thank you again, and I am sorry."

Smoke turned his smile to a friendly one. "It's all in where you grew up."

That night, everyone slept soundly for the first time since the herd had been rustled. Smoke Jensen would soon find how beneficial that had been.

"We'll do it the way we did before," Reno Jim Yurian informed his gang. "It worked then, no reason it won't now. What we're after is the horses. Never mind the men, unless they offer resistance."

Yancy Osburn scoffed. "What kinda resistance can one man and some brats give us?"

"You have a point, Yancy, but from the tracks we've seen, it looks like Jensen picked up some replacements somewhere. Be prepared for trouble."

Hub Volker addressed the men who would be with him. "We'll split off now, swing around on the flanks. When the boss is in place in front of the herd, he and five of the boys will charge the herd. We swing down from the side and start pushin' them back along the trail. Those on the other side will hit at the same time. Get a movin'."

They departed in silence, with nothing to say until the fighting ended. Each of the outlaws had wrapped himself in his private thoughts. Ainsley Burk wondered about that pretty saloon gal who had waved to him back in Muddy Gap while they were robbing the stores. Maybe he'd drop in on her and spend some of his take.

Prine Gephart astounded himself by recalling the face of the wife he had left behind in Missouri and his three freckle-faced boys, stair-stepped between five and nine. He hadn't wanted to abandon his sons, but his wife had turned into a shrew, always complaining about not enough money. And when he had some, getting on his case about where he got it and how. Danged woman, she had driven him to robbing to supplement the meager income from their hardscrabble farm. Well, he'd shown her.

Virgil Plumm visualized the old, weathered ranch house in Texas where he had been born and raised. With the stake he would have, he could fix it up, paint it even. Then find him a good woman and raise a batch of young 'uns. Ranching was in his blood. His paw had put him atop a horse before he could walk proper. He had tried to rope calves the first time when he was five.

Awh, what the hell was he thinking? Outlawing was the only thing he had known since the age of sixteen. He'd never change now. The gray, warped siding of the house faded. He would just go get drunk, gamble away his profit and visit the bawdy houses until the last dime had been spent. Oh, and get his six-gun fixed. It had been hanging up of late. The recoil plate must be worn.

Bittercreek Sawyer saw a world entirely different from any of his fellow thieves. The soft yellow glow of gaslights played through his mind. Attractive young Creole women all in white lace and lawn hoopskirt dresses graced the wrought-iron galleries of the French Quarter and cast admiring glances at him as he rode in a spanking bright, black lacquered carriage along Saint Peter Street. A cotton-haired darkey drove the rig. Bittercreek wore a frilly white shirt, paisley vest, cutaway coat and top hat. A silver-headed cane rested in one gloved hand. The rich aroma of Cajun cooking wafted on a light, moist breeze up from Jackson Square. The bass hoot of a riverboat steam whistle startled pigeons off their eve roosts. All was well with the world.

With the impending fight drawing nearer, Lucky Draper concentrated on the scene of a smoky saloon, where he stood surrounded by his friends, who slapped him on the back and whooped for joy. He had just broke the bank. The faro dealer looked at him with a gaping mouth. Lucky's pockets bulged with doubleeagles. He ran more through his fingers like grains of corn. A tall, willowy blonde ankled over, hips swaying in a skimpy dancer's costume.

She twined her arms around his neck and planted a big, wet kiss on his lips. Another lovely handed him a brimming glass of good rye. The cheering went on. Lucky tucked a twenty-dollar gold piece into the cleavage of each girl.

"Hold up!" came a low, but emphatic command.

It brought them all out of their dreams. Hubble Volker pointed at a low rise ahead. "Them horses are right beyond that ridge. We wait until we hear the first shots, then ride like hell."

Smoke Jensen's confidence continued into late afternoon. Then, before he knew what to expect, five men appeared on the trail ahead of them. They reined in momentarily, then came on at a gallop, weapons out and ready. The moment they came within range, they opened fire.

Tommy Olsen understood it all in a flash. "They're back!"

In a storm, the outlaws rushed beyond those in the lead of the herd. Smoke Jensen shot one out of the saddle, and then the horses stampeded. Gunfire broke out on the right flank of the panicked animals, driving them back on those behind. Eleven men streamed over the ridge in pursuit of the unsettled remounts. Most of them fired in the air, though a few directed bullets toward the hard-working drovers.

One of the Leaning Tree hands threw up his arms and wavered in the saddle. His horse scented the freely flowing blood and went berserk. It crow-hopped and sunfished until it dislodged the seriously wounded rider. Smoke Jensen swung in his saddle and fired directly at the shooter.

Smoke's bullet took him square in the chest.

He flew from the saddle and disappeared under the hooves of the shrilling, stamping remounts. A bullet cracked past Jensen's ear, and he looked to see that the five riders who had attacked from the front now seriously worked at killing every one of his hands, himself as well.

Eighteen

Reno Jim Yurian and the four men with him halted at the edge of the boiling mass of horses and took careful aim at the men who attempted to control them. Another Leaning Tree hand slumped on the neck of his horse. A bullet cut through the jacket worn by Smoke Jensen and burned a hot line across his shoulder. Damn, Smoke thought in a flash, that shoulder had only recently healed. Then he gave himself over to the battle that brewed around him.

There would be no containing the horses, Smoke realized at once. Already the outlaws pushed them down the trail in the direction from which they had come. Clouds of dust and powder smoke roiled upward to cut off clear vision of the violent confrontation. Heat became oppressive. Sweat ran down Smoke Jensen's forehead and stung his eyes. He wiped with a forearm to clear them. Suddenly an outlaw loomed directly in front of him.

Smoke saw the muzzle rise to center on his chest; then he triggered his Colt. The bullet smashed into the open, screaming mouth of the gang member. The back of Prine Gephart's head flew off with his hat, and his dreams died with him. Then his Smith American discharged, and a shower of stars exploded inside Smoke's head. Immense pain shot down his neck, and he felt himself slipping from the saddle. Swiftly, blackness overwhelmed him.

Caleb Noonan found himself facing three determined rustlers. He knew the horses had to be controlled, yet the threat to his life forced him to draw and fire at one of the men. His shot went wild, and he recocked his Colt. Another outlaw took a shot at Caleb.

An aching line of fire ran along the outer side of Caleb's right thigh. Then his mount surged into a frenzied leap as the slug burned into its belly. Caleb shot again and put a bullet into the meaty part of one outlaw's abdomen. Then a giant pain exploded in his chest. All strength left him, and his horse threw him.

He landed hard enough to cross his eyes. When he straightened them, he looked up into the muzzle of a .44 Winchester pointed at his head. He saw only the first flicker of muzzle bloom . . . then blackness.

Granger Bolt saw Caleb Noonan go down. He twisted in the saddle and brought quick retribution to the outlaw who had killed his friend. That brought immediate attention down on him. To his regret, the surviving member of the trio who had gunned down Caleb turned his way. He and Bolt fired as one. To his surprise, in the face of the certain knowledge of his impending death, the bullet cracked past Bolt's head. All around, the air moaned and crackled with flying slugs. With new wonder he saw the outlaw jerk, then slump in his saddle.

He might get through this after all, Granger thought to himself. Then nine more rustlers joined the fray. They rode in with cold determination. One sighted on Bolt and put a bullet through his head from a range of twenty yards.

Granger Bolt died without a sound. The fighting went on without him. By now, nearly half the herd had been started back toward Sheridan, Buffalo, and Bent Rock Canyon beyond.

Pulling out of the swirl of the combat, Ahab Trask decided that these rustlers were seriously trying to kill them all. It hadn't been that way the first time. He tried to rally his muddled thoughts and make sense of what he saw. There seemed to be gunmen everywhere.

Worse, they fired with deadly accuracy. Another of the Leaning Tree hands went to the ground, his chest bloodied from a shot in the back. Ahab Trask took the time he spent in observation to reload his six-gun. At such short ranges, it would serve well. Two rustlers charged straight at him, driving ten head of remounts before them. Trask raised his Colt and fired.

Unfortunately for him, the close proximity of the frenzied horses set off a fear reaction in his own mount. It jinked to one side and threw off his aim. Then the remounts surged all around him. To his horror, his horse reared and spun on its hind hooves. Trask felt himself slipping, and then a rifle butt drove out of seemingly no-where and slammed into his chest. He fell with a scream under the unshod hooves of the surging horses.

Ahab Trask's shrill cry quickly went silent. The remounts passed on. They left behind a lifeless ball of torn, bloodied clothes, bits of bone protruding from rents in the cloth.

A wicked smile playing on his lips, Reno Jim Yurian thought the whole plan had gone well. At the outset, not all of the men knew of his plan to kill everyone and leave no witnesses, or the chance of pursuit. Only those who rode with him, and those he placed on the left flank, had been aware of that.

He allowed himself a moment to gloat as those flankers crashed into the milling defenders. Two more drovers went down. One fell under the hooves of the remounts. Yes, well before sundown they would have the herd back together and under their control. Yancy Osburn rode out of the melee to join Reno Jim.

"They fight like wildcats, Reno. Ever'thing's so mixed up we're shootin' more air than men."

"So are they, remember. I don't see anything of Smoke Jensen."

"I think I saw him go down early on, Reno."

"Damn. I wanted him for myself."

"Anyway, he won't be a bother to us anymore. You have any spare cartridges?"

"In my left saddlebag. Take a box."

Yancy grinned. "If twenty rounds don't finish it, I'll eat my six-gun." Whistling lightly, he reached for the ammunition and returned to the fight.

"Give 'em hell, Yancy!" Reno Jim yelled after him.

Harper Liddy had a hard time keeping his mount between his legs. Gunshots cracked all around him. Ol' Reb, his trusty mount, constantly twitched his loose hide and made mincing side steps to express his discomfort. Everything was in such confusion. He could not prove it, but a moment ago it seemed as though the horses that had been driven off from the herd had started to return. How could that be? He had little time to speculate further.

A yowling rustler burst out of the miasma of dust and smoke and charged right at him. The hard case had a revolver blazing in each hand, his reins looped over the pommel. To Liddy's good fortune, the outlaw turned out to be a lousy shot. Hot lead flew past Liddy's shoulders, and one cracked overhead. A galloping horse provided a poor platform from which to fire a gun.

Harper Liddy took careful aim and ended Virgil Plumm's hopes of the good life in the French Quarter. Another, wiser, gunhand shot Harper Liddy from a standing horse. The bullet cut through Liddy's chest from front to rear. Bad hurt and knowing it, Harper fired point-blank at the charging outlaw, turned in his saddle and killed the man who had mortally wounded him before he himself fell dead at the feet of his mount.

* * *

Intent on protecting the Olsens, Jerry Harkness fought his way from behind the rustlers toward the wagon. He and the five men he had brought along arrived only seconds before the attack. Two of the men died in the effort to penetrate the gang. Jerry had taken another grazing wound. Now he dismounted and crouched beside the frightened family. From above him, a Winchester cracked, followed by a shot from a lighter weapon, a Marlin, Jerry thought. He added his own firepower to it and saw immediate results.

A surging roan went down right in front of him, yanked from its front hooves by its dying rider. Jerry cycled the lever action of his .44 Winchester and fired at another outlaw. *These bastards don't care about the horses, they're more interested in killing us,* he realized at once. He centered on another bandit and squeezed the trigger.

Jerry's slug took the man in his hip. He howled and turned away from the fight. Another of the volunteers Jerry had rounded up died as a trio of the rustlers discharged their revolvers into him from three directions, not more than four feet away. Jerry bit off a curse.

Two hard cases swept past him, and the weapons above went off in a roar. One gunman fell. The other turned back and pointed his six-gun at the occupants of the wagon. Too late to take aim, Jerry thrust himself upward, arms out to deflect the revolver. He got his hand on the barrel and succeeded in his purpose, only to have hot pain explode in his palm when the Colt discharged. A second later, a shot came from his left and bored through his chest, bursting his heart.

Head throbbing, Smoke Jensen regained consciousness to find an eerie silence blanketing the battlefield. Had the horses been taken and the gang gone from there? Slowly he roused himself, conscious of a steady seep of blood down the side of his head. At least, he thought, it was the side and not his forehead. Slowly, Smoke gained control over the focus of his eyes. He saw a number of the outlaws sitting their horses and staring in horror off across the plains. What were they looking at? Smoke raised himself farther.

When his gaze moved to the ridge surrounding them, his features mirrored the same shock as that on the faces of the outlaws. He blinked, then slowly, painfully, came to his boots. He could hardly believe what he saw.

Ringing the entire swale, a double circle of Cheyenne warriors sat their ponies. They looked down in silence while the dust and powder smoke drifted from the scene of conflict. The horses driven off earlier milled in front of those on the south side. While Smoke Jensen looked on in astonishment, Iron Claw raised his rifle, and the Indians began a silent, baleful advance down into the shallow basin.

Iron Claw looked down on the slaughter below. Of all the white men who drove the herd, only Smoke Jensen remained alive. He and the boy and a woman held weapons in their hands. Iron Claw's keen eyes caught movement in the bed of the rolling lodge, and he made out two small girl children. All of the others had died. Had he not made the decision to come here when sounds of the fighting reached his ears and those of his dog soldiers, even his friend, Smoke Jensen would have perished. He turned to his brother, Spotted Feather.

"We have come in time for our friend, Smoke Jensen."

"Not for the others," observed Spotted Feather.

Iron Claw shrugged. "They were white men. Now we will deal with the men who try to steal the horses of my friend. Then we will think on what is to be done next."

Iron Claw raised his feather-decorated rifle as a signal, and the Cheyenne began to advance.

Only Smoke Jensen knew the Cheyenne to be friendly. That resulted in utter chaos among the outlaws. Only escape filled their minds. The herd meant nothing now. Half a dozen took off to the north, to meet a wall of bullets and arrows. Recovered from his initial shock, Reno Jim Yurian shouted to the remaining outlaws.

"Band together, boys, we'll shoot our way out." He pointed the nose of his horse to the west and waited while the gang assembled behind him. When they had, with Utah Jack at his side, Reno Jim opened fire on the Cheyenne and spurred his horse.

Twenty-three hard cases began that fateful charge. Three got knocked from their saddles before they had covered fifty feet. The gang reached full gallop halfway across the slowly contracting ring of Indians. Abruptly, Reno Jim and Utah Jack reined in and let the others rush past them. As a result, the surviving outlaws took the brunt of the Cheyenne response.

Firing blindly at the Indians, the desperate hard cases crashed into the approaching ranks on a broad front. Rifles and revolvers fired an irregular volley that opened a narrow path through the Cheyenne ponies. Fighting at point-blank range now, the Yurian gang surged into the opening. More of the Indians moved to close the gap.

Before they could, Reno Jim spoke sharply to Utah Jack. "Now!"

They bolted forward and bulled their way through the rest of the gang, who struggled hand-to-hand now with the Cheyenne. Slowed to a walk, Reno Jim and Utah Jack shot two ponies out from under the last Indians blocking their escape. When the riders fell, the two white men spurred their mounts and broke into the open. They wasted no time. Turned to the south, Reno Jim Yurian leaned low over the neck of his horse and kept up a steady pricking with his big Mexican star rowels.

Back inside the contracting ring of warriors, Iron Claw started to call out for pursuit. Smoke Jensen stopped him with a raised hand. "No. Those two are mine."

Iron Claw nodded his understanding. "Go with good medicine, Smoke Jensen."

"I reckon I'll be needing some of that."

So saying, Smoke swung into Cougar's saddle and started south, after the outlaw leader and the traitor. The exertion of keeping in the saddle at a full gallop made his head spin again, and black spots rose before his eyes. Smoke had hastily tied a bandanna around his scalp graze, which had stopped the bleeding. For that he was thankful. Now all he had to do was catch up to his quarry.

Smoke ran Cougar about a mile, then slowed to a fast trot. It would be too easy to wind his mount and end up afoot. Considering the behavior of the fugitives, they might not take that factor into account, Smoke speculated. Ahead he could see the rising dust of their passage. With any luck, their horses would wear down soon and he could catch up. Only gradually did the realization of the effect of the attack register on him.

Too many good men had died back there. Jerry Harkness, Harper Liddy, Ahab Trask, Granger Bolt, Caleb Noonan and all those who had offered their help. The two he chased had a hell of a lot to account for. And Smoke reckoned to be the one to make them pay.

For a moment he felt an ache deep inside. It would grow, he knew, into an overwhelming sense of defeat . . . if he let it. No way he would do that, Smoke promised himself. He would track this pair to China and back if necessary. He looked forward to watching them hang.

Nineteen

Inexorably, Smoke Jensen traced the fleeing men across the high plains. Slowly he closed the gap. When he finally caught a first sight of them, Grubbs and Yurian walked their horses out of necessity. Even at that far distance, Smoke could see the flanks of the animals heave. White lather lay in rolls along their necks and around saddle blankets.

Fools, Smoke thought. They had gotten their horses completely blown. All the better for him. He gave Cougar a light tap of his round knob, cavalry-style spurs and picked up the pace. In no time, he closed the space between them to less than a quarter mile.

Then, abruptly and unexpectedly, the numbing pain returned to throb and gouge through Smoke's head. He swayed drunkenly in the saddle, his vision blurred and the world spun around him. A sudden spasm of nausea twisted his gut.

Groaning, Smoke bent over and vomited up a thin, green bile. His hand trembled as he reached for his canteen to rinse his mouth. Another shaft of blinding agony pierced his head. Smoke felt his balance gradually slip away. Darkness washed over him as he pitched out of the saddle.

* * *

Up ahead, Reno Jim Yurian and Utah Jack Grubbs watched in silence while Smoke Jensen fell to the ground. Grubbs pointed to the prone figure.

"I'll go back and finish him off, boss."

"Yes. I suppose that's the best way. I wouldn't get any satisfaction out of killing a helpless man."

"Nor will I. How the hell did those Injuns get mixed up in this?"

Reno Jim considered that a moment. "Probably had their eyes on the herd."

Utah Jack frowned. "From what I saw at the end, they didn't harm a hair on Smoke Jensen. In fact, their chief rode right up to him, and they talked real friendly like."

A grunt burst from Reno Jim. "I saw that. The damned savages must be friends of his."

A grim smile formed on the face of Utah Jack. "That'll make doin' for him easier."

"I'll meet you in Sheridan."

Utah Jack nodded in reply and set off on foot, at a walk, back toward Smoke Jensen. Reno Jim continued on south, leading his winded mount by the reins. They had lost the horses, he thought bitterly. Worse, his men had been slaughtered by the damned Cheyenne. Only six men were left back in Bent Rock Canyon with the cattle. He spoke aloud his frustration.

"How can I recover what I've lost? What kind of leader lets his men get trapped like I did?"

Only the low moan of a soft southwest breeze answered him.

* * *

A crunch of gravel under a boot heel brought awareness back to Smoke Jensen. He lay still, slowly opened his eyes and fought to focus. Above him, Cougar snorted a challenge. Another horse skittered its hooves and answered shrilly.

"Woah there! Easy, easy," a familiar voice soothed.

Smoke took the opportunity to raise his head and verify his suspicion. Though his head throbbed monstrously, he focused on the boots and rawhide chap-covered legs of Utah Jack Grubbs. Smoke looked higher. Grubbs was turned away from him, some twenty feet away, arms up to calm his nervous mount.

"Down boy. Down."

His attention completely off the man he came to kill, Utah Jack sawed at the reins. His sorrel gelding had been frightened by the 'Palouse stallion, and he had all he could do to regain control. As a result, he failed to see Smoke Jensen thrust himself to a sitting position.

Another wave of dizziness swamped him, and he had to sit a moment until it passed. Then Smoke reached out and gripped the right stirrup. Slowly, he dragged himself upright. Another black pool of dizziness engulfed him. He drew a deep breath through an open mouth to prevent it being heard. His vision cleared almost at once. He glanced down and silently swore.

Both of his Colts had fallen from the holsters and lay on the ground ten feet from him. He had run out of ammunition for his Winchester and left it behind. Then his left hand brushed the haft of the tomahawk he habitually carried on his saddle. Slowly he eased it out of the thong that retained it. In the next second Utah Jack settled his irritable horse. He turned again to face Smoke Jensen.

"So, you old bastard, you're on your feet." He cut his eyes to Smoke's revolvers. "Too bad you lost your irons. Without them, you're nothin'," Utah Jack scoffed, his mouth twisted in an ugly sneer.

He took a menacing step closer. "In fact, this is going to be so easy I think I'll do it with my bare hands."

Feeling not the least himself, Smoke answered in a low growl. "When pigs fly and cows sing."

"You've got a smart mouth, Jensen. If it wasn't for the prospect of gettin' that herd of yours, I woulda driven you into the ground like a fence post the first day on that stinkin' ranch of yours."

Time. Smoke needed every bit of it he could buy to get back even a little of his strength. To do so, he decided to bait Grubbs. "How are you going to do that, you mouthy little pile of horse crap? You gonna beat me to death with your tongue?"

"You'll find out in about a second. First, I'm gonna have my say. You're pathetic, Jensen. All that lovey-dovey stuff with that wife of yours. Askin' her opinion of ever' little thing. It made me sick. Any real man knows a woman ain't got no brains. You have to yell at 'em all the time and beat her at least once a month to keep her in line. And another thing. You never lay a hand on that towheaded brat. Ain't a kid that grows up right lest he gits whipped regular every day."

Smoke used all his willpower to hold his anger in check. He put a twisted smile on his face. "You're such a prime example of that."

"Damn right I am. My paw beat my butt raw at least once a week, took a belt to me ever' day. What really galls me is that you don't know anything about handling livestock. Horses has got to be whip-broke to properly tame them. Any fool knows that."

Taunting again, Smoke laughed at Grubbs. "Yeah, *any fool*. Are you through running that open sewer of yours?"

"Damn right," Grubbs barked. He started for Smoke again. To his surprise, Smoke beckoned invitingly.

"Come on, Grubbs, get right up close. I'm going to enjoy tearing you a new bung hole."

Utah Jack took two fast steps to close the distance, and he swung a slow, looping right. The moment he did, Smoke Jensen eased away from the support of Cougar and brought the tomahawk into sight. He swung it as Utah Jack's fist hurtled toward his jaw.

At the last second, Smoke jinked his head to the side as the keen edge of the blade sank into the arm of his opponent an inch above the elbow. It ground against the bone, dislodged a chip and then came free. Hot agony burned through Utah Jack, and he howled in anguish. Then numbness began to spread along his injured limb.

Grubbs backed off a few paces and fumbled the bandanna from around his neck. Clumsily he used it to bind his wound. Smoke Jensen came on. His arm useless, Utah Jack could not draw his six-gun. Smoke closed with him; blood dripped from the edge of his warhawk.

"You're fast for an old fart."

"Not so old by half, you traitorous dog."

Smoke felt new strength surge through his body. It lifted him. He reached Grubbs and pounded him in the chest with a hard right. Utah Jack backpedaled. Smoke came on. The menace of the tomahawk remained, cocked and ready. Smoke's right lashed out again.

Blood sprayed across the outlaw's face as hard knuckles crushed his nose. His eyes crossed, and he momentarily lost sight in the left one. Mopping at it with his left hand, he tried to block the next blow. His effort failed, and his lower lip split in a searing flash of pain. Smoke pressed his attack.

Utah Jack tried to dodge to his right and felt the fiery bite of the 'hawk against his ribs. Then the darting right fist of Smoke Jensen drove sharply into the solar plexus of Utah Jack. Air gushed from his bloody lips, and for a while Jack Grubbs saw black.

Doubled over, Utah Jack's vision cleared, and he grasped feebly at the hilt of a knife in the top of his boot. Groaning, he came upright as far as he could and drove the blade with lightning speed toward the exposed loin of Smoke Jensen. Cold steel skidded across Smoke's cartridge belt and punched into his side.

Gasping, he fell away from his attacker. He landed on the ground and rolled toward his six-guns. Utah Jack advanced on him. Smoke's hand closed over the butt-grip of one .45 Colt, and he whipped it upward. Close to blacking out, he cocked the hammer and tickled the trigger.

"Noooooo!" Utah Jack wailed as he realized what Smoke had accomplished.

Smoke's bullet smashed into the chest of Utah Jack Grubbs. It drove rib bone ahead of it into his heart. The powerful organ spasmed, then began to rapidly pump in an erratic rhythm. Eyes bulged, Utah Jack looked down to witness his demise.

Grubbs fell dead as weakness washed over Smoke Jensen. He had to get the stab wound cared for. From the feel of it, the blade had missed his liver. How, he didn't know, but his gratitude to his Maker was genuine. Carefully, Smoke dropped his tomahawk and tugged his shirt from behind his belt.

New pain radiated through his torso as he pulled it higher. Another whirl of dizziness staggered him. He looked down, expecting to see the worst. He saw instead a small, two-inch incision. A thin ribbon of blood trickled over the bluish lips. Gently, he probed the pale flesh surrounding it. Little pain followed. Head still aching at each step, he returned to his horse.

From a saddlebag, he took some of the remaining moss that had been collected a week ago for the drawing poultice Smoke had used on Jerry Harkness. He wet it from his canteen, packed it in the wound and retrieved a length of buckskin strip from the bag. That he wound around his body and tied tightly. Then he washed the bullet gouge on his head again and rebandaged it.

Hobbling away from Cougar, he stripped the

weapons from the corpse of Utah Jack. Smoke found the cartridge belt and revolver empty and five rounds in the Winchester. He gathered up his second Colt and replaced the expended cartridge in the right-hand one. He did not have the strength to throw the outlaw over his saddle, but he would not leave the horse out there to fend for itself. He led it back to where Cougar waited, mounted gingerly and put the 'Palouse in motion. With one rein around the pommel of Smoke's saddle, the sorrel trotted along peacefully beside Cougar.

Despite his recent head wound and the new cut in his side, Smoke began to feel stronger with each passing mile. He picked up the trail of Reno Jim Yurian readily and followed along at a fast trot. He had little doubt that Yurian intended to pass through Sheridan. Smoke wanted to catch him before then. Any hotel room or saloon front could become an excellent ambush spot. In a thoughtful mood, Smoke reached under the skirt of his saddle and extracted a softened piece of bison jerky.

He had obtained the dried meat from Iron Claw before setting out after the fleeing outlaws. "It will be good for your head," Iron Claw told him, pointing to the bandaged gouge with his chin.

"I doubt I'll need six strips."

Iron Claw insisted. "Eat them all. Then we get some hump meat. It will make you strong."

Smoke accepted this. He often recalled the story of the Kiowa war chief, Two Moons, who as a young man was reported to have taken thirty-six rifle and revolver wounds in one fierce battle with the cavalry from Fort Sill. At least two of them had struck him in the groin. The Kiowa subsisted almost entirely on bison. Not only did Two Moons heal up, but he sired seven children, and died at the age of eighty-three. That was enough to convince Smoke Jensen. There would be bison at the Crow Agency. He would get his hump meat.

Smoke bit at his lower lip to snap his focus back on what he had started out to do. His keen eyes fixed on the spot where Yurian had remounted. The depth of the hoof prints increased, and the space between them elongated. This time the rider kept to a trot. Despite the throbbing in his head, Smoke gigged Cougar into a canter. A mile farther, the tracks veered from the trail. Smoke looked back. He could not see the place where he had fought with Utah Jack. Reining Cougar to the left, he followed Reno Jim's sign.

Muted and made flat by distance, Reno Jim Yurian had heard the single shot. He knew it had to have been fired by Smoke Jensen. Utah Jack Grubbs would have pumped at least three slugs, as insurance, into so famous a gunfighter as Smoke Jensen. Accordingly, he left the trail to Sheridan and broke a new path cross-country. He knew that Jensen would be coming after him.

Deliberately he did not make any effort to cover his tracks. He had a definite plan. Reno Jim fixed his eyes on a distant line of trees that denoted a streambed. There he would find what he wanted.

When Reno Jim located it, he smiled a mean, thin-lipped smile. Perfect for what he had in mind. A deep, wide, twisting ravine ran perpendicular to the creek. Cut into the prairie by ages of runoff, it had grown to a depth he gauged to be fifteen or more feet. Quickly he backtracked to where he could negotiate the sloping side. Then he dismounted and led his horse down into the gully. He found the winding course to be ideal. It offered several places for a man to hide in wait.

Reno Jim picked his ambush site carefully. A limestone outcropping created a wide, gentle bend, and beyond it, a granite shelf forced a sharp turn in the dry waterway. The outlaw leader took his mount well beyond this and screwed a ground anchor into the sidewall. He tied the reins to this, pulled free his Winchester and returned to the angled curve. Then he settled in to wait.

Trees ahead, Smoke Jensen noted as he dogged the tracks left by Reno Jim Yurian. It would be the creek where they had camped two nights before. The place where the Cheyenne had tried to take the herd would likely be a couple of miles south. The irony was not missed by Smoke. Abruptly he made note of an overlay of tracks, one set returning across those that led to the distant creek.

A small alarm began to tingle in the back of his mind. If Reno Jim wanted to backtrack him—

self, he surely knew enough not to do it on his fresh trail. Not unless he wanted it noticed, Smoke's experience told him. Now, why would that be? He looked around, farther from the sign he followed. There, the return tracks cut away at a right angle from the trail he followed.

Then Smoke saw the broken ground at the lip of the ravine, where Reno Jim had descended. So that's it, Smoke thought grimly. He wants to lead me into an ambush. Might as well oblige the wily jackal. Smoke dismounted and tied Utah Jack's horse to a hawthorn bush. With that accomplished, he returned to Cougar and headed the animal down into the fissure.

Immediately, Smoke took in the nature of his new surroundings. Fine sand and small pebbles formed the bed of the cleft, its course a series of turns and bends. It had been carved out over what must have been centuries as water ran toward the creek. He judged himself to be close to eighteen feet below the level of the prairie. Reno Jim had left clear impressions of his boots as well as the hooves of his mount. Had the man wanted to hide his whereabouts, he would have come back and wiped out those telltale signs.

For all the harm done him today, Smoke could still smell an ambush in the making without effort. He chose to remain mounted, walking Cougar along slowly. He kept alert, his eyes moving constantly to detect any change in surroundings, or the glint of sunlight off a gun barrel. Man and horse rounded one twist in the defile and progressed along a relatively long straightaway. Another bend, wider than the previous one, waited beyond. For all his caution, it was not Smoke, but Cougar who gave the first alarm.

A sudden shift in the wind brought the scent of Reno Jim's roan to the nostrils of the spotted-rump stallion. Undirected, he halted abruptly near the center of the curve, jerked up his head and snorted a challenge. A fraction of a second later, Smoke Jensen saw a puff of powder smoke beyond the second part of the double bend. Immediately he felt the sting of shards on his face from limestone blasted loose by a bullet impact six inches from his head.

The slug had struck the rock at the exact point where Smoke's head would have been, had his horse not pulled up so short. At once, Smoke jumped the 'Palouse stallion to the left, behind the shelter of the rounded wall of the gorge. Quickly, Smoke dismounted and slid his rifle from its scabbard. He cycled the lever action and chambered a round. Then he eased the barrel out in the open.

He sighted at the spot from where the smoke had come and triggered two fast shots. They sang an evil duet as they ricocheted off the solid granite. Yurian fired again, this time hastily. A clump of dirt from above fell on the brim of Smoke's hat.

Then he answered the outlaw leader. One slug moaned off the slab and the other passed beyond. Reno Jim Yurian's shout sounded a bit strained. "I'm gonna get you, Jensen, you rotten bastard."

Twenty

"Plenty have tried," Smoke answered flatly.

Yurian changed subjects. "What did you do to Utah Jack?"

"I shot him. Left the carcass for the coyotes."

Reno Jim swore viciously, then concluded with, "I suppose I shouldn't be surprised."

"You're wrong, Reno. Like you were wrong about taking my herd. If he hadn't stabbed me in the side, I could have put him on his horse and brought him along."

A long silence followed that revelation. Smoke Jensen strained to hear any sound of movement. After the early exchange, he knew he had only two rounds left for the .44 Winchester, and a cylinder load in each of his .45 Colts. He reckoned Reno Jim to be no better off. He looked sharply down the crevasse at the click of one stone against another.

Funny, it had come from farther down the watercourse. Smoke took another quick shot, then risked a dash to the sharper bend. He reached it without drawing fire. So far, so good. One round left in the Winchester. He grasped it by the receiver and let it hang from his left arm. Six-gun drawn, Smoke rounded the acute angle and found the ambusher's vantage point vacant. It would have to be the hard way. Making the best time he could, Smoke sprinted back to Cougar and put away his rifle. Then he led the animal back toward where Reno Jim had disappeared.

Standing beside his horse, Reno Jim Yurian stared with disbelief at the empty saddlebag. That left him with only the ammunition in his Smith Americans. A dozen rounds. He turned at the sound of a hoof striking a rock and drew with smooth speed. Before he could stop himself, the hammer fell, and he wasted one of those precious cartridges.

His bullet struck nothing. From beyond the turn he heard a soft, mocking laugh. Reno Jim moved away from his mount and fired again when he had a clear view. That slug struck the rock ledge above Smoke Jensen's head. Deformed by the impact, it moaned off harmlessly. A fraction of a second later, a .45 round cracked past Reno Jim's head, so close he could feel the heat. He dived for the ground. Slowly, the realization came to him that he had two choices. He could stay here and trade shots until they both ran dry. Or he could head for the creek and attempt to escape pursuit. The latter course sounded best.

Except that the only way to insure success would be to make certain Smoke Jensen lay dead in this gully. He would have to out-wait Jensen. Time slowed down. It appeared to Reno Jim that hours dragged past before he sensed movement. At once, he fired in that direction.

The derisive laughter came again. That broke his nerve.

"Goddamn you, Smoke Jensen. Show yourself and fight like a man."

Two shots crashed from beyond the curvature of the wall. One bullet kicked up shards of rock from the boulder Reno Jim crouched behind. The other burned a hot gouge across his right shoulder blade. A taunting voice followed.

"Show yourself, Reno, and fight like a man."

All reason abandoned, Reno Jim emptied his right-hand revolver in an attempt to banish his broken spirit. Quickly he changed over to the one on his left. A return to silence ridiculed his outburst.

For a long, sweaty hour, Smoke continued to toy with Reno Jim. He changed positions and used his ammunition sparingly. To keep the pressure on, he had to expend part of his dwindling supply. His strength increased steadily while he watched his enemy unravel. Suddenly Yurian appeared in the open, his face slack, eyes wild.

"I'm coming after you, Jensen. I'm going to leave your brains on this sand."

In a rush, Reno Jim charged, firing as he came. Smoke returned shots. Reno Jim jinked from side to side. One of Smoke's rounds clipped the heel from one of Reno Jim's boots. He sprawled in the sand and scrambled to get behind a boulder. With his body out of danger, he thought furiously for a means to gain an advantage. Slowly it came to him. He weighed it. Yes, it would work.

"Jensen? Can we talk?"

"I'm listening."

"Can we work this out? I can tell you where the cattle the gang rustled are located. I can tell you something else, too. Real important."

"What's that?"

"I have a partner. A very influential man, a regular pillar of the community."

Smoke Jensen kept his voice neutral. "What do you expect in return for this?"

Reno Jim Yurian's voice broke with the intensity of his emotion. "I—I want to live. I don't want to be shot down in this miserable wilderness. And I don't want to hang. I want to work a deal. Maybe a few years in prison in exchange for my information?"

Smoke thought it over a second. "I'll promise you this for now. You be straight with me and I'll not kill you."

"Remember this, I want to come out of this alive."

"Tell me what you have and we'll see."

"That's all I get?"

Smoke spoke drily. "For now. Give."

"All right—all right. The cattle are in Bent Rock Canyon, down near Muddy Creek. There are six men watching them."

"And this partner of yours?"

Reno Jim choked back his anxiety. "I'll really get to live?"

"I gave my word. I'll not kill you."

"All right—all right. You won't believe this, but it's true. He's—he's Boyne Kelso. The cattle broker in Muddy Gap. A deacon in his church, of all things."

Smoke blinked. He considered Kelso a wind-bag, overwilling to depreciate the criminal inclinations of his delinquent son, and prone to make too big a show of his rectitude. Yet a partner to Reno Jim Yurian?

"Tell me that again."

"My partner is Boyne Kelso. He has been for the past six years."

Smoke mulled it over in silence. "All right. Throw out all your weapons. Do it now."

Two nickle-plated Smith and Wesson Americans thudded out on the sand. A .41 rim-fire derringer followed. Then a knife. Slowly, Reno Jim Yurian rose from his shelter.

"Step out in the open."

When he had, Smoke Jensen came from his own cover and walked up to the gang leader. A fleeting smile flickered on his face as he held his Colt casually. All of a sudden, he balled his left fist and slammed a powerful knockout blow to the jaw. He looked down at the senseless man and spoke aloud.

"I didn't say anything about not hitting you."

Tommy Olsen and Iron Claw followed the tracks left by Smoke Jensen. The war chief studied the horizon after three hours at a moderate trot. He nodded and pointed with his chin.

"Up ahead. It is our friend, Smoke Jensen."

Tommy gaped at him. "Gosh, you can see that far?"

Iron Claw nodded. "I used to be able to see farther." He tapped his cheek, near his left eye. "The eyes get weaker with age." He laughed.

"We gotta hurry," Tommy urged.

Sage advice came from Iron Claw. "We will get there faster if we do not run the horses."

Tommy looked blank. "Oh. Yeah. Smoke said something like that, too."

"He learned well from White Wolf."

"Who?"

"The man your people call Preacher."

Less than a hundred yards separated them now, and yet Smoke came on at the same pace. "He is leading two horses," observed Iron Claw.

"I can see that. One has a tied-up man on it; the other has one across the saddle."

"That one is dead, I think," Iron Claw told Tommy.

Smoke hailed them and finally increased his gait. When he rode up, he explained the burdens tied and slung over the saddles. "I've got Reno Jim Yurian. Jack Grubbs is dead. And I have unfinished business in Muddy Gap."

"What kinda business?" Tommy queried.

Smoke canted his head. "I think we might get back your cattle, Tommy. Among other things. First, though, we have to get those horses to Fort Custer."

"Before that you have to have those wounds treated," Iron Claw injected as he looked at the bloody cloth at Smoke's side. "And we have a feast."

Tommy Olsen enjoyed the feast every bit as much as their Cheyenne hosts. Smoke Jensen appeared impatient throughout the affair. Upon the return of Smoke and the others, six of the warriors became hunters. They rode off from the herd, in search of bison, while Smoke supervised the burial of the dead. A surprise had awaited Smoke in the form of Luke and five volunteers, all deputized by the sheriff in Sheridan.

"I thought you would be strapped down in a hospital bed," Smoke told Luke.

Luke shook his head in rejection of the idea. "Ain't a doctor born who can put me down a minute longer than I want to be. 'Specially when my friends are in trouble." He pulled a long, sad face. "Smoke, I'm right sorry not to have gotten here sooner. We coulda swung the balance."

"I'm not so sure, Luke. There were near to forty outlaws, before the Cheyenne got here and took a hand. By then it was too late for most of us. The Olsens and I survived only because of Iron Claw."

"Well, then, I'll not belabor the point. But I still feel bad about it. What really hurts is losing Jerry. He was a friend."

Nodding agreement, Smoke added, "And a fine horse handler. We'll all miss him."

Smoke Jensen turned away from the last grave when the Cheyenne hunting party returned with a fair-sized bison calf. There came a moment of tension when they made it clear they expected Della Olsen, as the only woman in camp, to dress out the animal and prepare it for cooking. Smoke stepped into the breech.

He spoke in the musical language of the Cheyenne. "She is a white woman; she knows nothing of how to properly clean a carcass. It will take her forever. If you want to eat of it before it spoils, have two of your apprentice warriors skin and cut it up."

They thought that over awhile and decided it might be a good idea. Boys too young to join on the hunt often worked with their mothers at the preparation of the meat, which taught them the techniques needed. Spotted Feather selected two lads about thirteen years of age and assigned them to the task. They looked unhappy about it, but did a satisfactory job.

Meanwhile, other warriors built a fairly large fire for such open country and added wood to it periodically to produce a deep bed of coals. When only a few tiny blue flames flickered over the glowing orange mass, the hump and ribs went onto grilling racks, taken from the gang's improvised chuck wagon. In no time, fat from the hump began to drip and flare up on the embers. That released a delicious aroma that filled the camp. One warrior produced a small drum and began to compose a song of the battle.

"Dog soldiers came. See us! See us! Dog soldiers came. The dark ones came. See them! See them! The dark ones came. My friends of dog soldiers die in big fight. See it! See it!" The song continued as Della Olsen came to Smoke Jensen.

"Smoke, what did you tell them to get them to stop insisting I deal with that small beast?"

Smoke's eyes twinkled when he answered, neatly circumventing the exact truth. "I suggested that white people did not know the medicine of the bison and it might spoil the meat if you were to touch it in an uncooked condition."

"And they believed that?" Smoke nodded, and she went on. "That's outrageous, though close to the truth. I could have easily pierced the entrails and contaminated the meat. Sven always did the butchering for our family."

Smoke looked relieved. "Then nothing was harmed."

Della opened a new topic. "Tommy tells me you are going to Muddy Gap. When do you plan to leave?"

"After the herd is delivered."

Della looked anxious. "Would you . . . I know it is a lot to ask, but . . . would you allow us to accompany you?"

Smoke's expression did not hold encouragement. "I will be traveling fast. I'll be taking Luke and the men he brought with me. They have something else to tend to. I don't see any way you can keep up."

Disappointment clouded Della's eyes. "We know no one north of here, nor in Sheridan for that matter. Could you at least let us come with you as far as Buffalo? I have a shirttail relative there."

For a moment, Smoke considered this. "We'll see how fast the herd moves."

After she departed, Iron Claw came next. "You are going to need help moving all these ponies, old friend. Some of my younger warriors, and of course the boys, are excellent herdsmen. They will go with you."

Smoke visualized what that would be like: a herd of remounts, driven to an army post on a Crow reservation, by seven white men, and probably four times that number of Cheyennes. It beggared description. At last he clapped Iron Claw on the shoulder.

"Sally will never believe this, Iron Claw."

Only an isolated summer thunderstorm delayed the forty-mile journey to Fort Custer. And then by only half a day. The Olsens kept up and did not complain. Colonel Abernathy, newly appointed to command at the post, accepted the herd after only cursory inspection. His face registered cordiality, though his eyes betrayed his apprehension at the presence of so many technically hostile Cheyenne at the fort.

"You've made good time, although we did expect you some three days ago. Your explanation of the reason is quite satisfactory, and please accept my condolences over the loss of your men." He brightened, returning to the subject at hand. "The remounts are in excellent shape. Here is a draft on the government, Department of the Army, for the agreed amount, Mr. Jensen. You may present it for payment at any major bank that has accounts with the government."

"In Denver?" Smoke asked.

"Yes, certainly. The First Mining and Milling handles our payroll as a matter of fact."

"Fine then. I wish you good luck, Colonel. Those men who came out here with you look mighty green."

"They are. Never fear, my sergeant major will whip them in line in no time. Now, may I offer you the hospitality of the post for the night?"

"No, thank you. We have urgent matters south of here. Every hour is important."

Abernathy looked relieved. That meant the Cheyenne would be leaving soon. "I can appreciate that. The man you have as a prisoner. He looks dangerous."

Smoke answered levelly. "Believe me, he is. He and his gang nearly took your remounts from us."

That set Colonel Abernathy back a bit. "My word."

Smoke's cool, golden gaze fixed the colonel. "Yes. And now, if I have anything to say about it, he has a date with the hangman."

Along about ten miles outside of Buffalo, Smoke Jensen learned that the shirttail relative of Della Olsen was a stern, uncompromising brother-in-law. "He has never really accepted me. Bjorn believed that Sven married below his station. What did it matter that we loved one another? *He* was the older brother and expected Sven to do as bid."

Smoke looked her straight in the eyes. "Then the chances of a warm welcome are . . . ?"

"None. But I have nowhere else to go. And the children are his brother's."

"I've known my share of proud, stubborn men. My bet would be that it won't count for much with this Bjorn."

"So, then what?" Della had reached the limit of her hope.

Smoke hesitated only a moment. "How does Muddy Gap sound to you? There are people there beholden to me. I can put in a good word better there than in Buffalo."

Joyful optimism lighted Della's face. "Oh, Smoke. I—I don't know what to say. We—I've been such a burden. I would never be able to thank you enough."

"You already have. Your cooking has kept my hands' spirits high; Tommy has become a good friend. It will be my pleasure to extract some gratitude out of the good folks of Muddy Gap."

Della smiled radiantly. "Well. Now I can hardly wait to get there."

Smoke cut his eyes to the bound figure of Reno Jim Yurian. "Nor can I. I want to get this lizard behind bars and scoop up his partner in crime. Then we'll go recover your cattle. The sale of them will give you a nice little stake, I'm sure."

On the main street of Muddy Gap, which much to Smoke's surprise had been renamed *Jensen Avenue,* as proclaimed by newly painted and displayed signs, the small band of travelers split up. At Smoke's suggestion, the hands went to the Sorry Place saloon. The free lunch would provide them with food they had not tasted in a while. Della Olsen and her children went to the hotel to take rooms for the interim. Smoke, accompanied by the bound Reno Jim, headed to the jail.

There, he dismounted and dragged Reno Jim Yurian from the back of the outlaw's horse. Smoke frog-marched him up the steps and into the sheriff's office. Marshal Grover Larsen looked up with surprise and pleasure on his face.

Smoke spoke directly to the point. "Marshal, this is the man who murdered a rancher named Olsen and rustled his cattle, he also took a number of other beefs. And, he's the one who stole my herd for a while. There are six men, all that are left of his gang, out at Bent Rock Canyon. My men and I are going after them when I've rounded up his partner."

Larsen blinked at the finery worn by the prisoner. "Why, that's Reno Jim Yurian. He's a former gambler who has turned to ranching. Quite prosperous, too. He does a lot of business with Deacon Kelso."

"I'll bet he does," Smoke said drily. Then he shoved Yurian into a chair. "Now, he has a story to tell you, Marshal."

When Reno Jim Yurian concluded his tale of robbery, rustling and murder—prompted by the efforts of Smoke Jensen—Marshal Larsen sat staring at the man as though witnessing for the first time the presence on earth of one of the imps of Satan. A sweating Jim Yurian cut his eyes from Grover Larsen to Smoke Jensen.

He lowered his gaze when he asked plaintively, "I've done what you've asked, and said what you wanted me to say. Now am I free to go?"

Marshal Grover Larsen screwed his full lips into an expression of pure disgust. "Nope. For starters, what you did to this town is enough to get you an appointment with the gallows. Then there's Sven Olsen. Oh, I knew him all right. A fine man. Horse thievin' and cattle rustling are hanging offenses, so's murder of express agents and shotgun guards. No, Reno, it looks like you'll swing, for certain sure."

Reno Jim Yurian turned to Smoke Jensen to plead his case. "But, you promised."

Smoke looked at him, mischief alight in his

eyes. "Yes, I did," he allowed. "That only applies to what you did to me and my men. I don't speak for Muddy Gap, or for the territorial attorney."

Reno Jim tried to come to his boots, hampered by his bonds. "You can't get away with this! It isn't fair! I'll beat this easy. I've got money, power, influence."

Smoke Jensen shook his head in refutation. "Right now it looks like all you have is a trapdoor in your future. Now, Marshal, let's go get his partner."

"And who's that? He didn't say."

Smoke produced a grim smile. "It's Boyne Kelso."

"I'll be damned. I'm with you, Smoke," Marshal Larsen added, as he reached for his shotgun.

Twenty-one

A highly agitated Slick Killmer, one of the six men Reno Jim Yurian had left to tend the cattle in Bent Rock Canyon, stood with hat in hand before the desk of Boyne Kelso. Oily beads of sweat had popped out on his forehead. He cut his eyes rapidly from corner to corner of the room and started violently when a noise came from out in the hall.

"That's right, Mr. Kelso I saw 'em with my own eyes. I was in for supplies, and a little Red Eye for the boys, when they come ridin' into town. Smoke Jensen, big as life, an' he had the boss as a prisoner. They went direct' to the marshal's office."

Boyne Kelso's eyes narrowed. "You could not have made a mistake?"

"No, sir. I told you jist what I saw. If I'd had more fellers to back me, I'd 'uv braced them right then."

"You keep saying 'them,' Killmer. Why is that?"

"Jensen had some rough-looking drovers along with him. Though they carried themselves like gunfighters."

A sudden chill filled Kelso. "How many?"

"Six, all together. An' there was a family

along. A woman and three young 'uns. A boy half-growed an' two little girls."

Kelso sought to form a plan. With Jensen in town, and Reno captured, he had a good idea what would come next. "Where did the family go?"

"I dunno. I reckon to the general mercantile. They had a wagon with them. Funny thing, it looked jist like the one the boys took with them when they went after them horses."

Boyne Kelso stifled a groan. That meant the gang had been wiped out, or at best scattered. Which could only mean Jensen's horses had not been rustled.

"Think, man. Where is that woman, and those kids?"

"Well—ah—they coulda—coulda gone to the hotel."

Kelso thought quickly. "Go to the Trailside. You know Butch and Docking and Unger? Tell them I want them to come here. There's work for them to do."

Slick Killmer gave him a fish eye. "What makes you think they'll drop everything an' come do your bidding?"

"You idiot, *I own* the Trailside. They work for me."

Not the brightest of all outlaws to have taken the owlhoot trail, Slick scratched at his noggin. "You do? Why, you're a deacon in the church. Ain't you Christian folk again' likker an' wimmin?"

Kelso brushed at the front of his coat. "There's some in our flock that take such things seriously, yes. I don't happen to be one of them. Now, do as I say. We have to find a way to get Reno out of that jail and finish Smoke Jensen."

Smoke Jensen and the marshal went directly to the office of Boyne Kelso. On the way up the outside stairs on the bank building, Smoke gave terse instructions.

"Cover me from the upper landing. I'll go in after Kelso alone."

Grover Larsen added a bit of caution. "He may have help in there."

A fleeting grin flashed on Jensen's face. "From what you tell me of that office, there can't be more men in there than I can handle."

Frowning, the lawman nodded. "It is small."

At the top, Marshal Larsen took a position that let him see in through the glass pane in the door and cover the alley as well. Smoke put his hand on the knob, turned it and went through into the hall. He unlimbered his .45 Colt as he stepped over the threshold. No resistance met him.

Five long strides brought him to the frosted glass panel in the door to Kelso's office. Here he stood to the side, reached over and freed the latch. When the portal swung inward, three rapid shots answered the movement. One struck the glass and shattered it; the other two smacked into the wall across the corridor.

Smoke Jensen bent low and entered in a rush, his Peacemaker leading the way. He saw the bulk of a man hunched behind the desk and the muzzle flash. A bullet cracked over his head. Then his Colt spoke.

His first round hit the man scare in the chest.

Driven backward by the powerful thrust, Art Unger crashed both elbows through the window panes before arresting his movement. He tried to cock his six-gun.

Another .45 slug drove into his belly, a fist's width above his navel. It doubled him over, and he pitched onto his face. The Colt Frontier in his hand slid across the floor. Smoke crossed to him. Large exit wounds made ugly blossoms on the man's back. Smoke rolled him over.

"Who are you and what are you doing in Kelso's office?"

"Art . . . Unger. The boss put me here to . . . stop you."

"Don't look like you did it."

Unger gasped, his death rattle already clear in his throat. "N-no. But, it's too late for you anyway. Mr. Kelso an' a couple of the boys has got that woman friend of yours, and her brats. He— he's aimin' to make a trade."

"What's that?"

"Them for him an' Reno Jim goin' free."

Smoke bit off his words harshly. "That'll never happen."

Wincing at the pain, Unger screwed his face into an expression of defiance. "Th-then they're dead meat. An' so are you if you go after them."

Cold fury froze the face of Smoke Jensen. "Where are they? Where did Kelso take them?"

"That—that's for you to find out." With that, Unger went rigid, shuddered violently and died.

When Della Olsen answered the knock and found two men standing outside the door to her room, she did not know what to think. One of them touched the brim of his hat politely, then removed it.

"Mizus Olsen?"

"Yes, I am she."

"Smoke Jensen wants to see you and your young 'uns right away. We're to bring you to him."

"Why, whatever? Don't tell me he's found us a place to stay already?"

"I don't know, ma'am. Only that he said to come at once. We'll show you the way."

Della cast a glance over her shoulder. "Come on, children. We have to meet Smoke."

When they turned into a saloon, Della had immediate misgivings. By then it was too late. The two men fell back and blocked the doorway. Ahead of her at the bar stood a man she had not seen before. He wore the clothing of a prosperous businessman, and a satisfied smile that could almost be called a smirk. He nodded to her and waved a hand to encompass the room.

"Welcome to the Trailside, dear Mrs. Olsen."

"What? Where is Smoke Jensen?"

"No doubt searching my office for me about now."

"You're—you're Boyne Kelso?"

Kelso sighed. "Ah, it's a true pity that our Mr. Jensen has chosen to confide so much in you. I was afraid that might be the case. Whatever, you are to be my ace in the hole. You and the three jokers."

Anger suddenly drove away fear, and Della

stamped her foot. "I'll thank you to explain yourself in a manner that makes sense."

Kelso smiled and nodded jovially. "I have a friend, a business associate, who is currently languishing in the jail. Mr. Jensen put him there. I intend not to suffer the same fate. In fact, I expect to be trading you and your offspring for his release and our continued freedom. Is that clear enough?"

Della's eyes narrowed. "Smoke Jensen will track you down no matter how far you go."

Kelso shrugged, indifferent to her threat "Not if he is residing on that hill above town."

Eyes wide in horror, Della spoke the obvious. "You can't get away with that. The law would have you in an instant, rest assured."

A nasty sneer on his face again, Kelso advised Della. "The law in this town is an old man and a green deputy. With Smoke Jensen out of the way, they would do well to successfully swat a fly." He gestured to his henchmen. "Tie them up and put them over at that table."

"The Trailside." Smoke Jensen spoke the two words crisply as he came out onto the landing.

"Right. I heard the shots. Who is it?"

"*Was.* Someone named Art Unger."

Grover Larsen nodded. He had no doubt how that exchange had come out. Together they went down the steps to the walkway. Smoke used the descent to eject spent cartridges and slid in fresh ones.

Tersely Smoke told Larsen what he had learned from Unger. "Kelso has Della Olsen and her children. He intends to trade them for Reno and his freedom."

He and Larsen turned onto Jensen Avenue and started for the Trailside. Smoke motioned across the street.

"Over there, where you can cover the whole front."

Marshal Larsen was relearning things he had forgotten about being a lawman. He knew at once what Smoke had in mind. From across the way, he could cover the entire front of the saloon while Smoke went through the batwings. For a moment, Grover wondered why Smoke had not chosen for them to go in by two entrances at once, catch those inside in a cross fire. Then it came to him. First, the Olsens were inside, and second, Smoke had no idea exactly how many gunmen Kelso had in the barroom. He crossed the street.

Already, gawkers had begun to gather, careful to give the front of the saloon a wide berth. When the marshal reached the right position, Smoke cut to the center of the street. He strode to a position directly in front of the open door to the Trailside. He faced the liquor emporium and crossed arms over his chest. Then he called out to those within.

"Boyne Kelso! I know you're in there, and I know what you have in mind. Why don't you come out here and face me like a man."

"You can go to hell, Smoke Jensen."

"What? Are you going to hide behind a woman's skirt, Kelso? Do you expect those children to protect you from what I'm going to do to you?"

Silence held for a while, during which more townspeople clustered in the dual crescents of curiosity seekers that extended out into the street. Then an aggravated Kelso offered a challenge to Smoke Jensen. "How'd you like it if I killed 'em one at a time and threw them out to you?"

Smoke gauged the likelihood of that. "Do you have any idea of what would happen to you after the last one got used up?" He paused a few seconds. "Have you ever seen what the Cheyenne do to someone who has deliberately harmed their women and children? Well, I'll tell you.

"They find themselves a bee tree and get some honey; then they find an ant hill, nice, big, red ants. Then they strip the ones who violated their families and stake them out over that ant hill. Next comes the honey. They smear it in every body opening. With a special lot around the eyes and the groin. Then they stand back and let the ants handle it for them. Sometimes they make jokes about the way the victims scream and writhe."

Smoke paused a long, dramatic five seconds, then threw back his head and bellowed, "THAT'S what I will do to you, you son of a bitch!"

No one spoke for a full, tense minute. Then Kelso called out, his voice colored by uncertainty. "You'd never do that, Jensen. You're too law-abiding."

"Don't try me, Kelso, because I swear by the Almighty that I'll make an exception in your case."

That did it for Boyne Kelso. His nerve broken,

he pointed to Butch Jones and Ham Docking. "You two, take him. Do it now."

Ham Docking had second thoughts. "Mr. Kelso, I don't think . . ."

Driven by the power of his anxiety, Kelso snapped, "You aren't paid to think. Now get over there and kill that bastard."

Both of his henchmen started for the swinging doors. Della drew a deep breath and shouted. "Look out, Smoke, there's two of them coming at you."

"Shut up, woman," Boyne Kelso bellowed at the same instant that Smoke Jensen drew with his usual blinding speed and put a bullet precisely three inches to either side of the doorjamb.

Butch Jones shrieked in agony and went to his knees, his belly pierced by splinters and hot lead. Ham Docking howled a curse and spun away. Shards of wood protruded from his left arm. The slug had missed. Boyne Kelso blinked. It had all happened so fast. Enraged, he drew a nickle-plated .38 Smith and Wesson from a shoulder rig and took a step toward the huddled Olsens.

"I warned you, Jensen. I'm gonna start with the little girl."

"No, you won't." All at once, Smoke Jensen stood in the doorway, a .45 Colt in his rock-hard fist.

Boyne Kelso spun toward the opening as a moaning, terrified Ham Docking darted past Smoke Jensen to escape certain death and ran out the door. A shouted command came from outside. "Halt!" It was followed by the boom of a shotgun. The moaning ceased.

Smoke directed his attention to Kelso. "You have a gun. Use it."

Indecision caused Kelso's arm to sway between the Olsens and Smoke. "Nooo. I'm not going to try to take you, Jensen."

Smoke casually fired a round between his legs. "Use it, you gutless piece of dung."

Driven by mindless terror, Kelso swung back toward the Olsens and raised the Smith. "I'll kill them all, I swear it."

In a flash, Smoke Jensen shot Boyne Kelso through the side of the head. His brains sprayed on the rank of bottles on the back bar. For a moment, Kelso swayed on his boots, took half a tottering step, then fell face-first into the sawdust. Without a word, Smoke Jensen stepped over to the Olsens, freed them from their chairs, and escorted them to the door.

Outside, he took note of the crowd for the first time. Among them he spotted Ginny Parkins. Gasping, she rushed to his side and vied with Della Olsen for the privilege of first hug and kiss. In the end, Smoke got soundly bussed by each of them. Then Ginny spoke up, riveting Smoke with her words.

"I—I received your gift. And—I—I—ah—used it. I shot Brandon Kelso in the knee with it. He and his loutish companions tried to compromise me," she explained with a blush. "It has profoundly changed me. I have a different view of the use of force. Violence, I now believe, is sometimes necessary to the preservation of order and for self-protection. I've grown up some, Smoke. For that, I am grateful to you. You saved my life again, it seems."

Della Olsen took center stage then. "Smoke, we're going to stay in Muddy Gap. Somehow I think your coming to our rescue is all the recommendation we'll need."

"Well then," Smoke declared as he ruffled Tommy's hair and gave Ginny a friendly squeeze, "it looks as though I'm leaving the town in good hands."

Traveling alone, except for the burden of sorrow over the loss of so many good men, some who had been close friends, Smoke Jensen reached the Sugarloaf in only five days. His dark mood lifted when he saw Sally's raven hair bent over the kitchen sink. Before he could dismount, she sensed his presence and hurried out on the porch, wiping her hands on her apron.

"Oh, Smoke, it's so good you're back."

Smoke stepped from the saddle and produced a warm, genuine smile. "You've no idea how good it is for me. I've missed you Sally-girl."

"It's good you're home." A bubble of laughter rose in Sally's throat. "I see you planned your arrival to be time for noon dinner."

Smoke produced a fleeting smile. "I surely did. I've been dreaming of one of your pies since I left Muddy Gap."

Her initial joy passed as Sally noted the air of sadness about her man. Then she looked beyond him to where the returning hands should have been near the corral. "Did you ride on ahead? Where are the others?"

Smoke's delight at being home dissolved.

"They—they're gone, Sally. Killed by rustlers. Let's go inside and I'll tell you about it."

Seated at the kitchen table, coffee mug in hand, Smoke related to his beloved Sally the ordeal he and his friends had undergone since they had left the Sugarloaf. When he concluded, Sally brushed a tear from the corner of one eye and cleared her throat.

"They're at peace now. Oh, Smoke, I'm so sorry." She went to him then and hugged him tightly, giving him the compassion and consolation he needed so badly, though he would never ask for it.

By then, the working hands had ridden into the ranch yard. All but one headed for the hot meal awaiting them. Bobby Jensen, who had seen Smoke Jensen's horse at the tie rail, broke from the rest and raced to the main house. He burst through the kitchen door and threw himself at Smoke.

"You're home! I jist knew you'd be here today," the boy said.

"Did you now?" Smoke tousled Bobby's white blond hair.

"Are you gonna take me along the next time?" Bobby asked through his pleasure at seeing Smoke again.

Suddenly Smoke's thoughts rebounded to Tommy Olsen. He reflected on how the boy, only a year older than Bobby, had become a man in the crucible of their shared hardship. He wanted so much that such suffering would never visit Bobby. But then, the lad was growing up. He held Bobby out at arm's length.

"Bobby, it is sometimes wise to be careful

what one wishes for. You might just get it. As to going with me . . . not the next time. I think when you turn fourteen will be soon enough. We'll go find us an adventure then." *And a tame one at that,* Smoke promised himself.

Sally Jensen joined her husband and adopted son and embraced both her men. Smoke was home and wise as always, and all was well in her world.

THE MOUNTAIN MAN SERIES BY
WILLIAM W. JOHNSTONE

__The Last Mountain Man	0-8217-6856-5	$5.99US/$7.99CAN
__Return of the Mountain Man	0-7860-1296-X	$5.99US/$7.99CAN
__Trail of the Mountain Man	0-7860-1297-8	$5.99US/$7.99CAN
__Revenge of the Mountain Man	0-7860-1133-1	$5.99US/$7.99CAN
__Law of the Mountain Man	0-7860-1301-X	$5.99US/$7.99CAN
__Journey of the Mountain Man	0-7860-1302-8	$5.99US/$7.99CAN
__War of the Mountain Man	0-7860-1303-6	$5.99US/$7.99CAN
__Code of the Mountain Man	0-7860-1304-4	$5.99US/$7.99CAN
__Pursuit of the Mountain Man	0-7860-1305-2	$5.99US/$7.99CAN
__Courage of the Mountain Man	0-7860-1306-0	$5.99US/$7.99CAN
__Blood of the Mountain Man	0-7860-1307-9	$5.99US/$7.99CAN
__Fury of the Mountain Man	0-7860-1308-7	$5.99US/$7.99CAN
__Rage of the Mountain Man	0-7860-1555-1	$5.99US/$7.99CAN
__Cunning of the Mountain Man	0-7860-1512-8	$5.99US/$7.99CAN
__Power of the Mountain Man	0-7860-1530-6	$5.99US/$7.99CAN
__Spirit of the Mountain Man	0-7860-1450-4	$5.99US/$7.99CAN
__Ordeal of the Mountain Man	0-7860-1533-0	$5.99US/$7.99CAN
__Triumph of the Mountain Man	0-7860-1532-2	$5.99US/$7.99CAN
__Vengeance of the Mountain Man	0-7860-1529-2	$5.99US/$7.99CAN
__Honor of the Mountain Man	0-8217-5820-9	$5.99US/$7.99CAN
__Battle of the Mountain Man	0-8217-5925-6	$5.99US/$7.99CAN
__Pride of the Mountain Man	0-8217-6057-2	$4.99US/$6.50CAN
__Creed of the Mountain Man	0-7860-1531-4	$5.99US/$7.99CAN
__Guns of the Mountain Man	0-8217-6407-1	$5.99US/$7.99CAN
__Heart of the Mountain Man	0-8217-6618-X	$5.99US/$7.99CAN
__Justice of the Mountain Man	0-7860-1298-6	$5.99US/$7.99CAN
__Valor of the Mountain Man	0-7860-1299-4	$5.99US/$7.99CAN
__Warpath of the Mountain Man	0-7860-1330-3	$5.99US/$7.99CAN
__Trek of the Mountain Man	0-7860-1331-1	$5.99US/$7.99CAN

Available Wherever Books Are Sold!

Visit our website at **www.kensingtonbooks.com**